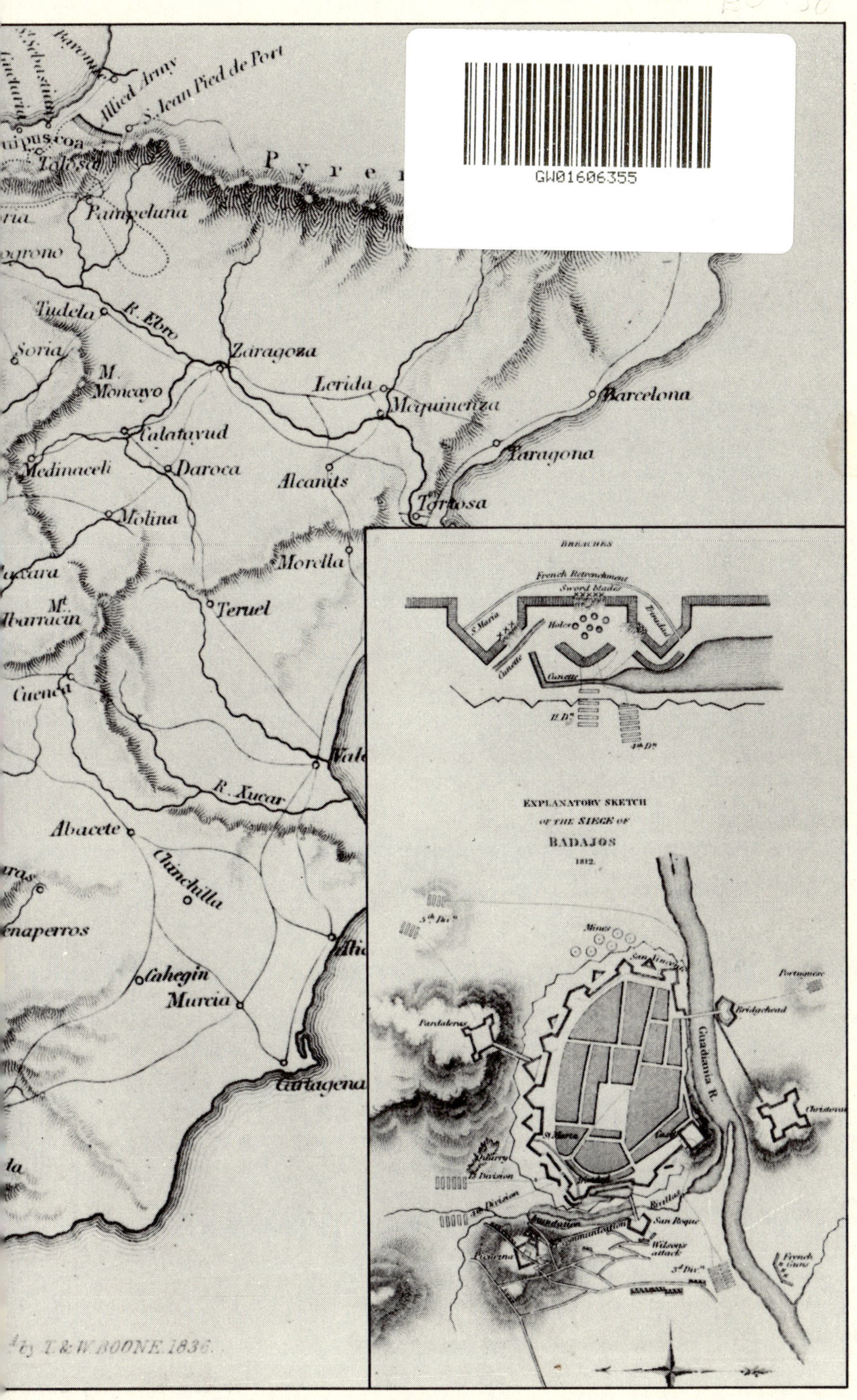
S. Sebastian
Allied Army
S. Jean Pied de Port
Tolosa
Pyren
Pampeluna
Tudela
R. Ebro
Soria
M. Moncayo
Zaragoza
Lerida
Mequinenza
Barcelona
Calatayud
Daroca
Medinaceli
Taragona
Alcanits
Tortosa
Molina
Morella
Teruel
Cuenca
R. Xucar
Abacete
Chinchilla
Cahegin
Murcia
Cartagena
by T. & W. BOONE 1836.
BREACHES
French Retrenchment
Sword blades
S. Maria
Holes
Trinidad
Cunette
4th Dn
EXPLANATORY SKETCH
OF THE SIEGE OF
BADAJOS
1812.
Mines
Portuguese
Bridgehead
Guadiana R.
Pardaleras
St. Maria
Quarry
Division
Inundation
San Roque
Wilsons attack
Picurina
3rd Divn
French Guns

THE OTHER SIDE OF THE HILL

Also by Peter Luke:

Plays

HADRIAN THE SEVENTH

BLOOMSBURY

RINGS FOR A SPANISH LADY
(translated from the Spanish of Antonio Gala)

PROXOPERA
(adapted from the novel by Benedict Kiely)

Fiction

TELLING TALES
(Selected Short Stories)

PAQUITO AND THE WOLF
(for children)

Non-fiction

SISYPHUS AND REILLY
(autobiography)

(ed.) ENTER CERTAIN PLAYERS:
Edwards-Mac Liammoir and the Gate, 1928–1978

THE MAD POMEGRANATE AND THE PRAYING MANTIS:
Adventure in Andalusia

The Other Side of the Hill

A NOVEL OF THE PENINSULAR WAR

by

PETER LUKE

LONDON
VICTOR GOLLANCZ LTD
1984

First published in Great Britain 1984
by Victor Gollancz Ltd,
14 Henrietta Street, London WC2E 8QJ

British Library Cataloguing in Publication Data
Luke, Peter
The other side of the hill.
I. Title
823.'914[F]   PR6062.U4

ISBN 0-575-03490-4

Typeset at The Spartan Press Limited, Lymington, Hants
and printed in Great Britain by
St Edmundsbury Press, Bury St Edmunds, Suffolk

TO

MY BROTHER-RIFLEMEN

WITH WHOM I HAD THE GOOD FORTUNE TO SERVE

1940 TO 1946

All the business of war, and all the business of life, is to endeavour to find out what you don't know by what you do; that's what I called 'guessing what was at the other side of the hill'.

THE DUKE OF WELLINGTON

FOREWORD

In book trade terminology the work between these covers is what is called an 'historical novel'. But this description somewhat distorts my idea not only of what I set out to write, but what I think I have written. In the first place all my main characters are true characters. I am telling the stories of people who actually lived. All I have done to make 'fiction' of it all is now and again to give shape to events, occasionally to alter time-sequences, and sometimes to fill in lacunae with a bit of imagination—this is in order to give the book a form more acceptable to the reader.

As to the matter of eye-witness accounts: these, to me, are the most fascinating aspects of history and I have used them throughout for the sake of authenticity and verisimilitude. In doing so I feel I would have had the approval of my protagonist, Harry Smith, even though he quite clearly stated in his autobiography that he would have liked the novelist Charles Lever (1806–1872), the writer of those gleeful and picaresque stories of Irish Dragoons in Spain and Galway, to have been his literary interpreter. But this was not to be. I usurped the role with little to claim the intrepid Harry Smith's assent beyond the fact that I had the good fortune to serve with his old regiment, The Rifle Brigade, albeit several wars and many years later.

Jimena de la Frontera P.L.

PROLOGUE

"REMEMBER," CONCLUDED Uncle Sydney Beckwith, addressing the officers of the 95th Rifles, "the Regiment is part of all of us, but greater than any of us."

Harry Smith had no reason to disagree with this sentiment but he, like many of the other young officers present, had heard it before. The memory of the previous campaign and the bitter retreat through snow-bound Galicia, ending with the bloody evacuation of La Coruña, was fresh in the memories of most of them. Corunna, as Colonel Beckwith called it, had been a victory, but a Pyrrhic one.

It was now June 1809, six months since they had buried Sir John Moore on the ramparts of La Coruña. 'Uncle Sydney', as Colonel Beckwith was affectionately known, had been giving final orders to his regiment at Dover prior to embarkation for a return to the Peninsula. This was a moment all had been waiting for. The 95th had much unfinished business in Spain.

His homily at an end, the Colonel looked around at his officers before dismissing them to their duties. He had always held that it was easy enough for a soldier to behave well in victory, but to fight on a stricken field was another matter. The three weeks' retreat to La Coruña had given him plenty of time to assess the qualities of all ranks.

In front of him now stood the light-weight, dark-eyed Harry Smith. He was the quintessential Rifleman. Swift and bold in action, he was the *par excellence* thinking, fighting soldier, putting the needs of his men first and his own last at all times. If only, the Colonel reflected, Harry would exercise some control over his temper and his language. There had been times when his abrasive manner had caused offence to officers of other regiments—particularly senior officers.

Beside Harry, immaculate from his rakishly poised shako to his shining black Hessians, stood the exquisite figure of Lieutenant Dan Cadoux. In complete contrast to Harry, Beau Cadoux (he pronounced his name Cardo), or Dandy Dan as he was sometimes called, was by nature more an habitué of Bird Cage Walk or the coffee-houses of St James's than of the coverts and fields of the shires. Nevertheless, Dan Cadoux had done well in Galicia and had even managed to retain a certain elegance despite coming ashore at Portsmouth without his boots. He was still wearing his famous ruby ring, though, as the riflemen had not been slow to remark.

Charles Eeles was another subaltern who had been with the battalion through the last campaign. During the retreat Eeles had rejected the officer's sword as an obsolescent weapon and had armed himself like the men with the new Baker rifle. Thereafter he was never without it. One of the best shots in the battalion, Eeles was one of the new breed of officers to emerge with the formation of the 'experimental' Rifle Corps, a corps that was proud of its smart, but essentially practical, dark-green uniform as much as in the speed and accuracy of its marksmanship.

Standing a sandy head taller than Eeles was Johnny Kincaid, Harry's friend, who concealed a thorough-going professionalism under an insouciant manner, which last emerged strongly in his prose style when he took to writing his memoirs. It would never have occurred to the Colonel, or anybody else, not to trust Johnny. He was forever exposing his tall frame in the face of the enemy, but he could be depended upon always to be in the right place at the right time.

Of the new subalterns, Uncle Sydney had brought with him two of his nephews, Bob and Charlie Beckwith, who seemed to have been bred for life in a Rifle Regiment. Not so Lieutenant George Simmons. This rather portly young Yorkshireman did not wear 'rifle green' as to the manner born. He had been assistant surgeon to a Volunteer regiment but, for reasons which mystified everybody, he had abandoned the medical profession to apply for a commission in the 95th. Since policy was to increase the establishment of the Rifle Corps, and since George Simmons' credentials were impeccable, the Colonel accepted him, but his presence continued to baffle his fellow-subalterns.

Of the Company Commanders Captain Jonathan Leach, a good country-squire type of soldier, had developed a keen interest in pretty nuns in Spain and flirting with them had become one of his main off-duty diversions. Another rugged individualist, Patrick Uniacke, who was of the same Anglo-Irish background as Sir Arthur Wellesley himself, had gathered many of the Micks and Paddies to him and had created in 'C' Company a Hibernian dimension with its own inner *esprit de corps*.

The most senior Company Commander was Major Peter O'Hare who, despite his name, was not born Irish. According to Rifleman Costello, who was, O'Hare was the ugliest man that ever wore a green jacket—or any other jacket for that matter. The red-headed Peter O'Hare had risen from the ranks, a rough passage at any time, and one that was reflected in some of his ways. But, in the opinion of Uncle Sydney, who knew what really counted, he was the most valuable officer because there was no soldier in the regiment who would hesitate to follow where Peter O'Hare led.

As the officers went their ways to prepare for a dawn embarkation, Captain 'Rutu' Stewart, the Adjutant, approached the Colonel with a message from their Brigadier 'Black Bob' Craufurd. On landing at Lisbon, the Brigadier said, the Light Brigade was to make all possible speed to join Sir Arthur Wellesley wherever he might be.

No sooner had Sir John Moore left the Iberian Peninsula by one door, as it were, than Sir Arthur Wellesley entered by another. The bold Irishman had a flair for taking the tide at the flood and on this occasion, as on many other, his timing was good. Napoleon, having pushed a British army into the Bay of Biscay, had now returned to France to attend to more pressing matters.

"Depend on it, Fitzroy, we'll not be seeing Boney again in the Peninsula. He's got other fish to fry."

The person thus addressed was the Military Secretary, Captain Lord Fitzroy Somerset. Together with Captain Alexander Gordon, the General's ADC, and Brother James Doyle, an Augustinian friar, these three made up what the Commander-in-Chief called his 'family'.

The inclusion of Jimmy Doyle in the family may have seemed a curious one, but in fact he served a valuable purpose. Studying for the priesthood in Coimbra, Doyle, who was a scholar and a linguist, served as the Portuguese end of an espionage triangle which straddled the French lines of communication as well as the main roads between Madrid and the Portuguese frontier.

The instigator of this spy network was another Irishman, Monsignor Patrick Curtis, head of the Irish College in Salamanca. The third point of the triangle was yet another religious, Madre Soledad, Superior of the Convent of Nuestra Señora de La Soledad in Badajoz. But only to Monsignor Curtis were known the individual links in the chain.

Between Coimbra and the important border-town of Badajoz communication was maintained by a seminarian colleague of Doyle's called Cristóbal De Los Dolores de Leon who, when not at the University of Coimbra, lived with his two sisters, Victoria and Juana Maria, in Badajoz. The link between Badajoz and Salamanca was another rather mysterious cleric by the name of Padre Julián, while communications between Salamanca and Coimbra were operated by a variety of seminarists from the Irish College whose names almost invariably began with an O' or a Mac.

All these sources fed their intelligence into the headquarters of Sir Arthur Wellesley, and Sir Arthur used the information to the full.

At the time of the Light Brigade's embarkation at Dover, Wellesley, acting on information received through young Cristóbal De Los Dolores, turned north and made a lightning strike at Oporto. With the luck that often attends the courageous, Wellesley crossed the seemingly uncrossable Douro river and inflicted a crushing defeat on Marshal Soult, now sporting the airy title of Duke of Dalmatia. Soult and what was left of his army were sent packing back into Galicia, and thus was Sir John Moore avenged.

CHAPTER ONE

AMONG THE CANES and tamarisks beside the Tagus a hundred thousand frogs were croaking away the amorous night. Under a waning moon the frog-chorus drowned the snores of the riflemen sleeping along the bank. It was half-past one in the morning of 3 July, the Light Brigade's third morning in Portugal.

Anticipating 'Rouse' by a few moments, Harry Smith, opening his eyes, could see in the moonlight the dark form of a sentry cross to where black lumps of men lay sleeping; he saw him bend down and heard the incoherent mutter of voices before he straightened up again to move purposefully on elsewhere.

Turning on his back Harry looked upwards to see the tall eucalypts above his head swaying slightly in the first breeze of morning. Then the tremulous quaver of the bugle-horn sounding 'Rouse' splintered the air and the army of frogs went silent.

Now the dark horizontal shapes gradually became perpendicular as the soldiers, grunting, groaning, and cursing rose and accoutred themselves for the day's march.

Someone near Harry farted loudly. "Better out than in," said Rifleman West, Harry's soldier-servant, cheerfully. Rifleman West was an old soldier of about forty who had served under Sir Arthur Wellesley in India. He had a touch of grey in his hair now and his attitude towards Harry was a mixture of the respectful and the avuncular. "Have you finished with your portmanteau, sir?" Getting the answer 'Yes', West rolled up his officer's boat-cloak, strapped it into the valise, and humped it together with his own greatcoat towards the baggage lines.

"See you at the first long halt, sir," he said, then added, "Come on, sir. Show a leg!"

Soon afterwards the second bugle-call, 'Fall in', rang out bright and clear and immediately the many individual silhouettes coagulated into one black mass.

"Stand to your front—'A' Company!"

"Stand to your front—'B' Company!"

The familiar orders came down the line until Jonathan Leach called out, "Stand to your front—'I' Company! . . . Right turn! . . . By the left, quick march! . . . " And instantly more than a hundred men, including Harry Smith, were quick-stepping along the road to Abrantes.

Soon the word came down to march at ease. Loosening their collars and slinging their rifles, the men could see to their right the broad expanse of the Tagus shimmering in the pale moonlight as they bobbed along at the regulation 140 paces to the minute.

At the first village the bugle-major gave the word and thirty bugle-horns let rip with the regimental quick-step, 'Over the Hills'.

"The Rifle Brigade have gone away
Over the Hills and Far Away
And left the girls in the family way. . . . "

sang 'Sniper' Jackman of 13 Platoon.

"Three o'clock in the bleeding morning . . . that should make the dagoes shit blue lights," observed Rifleman Doubleday, referring to the bugles.

"How many times have I told you that Portuguese isn't bloody dagoes, you ignorant sod," answered Prickett. "Only bleeding Spaniards is dagoes—*Diegos*, got it?"

"Well they're all bleeding dagoes to me."

All down the line officers and men were beginning to feel the strain. Old sweats had allowed themselves to get soft in England and new recruits had yet to become hard.

"One pair of shoes, ditto soles and heels, two shirts, two pair of stockings, three brushes, box of blacking, razor, soap-box and strap, spare pair of trousers, mess-tin, centre-tin and lid, knapsack and straps, haversack and canteen, greatcoat and blanket, powder-flask filled, ball-bag and thirty loose balls, small wooden mallet, belt and pouch containing fifty rounds, sword-belt and rifle—and they call us 'Light Infantry!' Jesus, Mary and Joseph," said Rifleman Costello, a young soldier from Mountmellick in Queen's County, "You wouldn't do it to a Connemara donkey."

"You are carryin' the regulation sixty pounds' weight, Costello," said Sergeant Brotherwood, "as per regulations laid down for a rifleman—at least you were, but as it happens to be your day for carrying the bill-hook you're carrying six pounds on top. But you Paddies, you say, are the hardiest fighting men in Europe so I don't suppose you'll notice the difference."

By moonset the regiment had covered twelve miles. By the time the morning star had been extinguished by a pink dawn there were still eight more miles to go; these in the heat of the July sun. But for the moment there was a long halt, the camp kettles were out and soon everybody was refreshing himself with a brew of tea and whatever food there was in the haversacks.

Presently Harry noticed some activity up forward near battalion headquarters and saw a dragoon who presumably had come down the road from the direction of Abrantes. Later when the Adjutant, 'Rutu' Stewart, rode down the line to collect daily returns from Company Commanders, Harry called out to him, "Any news, Rutu?"

"Well, I don't know whether you can call it news, exactly," said the Adjutant, "but Sir Arthur seems to have joined up with General Cuesta and it looks as if there's going to be a bit of ball-dancing presently, so get your dancing-pumps on." And they marched on under the fierce July sun until, at about noon, they came to Abrantes where they bivouacked in the shade of some cork trees beside the river.

With a regiment in the field, even after a twenty-mile march, there are a hundred jobs to be done before food, rest, ablutions, or any other form of leisure activity can be enjoyed. But sooner or later, when rifles have been inspected, guards mounted, piquets posted, sick cared for, water and rations drawn, and all the other innumerable fatigues, the moment comes when each man can please himself.

As soon as Lieutenant 'Worthy George' Simmons considered his responsibilities to be over for the afternoon he went to the river to wash his feet and his socks which he put to dry in the sun. Then returning to the shade of a cork tree he removed his cap, or shako, and taking from its spacious interior a notebook he started to write a letter:

My Dear Parents,
After experiencing a very favourable voyage we came in sight of Lisbon and cast anchor before the town on the 28th June. I must confess I felt very much disappointed with the place, as a stranger seeing the town from a distance would conceive it a beautiful city. The people in general are dirty in the extreme, their houses are never white-washed and stink worse than an English pig-sty. All the nastiness is thrown out of the windows in the evening and in hot weather it is very offensive to the nose of an Englishman.

I went to see several churches which afforded me some amusement and excited my pity to see a people through ignorance and gross superstition duped by a set of worthless priests under the plea of religion.

I dined at an English hotel and afterwards went to the opera. The dancing was too indelicate to give pleasure—at least I felt it to be so and blessed my stars I was an Englishman. The Portuguese ladies seemed to enjoy a performance which must make a Briton turn with disgust and awake in his soul those refined sentiments for delicacy and virtue which characterize our British dames.

At Santarém, a large town on the river Tagus, we were billeted in the grounds of a monastery. I had lain down to sleep when a monk requested me to rise and follow him. He led me upstairs to a large apartment where a number of his brotherhood were assembled and soon had the table filled with rich food, fruit and good wines in abundance. I passed a few hours very agreeably with these hospitable monks who all appeared, from their rotundity of body, to pay more attention to feeding than to praying.

The weather is intolerably hot and today two men died from the heat of the sun when marching. We are often troubled to procure water but I always make a practice of carrying a supply for myself, also provisions in my haversack for two or three days' support.

Sir Arthur Wellesley, we hear, is rapidly advancing towards Madrid and we are endeavouring to join him as soon as possible. The army has great confidence in Sir Arthur and are exceedingly anxious for the day of battle. I am a young soldier but I hope I shall do my duty when put to the trial.

My love to my dear sisters. I hope Anne is now a comfort to her mother.

I remain with every good wish your dutiful son,

Geo. Simmons.

P.S. As I am continually on the move direct as follows: Lt Simmons, 1st Bn 95th or Rifle Regiment, Portugal or Spain.

A shadow fell across the page. Simmons looked up to see the tall sandy-haired figure of Harry Smith's friend Johnny Kincaid.

"Hullo George! Tell me, is Harry about?"

"Yes, he's over there," George answered, pointing to 13 Platoon lines.

Kincaid found Harry talking to his Company Commander, Captain Jonathan Leach, on the all-absorbing subject of rations.

"Damn stupid arrangement getting the Portuguese to supply us," said Leach. "The Whitehall Warriors can always be relied upon to think up a plan impossible to implement."

"Well, if the men aren't getting enough to eat nobody can expect them not to help themselves," said Harry.

"It won't do, Harry. You know as well as I do it's anything up to three hundred lashes for looting."

"Do you think that would stop men like Prickett and Doubleday? Poaching is a way of life to those fellows."

Johnny Kincaid suggested that they should take a look at the town. Accordingly, the two subalterns set off up the hill towards Abrantes.

Apart from some antique and abandoned fortifications the only building of note was a large edifice on the far side of the town which they decided to make for.

"Funny thing about old Jonathan," said Kincaid, referring to Harry's Company Commander. "Always chasing nuns?"

"This looks like a monastery, or something of the sort," answered Harry. "Let's see if there's anyone at home."

The entrance was unbarred and gave on to a large courtyard of some architectural distinction. The masonry had at one time been painted in ochre, but the decorated Manolino entablature surmounting the whole fabric had been left in its natural stone with excellent effect.

"Not much sign of life," said Harry. "Let's try down here."

A darkish passage of worn flagstones now presented itself. As they entered, they became aware of a sort of metallic squeaking. Making their way towards this sound they now heard the surprising sound of girlish laughter.

The cause of these muffled giggles was soon apparent. Leaning nonchalantly against the wall in front of an aperture that held some sort of revolving metal drum, stood the dashing figure of Harry's Company Commander, Captain Jonathan Leach, complete with low-slung sword, silver mounted cross-belt, and green and black-frogged pelisse hung from his shoulder. He seemed only mildly put out by this approach of the two subalterns.

"Well, well! How goes it, Jonathan?" said Kincaid.

"Satisfactory," said the Captain smugly. "Look at this."

He then reached out and pulled a metal handle in the wall which set going, not only the tinkling of a bell, but also the tinkle of happy female laughter.

"Now watch carefully," said Jonathan. And almost immediately the whirligig began to rotate revealing a sort of 'dumb-waiter' with shelves on which reposed three little sugary cakes tastefully arranged on crenellated paper saucers. Beside the sweetmeats lay another twist of paper in the form of a note, or *billet-doux*.

When the whirligig ceased its squeaky gyrations more titters could be heard, followed by some speculative whispering. As Smith's and Kincaid's eyes became accustomed to the gloom they noticed beside the 'dumb-waiter' a small iron grille and, behind it, framed in a white wimple, a pair of large, dark and beautiful eyes.

"Eat your cakes, boys. They are quite excellent," and smiling complacently, Jonathan picked up the note. "Like a little nest of doves, aren't they? I only wish I could understand what they say. . . . Ah, Harry you're the man. Read that."

There was a pause, then Harry began to read aloud.

Dear and honoured Captain,

My name is Sister Teresa, I am twenty-one years old and come of a good family of Lisbon. I have been told I was pretty before the nuns cut off my hair. But it will grow again if God wishes. My friend is called Sister Inmaculada. She is only nineteen but she is a very good and pretty and well-educated girl. We want, please, to come with you to join your army. We will look after you and we will wash and mend your clothes and will cook nice dinners (did you like the sweets?) for you if you will help us get out of here. We will be very useful and no trouble because we are strong and healthy. Only please, dear sir, write quickly to say that you take us with you. Perhaps we could come tonight.

May God preserve you for many years,
your humble sisters in Christ,
Teresa and Inmaculada

Jonathan Leach's fingers instinctively rose to brush up his silky moustache. "Very tempting, I must say."

"Poor little pastry-cooks," answered Kincaid turning towards the dumb-waiter. "Wouldn't it be rather cruel to leave them. . . ."

" . . . and put them on the ration strength? It wouldn't go down with the men at all."

"But if they're being confined against their will. . . . " At this point Harry butted in: "Johnny—it won't do. They are more or less safe here where they are. If they come with us you know perfectly well what will happen—sooner or later."

"It's a bit of a facer," agreed Leach.

"What I would like to know," went on Johnny Kincaid, "is why nice girls like that are put into convents in the first place."

"What I would like to know," said Harry, "is if they *are* nice girls why are they not more carefully chaperoned? I always thought that these sort of places were run by a lot of old gorgons—"

An alert expression now came into Jonathan Leach's eye.

"Don't look now . . . " he said; whereupon the two subalterns turned immediately and saw a small person in the full habit of a nun coming towards them. She was a lady of a certain age with a serene expression and dignified manner. The three officers knew a look of authority when they saw one and saluted respectfully.

"Good evening gentlemen," she said in English. "I think you are British officers?"

"We are indeed Ma'am," answered Leach, immediately on his best behaviour.

"I am Madre Maria Cristina and you are very welcome to our convent. You have a little refreshment? My nuns are good cooks. We train them here in a little especiality which we call *mantecado*. You like the *mantecados*?"

"The cakes—what you call 'em—were excellent, Ma'am," interposed Leach. "Would it be in order to ask what we owe?"

"Of course you owe nothing, sir," replied the Mother Superior. "It is a small thing. I wish only that we could offer you something more substantial but unfortunately the French—"

"Ah the French, Ma'am! There's the rub, as the poet said. But if we may not pay for the cakes," continued Jonathan Leach, catching Harry's eye, "we would like at least to write a little note of appreciation to the cooks."

Harry Smith was quick to take his cue but the Mother Superior was quicker.

"I regret but the writing of notes to the kitchen staff is strictly prohibited. . . . However," she added, observing looks of discomfiture on the faces of the young men, "on this occasion only I will make an exception since I assume"—and here the three officers thought they discerned a certain emphasis—"you will not be coming here again."

"Alas, I fear that is so, Ma'am," Kincaid replied. "You see, Sir Arthur Wellesley, our Commander-in-Chief, really can't do without us and we're hurrying along to help him out of a bit of bother he seems to have got into in Spain. By the way, you speak excellent English, Ma'am, if I may say so."

And, while Kincaid was making polite conversation, Leach took the opportunity to have a muttered aside with Harry.

"Write something quick, Harry."

"What shall I say?"

"Say, 'Very sorry, can't be done. Thanks for the cakes and good luck.'"

"Do you want to sign it?"

"No. Just put 'the greenjackets'."

Madre Maria Cristina then turned her attention to Leach and Harry.

"And now, gentlemen," she said, "perhaps you would care to see a little of our establishment before you go—if you will come this way please. Our chapel is quite famous. It was built to the order of King Manoel X in 1592 especially for his daughter who became a member of our Order. She was buried here and her tomb is considered to be of some merit. Also I will show you the east window which, as you will see. . . . "

Harry Smith, who was the last to follow Madre Maria Cristina down the passage, stopped for a moment to adjust a bootlace. As the footsteps of the others receded he was almost certain he could hear the sound of two young voices sobbing quietly behind the grille.

CHAPTER TWO

"DAMN HIS EYES!"

The sight of Peter O'Hare's ugly face distorted by anger quickly expunged any daydreams, lecherous, romantic or humanitarian, that Leach and company may have brought down with them from the Convent.

"Damn whose eyes?"

"Black Bob, of course," answered O'Hare, his red thatch sprouting out viciously from under his green cap. He waved a document in the air. "Fourteen pages of calculated insult: imagine telling someone like old Sydney Beckwith just how and where he should march in relation to his own regiment. And listen to this: 'Article III, para 4; Any man who, for the sake of avoiding water or other bad places, presumes to step on one side or quit his place in the ranks must be brought to a Court Martial. If ill, he must be tried as soon as recovered; but if not ill it must be done on the drumhead and the punishment be inflicted forthwith.'"

"Our Brigadier seems to be obsessed by puddles," observed Dan Cadoux.

Harry Smith looked at Cadoux's beautifully polished boots and refrained from making any remark.

Leach brought them back to the point at issue: "Damned staff having nothing better to do, of course, than concoct all this coggidge. Well, I suppose I better read it."

"You'd better do better than that," snarled O'Hare. "All officers are obliged to learn them off by heart."

George Simmons now appeared, his walk a side-to-side affair, half diffident, half arrogant, the suet whiteness of his face relieved by a red sun-blister on his nose. "Has anybody read the new Standing Orders?" he asked as if he had just stumbled on the Holy Grail.

Harry neither liked nor disliked George. He only felt instinctively that he did not belong.

"Strictly Line Regiment material—George," murmured Dan Cadoux in Harry's ear, and this annoyed Harry because it expressed precisely what Harry felt. He felt doubly irritated at finding himself in agreement with someone he disliked. Perversely, he began to feel sorry for George.

'Rouse' at half-past one in the morning. Shadowy branches of cork trees fingered each other in the dark. The smell of fennel bordering the road rose as the men, falling in, trod it underfoot. By midday two riflemen overcome by the heat were sentenced at the drumhead for falling out. Reanimated by twelve lashes apiece, they proceeded on their way carrying of necessity their packs on their heads. Black Bob Craufurd, author of the offending 'Standing Orders', and hitherto anathematized only by officers, was now making his oppressive presence felt by the rank-and-file. But they kept marching.

Cork trees and olive trees, each with its own dark shadow, dotted the plain, an undulating desert where only corn-stubble broke the surface of the dry earth. Harry Smith found it hard to imagine how anything as life-giving as wheat and barley could have come out of this baked earth, and his thoughts went back to damp Cambridgeshire and the green stalks of crops not yet ripe for harvesting.

They halted at Gavião and Johnny Kincaid declined an invitation from Harry to explore the Moorish castle. He was tired, he explained, because he found it impossible to sleep in daylight and the sun, he said, "took a damnable long time to go down and, once it's down, we're up".

At Nisa, which the regiment entered to a boisterous flourish from the bugles, they were greeted by a colony of storks crowded on steeples, walls and rooftops who greeted the soldiers with a loud clattering of their beaks: "The best welcome we've had in this bleeding country," said Doubleday.

Cork, ilex and olive and the long dusty road seemed to stretch forever under a relentless sun, over an endless plain.

But on 13 July the plain came to an end and the road, lined with tall eucalypts, began to zig-zag down through a rocky pass.

And suddenly, rounding a turn, deep and dark below them was the great Tagus once again. Beyond, linking the road to the village of Vila Velha, was a bridge of boats across which some of Stapleton Cotton's hussars, looking like toy soldiers, were already leading their horses.

From the crossing of the Tagus on the 13th until the 27th there was no further issue of bread. Notwithstanding, the Light Brigade continued to march a minimum of twenty miles a day on rations of goat, mouldy ship's biscuit and such 'beef' as a starved bullock rendered when too weak to draw its load. There were very few stragglers though three more men died of heat stroke.

"Must be something to be said for a man who can keep a whole Brigade operational under the circumstances," said Harry Smith as they lay down in an ilex wood just outside Navalmoral. George Simmons, looking very serious, took his little notebook out of the lid of his shako and made a diary entry: '27 July, 1809. Marched fourteen hours to Navalmoral, the weather very hot and no water to be obtained. The soldiers very much fatigued. I thank the Almighty that He has blessed me with an excellent constitution or I should now be numbered among those unfortunates who have perforce succumbed to Genl Craufurd's brutalities.'

The next day, the 18th, and the hottest so far, the Rifles were having their midday halt on the road to Oropesa when George Simmons heard a deep and distant sound.

"Listen!" he said. "Thunder. Thank goodness. A storm should reduce the temperature a bit."

The growling rumble occurred again.

"George, my lad," said Harry, his eyes bright and lively, "What you are hearing is not thunder."

"What is it then?" Comprehension came slowly to Simmons. "What? . . . You mean—guns?"

The long line of hot and tired men lying by the side of the road, sat up or turned over to listen.

"Well, lads, tomorrow it's breakfast off powder and ball," said Sergeant Brotherwood.

"What's that, then?" asked Rifleman Cochrane who, with his wife, Jenny, had joined the regiment at Shorncliffe. Brotherwood did not bother to reply.

"What's he mean, breakfast off powder and ball, Jackman?" persisted Cochrane. Sniper Jackman, whose trousers were bothering him, slowly got to his feet.

"When you smell powder for the first time, sonny," said Jackman easing his crotch, "just see what your appetite's like. Some have a taste for it, some don't. It's all according."

"What's the matter wiv you, Jackman?" said one, Palmer, known as the Bombproof Man. "Got the Salamanca clap?"

"What's the Salamanca clap then?" asked Cochrane again.

"Getting nearer to Talavera Vera," shouted a chorus of old sweats from Moore's campaign.

A Lieutenant of the 14th Light Dragoons on a sweating horse came pounding down the line asking for General Craufurd. Rumours began to circulate: the British had joined up with the Spanish army of General Cuesta. They were about to engage the French somewhere near Talavera. Sir Arthur Wellesley was or was not waiting for the Light Brigade before offering battle.

The Dragoon officer was soon seen coming back up at a hand-canter.

"What's the news, O'Malley?" shouted Harry Smith.

"You'll need to get a move on, my boy, or you'll be too late."

"Who said so?"

"Why, old Nosey, of course."

Up to this moment the riflemen had fallen in and marched because that was what they were trained to do. Now with the sound of gunfire in their ears, their perverse determination, despite heat, thirst and fatigue, was to push on. Suddenly from the opposite direction came first a few, then literally hundreds of Spanish soldiers including a number of officers. Some were walking wounded but the majority were not, and many had thrown away their weapons in favour of assorted loot. As they passed they all shouted at once, pointing behind them as if they could already see the bayonets of a bloodthirsty French army on their tail.

"Bloody dagoes!" growled Corporal Prickett, roughly shouldering a gesticulating Spaniard out of his way.

Following the runaway Spaniards came a number of British soldiers, some lightly wounded, some contriving to limp, others shamelessly deserting.

"It's no good up there, mates," shouted a thin man with froth in the corners of his mouth, "Sir Arthur's dead—the Guards is all done up, too. They're only just behind."

"Go shit in it, you mouldy bugger," shouted Doubleday raising a laugh from the sweating riflemen.

"I'm telling you, you won't do no good going on up there," croaked the man again, and moved on in a shuffling sort of run.

Then came a pale young officer on a poor-looking horse. He was bare-headed and held his head rigidly averted from the column of riflemen.

"And where, sir, might you be off to?" shouted Harry Smith.

"I'm going—I have to go to—I've been sent. . . . " And the young man urged on his nag without looking to right or to left.

At Oropesa they stopped long enough to cook a meal. Thereafter with only mandatory halts, they marched on for the rest of that day and right through the night. They marched forty-two miles in twenty-six hours. But when they marched on to the field of Talavera just before nine o'clock in the morning the battle had already been won.

Many of the rank-and-file of the British army there did not as yet know they had won.

They just stood, haggard and red-eyed after two days' fighting, their own and the French dead lying round them as they had fallen. No doubt many, as the new day dawned, expected to hear once again the French drums beating the dreaded *rataplan* of the *pas d'attaque*.

But instead they heard the bugle-horns of the 95th *andante con brio* as on to the field marched the Light Brigade in one compact body. Seeing the old familiar regiments again: the 43rd, the 52nd and the 95th Rifles, the battle-weary men gave out a great spontaneous cheer, a cheer which was taken up all along the line.

When Sir Arthur Wellesley, shaven and as matter-of-fact as on any other day of the year, invited General Craufurd to take over all picket and outpost duties it seemed to the Light Brigade as a whole the most natural thing in the world. The question of tiredness did not come into it.

To Harry's fury, however, the French had withdrawn in the

night behind the river Alberche. He therefore turned his aggression towards the enemy within the gates. Making his way to pick a fight about rations with the Commissary, a strange sensation came over him. He turned suddenly to look behind him. And there grinning as he approached was his brother Tom.

So great was their mutual pleasure at seeing each other again that the brothers just stood there grinning and pumping each other by the hand for an exaggerated length of time.

Museums and galleries, military clubs and many private houses are adorned with paintings which make battlefields seem to be the most agreeable places on earth. At best these battle scenes appear like healthy games for boys. At worst they have a cosy domestic atmosphere about them, where drummer-boys succour their fallen comrades with canteens of water, kilted highlanders bandage each other's cuts and bruises, and the moribund in decorative poses proudly salute their Commander-in-Chief as he saunters by. In this respect Lady Butler's *Scotland for ever!* and Frith's *Derby Day* have much in common.

The reality is somewhat different. On the morning after Talavera, at the moment when Tom and Harry Smith were reunited (a pretty enough scene), there lay on the ground 840 British dead, more than nine hundred dead Frenchmen and perhaps two or three hundred Spaniards. In addition, there had been much cavalry action on the previous day and the field was strewn with dead and wounded horses. Furthermore, the dried grass and scrub had caught fire and both dead and wounded had been roasted in flames fanned by the wind. As the July sun rose to its zenith on that morning of the 29th the stench of putrefying and burning flesh, both animal and human, became intolerable.

To dispose of this problem as quickly as possible an order was given to burn all dead. But the men, particularly of the regiments who had had most casualties, growled and would have none of it.

"It's not right, is it?" said Doubleday. "I mean to say, a covey what's died for his country is entitled to a Christian burial, ain't he?"

"Since when was you so holy, you horrible sinful creature?" answered Corporal Prickett. "Got a bad conscience, have you?"

But most men in the army agreed with Doubleday, and Sir Arthur knew when not to enforce an order.

"Then get your shovels out and dig," said Craufurd. And all that day the men of the Light Brigade, and hundreds of others besides, stripped to the waist, dug the hard-baked earth under the burning sun. And since the British were left in possession of the field of battle, in conformity with long-established accord between respectful enemies, they buried the French dead too.

"Army life has its little compensations," said Doubleday, pocketing a gold locket found on a captain of Chasseurs whose body was about to be dropped into a pit.

"Oh, yes?" responded Prickett. "Now we know, don't we? That's why you was so keen on decent Christian burial, you thieving bloody vampire. Make sure that locket gets lodged in our joint account."

While everywhere men of the Light Brigade were joyfully encountering old friends, let alone brothers, on the field of Talavera, Craufurd's encounter with his chief was less felicitous. Black Bob had been the bearer of a bundle of despatches from England and these were far from welcome. Sir Arthur's relations with Cuesta and the Spanish Junta were difficult enough on both military and political levels. On the aftermath of a hard-won battle he could well do without muddle-headed, two-month-old directives from Whitehall.

In order to gild, as he thought, the pill, Craufurd now produced a letter.

"Here, sir. I've brought you a letter from Lady Wellesley. She gave it to me herself."

Sir Arthur took the letter, saw with dissatisfaction Kitty's faint and spidery writing, and grunting, stuffed it unopened into his pocket.

"Sorry you missed the fight, Bob," he said. "But I'll tell you one thing: if Boney had been here we should have been beat. As it is we shall have to withdraw."

"Withdraw, General?" Craufurd's temper rose easily to the surface. "We haven't just marched sixty-two English miles in twenty-six hours in the hottest season of the year just to withdraw." Wellesley's warm voice turned cold: "General

Craufurd, the efforts you have made to rejoin the army promptly are commendable. You will receive detailed orders for future operations as soon as my staff have had time to prepare them."

As Craufurd was leaving headquarters he passed the Military Secretary, Lord Fitzroy Somerset. "Your master's damned crusty this morning," growled the Light Brigade Commander and passed on without another word.

Soon after Craufurd's departure Sir Arthur called for his horse. Before leaving he checked his pockets and came across the letter from Kitty. With scarcely concealed irritation he skimmed through it: ' . . . rose this morning very late from fatigue . . . heard little Arthur's catechism . . . I fear indolence is again creeping about me . . . I am fatigued by a regular course of insignificant occupations and am dissatisifed with myself when idle. . . . ' Impatiently he rolled the letter up in a ball and threw it in the fireplace.

Gordon came to say the horses were ready.

"Where are we going to, General?" asked the ADC.

"Badajoz," came the answer. "It's the only place to go."

CHAPTER THREE

If Lord Wellington, as the Commander-in-Chief had now become, had gone to Badajoz because it was 'the only place to go', Captain Gordon and Lord Fitzroy Somerset had billeted themselves on the De Los Dolores family because it was the *best* place to go. It had been Cristóbal's suggestion and they welcomed it.

The house, built like many Spanish town-houses in the Romano-Arabic concept round an atrium, had considerable charm. The atrium or patio, half-enclosed like a cloister, contained a tall palm tree, a purple bougainvillaea and a number of other climbing plants and shrubs such as jasmine and *la dama de la noche*, these last having been planted for their sweet scents as much as for their flower and foliage. In the middle an old fountain, green with moss, released an imperceptible trickle of water to mitigate the heat of summer.

"No wonder the Moors," said Lord Fitzroy when he first saw the place, "were so reluctant to leave Spain."

For the two young staff officers the house had many advantages. It was only two minutes' walk from the Plaza de España where Lord Wellington had his headquarters, and it contained two charming daughters, one of whom was a rare beauty. An additional bonus was the old servant, Frasquita, who was a good cook, not too heavy-handed with the oil.

Olive oil had in fact been the basic source of income to the family until recent years and their two farms, one at Olivenza and the other on the road to Albuera, were models of good husbandry—at least until Don Eusebio, the father of Victoria, Cristóbal and Juanita, died. Nevertheless, despite the war the olive groves had not been despoiled by either army, and the family, including the uncle, a grandmother and several maiden aunts, still managed to live quite comfortably.

Alex Gordon, twenty-five at the time of arriving at Badajoz, was delighted with his new quarters, a paradise after the hard-lying of the recent campaign. The only drawback was the presence of Victoria, whose beauty he found vaguely disturbing. But Victoria, a young bride whose husband, Jacinto, was away fighting for his country, was out of bounds.

Fitzroy Somerset, two years younger than Gordon, had had a horse shot from under him in the last battle and had been given the honour of taking the Talavera despatches to London. This was an exceptional distinction at a time when it was customary for the chosen messenger to bear important news direct to the monarch himself. With this privilege went the perquisite of a week's leave and the young Captain lost no time in making the most of it. One night at Almack's he met Emily Wellesley, Lord Wellington's niece, and by the end of the week there was a certain understanding between them. On his return to Army Headquarters at Badajoz, therefore, Lord Fitzroy's head and heart were full of English roses. In consequence Victoria's charms, which were more of the jasmine and carnation variety, made little impression on him, not that the gravely formal Victoria would have done anything to encourage either of her lodgers.

In their leisure hours both young men therefore turned their light-hearted attention to the younger sister Juanita, though she was still only a schoolgirl of eleven. For her part lively Juanita, who had no inhibitions about performing, was always ready to oblige with a regional or traditional song. These she sang with great attack and, as Victoria explained, an unusually sophisticated control over the tricky 'arab' quarter-tones.

Even more to the taste of the young British officers were the various dances such as the *sevillanas* and *jotas* which Juanita performed with skill and panache.

Victoria, in Jacinto's absence, could seldom be persuaded to join in these entertainments. But one evening Cristóbal came home with a crowd of friends who were *tunos*: student musicians who, dressed in the traditional costume of an earlier epoch and adorned with multi-coloured streamers, busked with guitars and lutes round the bars and eating houses for pocket-money.

In no time at all they had swung into the irresistible rhythm of a *sevillana Rociera*. Two more took up their positions with arms raised challenging the sisters to dance.

There is no Spanish girl who has not got her native dance in her blood, bones and understanding. The De Los Dolores sisters were no exception. The *sevillana*, as its name suggests, is indigenous to Andalusia but there are few women, at least in the southern half of the Peninsula, who do not know it. It is a formal precisely-choreographed courtship ritual and Victoria, like her sister, could perform it well.

With the intensification of the war the lives of most people in Badajoz had changed. Cristóbal, for one, had left Coimbra, not because of lack of vocation for the priesthood, but because Victoria had persuaded him that his place was at home. In any case his usefulness to the British military headquarters had ceased when the army had moved into Spain. Cristóbal therefore enlisted in the local militia which General Menacho had sensibly formed from the able-bodied *Pazenses*, as the citizens of Badajoz called themselves.

"Joining the militia," Juanita confided to her friends Gordon and Somerset, "has made Tobi much nicer these days. I mean he actually talks to me now and again. I suppose it's only because of you, though. I mean, you're real soldiers and you talk to me, so I expect he thinks it's the smart thing to do."

"Oh, I don't know about that," answered Lord Fitzroy diplomatically, "I think it's because you have become more grown up and he finds you more of a companion—not just a tiresome little sister."

"I think you like Cristóbal better nowadays," said Alex Gordon, teasing, "because he often brings boys round to the house."

"*Ay, que cara dura! Quelle effronterie!*" said Juanita, pretending to be offended. "I hate boys. They are so stupid. Always laughing ja-ja-ja and braying like donkeys!"

Juanita and the two British officers habitually spoke in the only language they had in common, French. Juanita attended the convent of La Señora de la Soledad near the Castle where she had shown promise as a linguist under the instruction of the Basque Sister Rosario. She was *sobresaliente*—outstanding—in French.

"Sister," said Juanita one day, "you love the French language so much, you must like the French, too."

"Oh, yes. I know I'm not supposed to, but I do. You see I went to school in Pau and, well. . . . " And tears came glistening into her blue eyes at the thought of the good nuns and all the other French men and women she was supposed to hate but couldn't.

One day as the girls were tumbling out of school twittering like skylarks Juanita heard the Mother Superior's voice: "Juana Maria . . . Juana De Los Dolores, come here, child!"

Juanita shouted some quick '*hasta luegos*' to her friends and ran back to where the Madre Superiora was standing with a priest.

"Juana Maria, I want you to take the Reverend Father here to your house. Padre Julián wishes to speak with *el capitán inglés* who is staying with you."

"Yes, Reverend Mother," replied Juanita, on her best behaviour.

"El Capitán Gordón," said Julián, taking Juanita by the hand, "*o el otro señoría*, Feezroy Esomerset."

Indifferent as she was to most priests except for her respect for their cloth, Juanita could not help feeling the friendly warmth that emanated from this man. There seemed to be missing that elderly neuter thing: that odour of sanctity—that faint whiff of candle-grease, altar wine and incense—that unconsciously she associated with the generality of clergy. Instead Don Julián gave off a distinct effluvium of saddle-soap, horse-sweat and tobacco smoke which, on the whole, she thought she preferred.

"Why do you keep looking at my boots, Juanita?" said Julián presently, as they were making their way through the narrow streets between the convent and the Plaze de España. Juanita blushed.

"Oh, was I Father? I don't know," she lied. "Perhaps I wanted to see if you were wearing spurs."

"Why should I be wearing spurs?" asked Julián holding out a foot encased in conventional black shoes.

"Well, I know you don't come from here, so it would be quite reasonable. Where do you come from, Father?"

"A small village called Santíz near Salamanca."

"That is a long way. So I was right, wasn't I?"

Julián took a good look at Juanita and nodded.

"You're a bright girl, Juanita. I can see I shall have to be careful what I say to you."

"I don't know why. I'm very reliable you know."

"Hmmm . . . I dare say you are. Another Condesa de Bureta in the making, perhaps."

"Who's the Condesa de Bureta?"

"Don't tell me you've never heard of Doña Agostina, the heroine of Zaragoza?"

"Of course I have but I never knew her other name. Do you know her?"

"I met her once when I was in Aragón."

"Oh, how I envy you. I've often imagined her manning the barricades with her musket and inspiring the Zaragoza men to fight the French. Is she pretty?"

Julián laughed. "That's a typical woman's question. I don't suppose she would have inspired the men too much if she was a scarecrow. What would you do if the French attacked Badajoz, Juanita?"

"Oh, I'd like to be like Doña Agostina—but I'm not pretty enough, I'm afraid."

"You will be, Juanita. You will be."

"Ha! I doubt it. But thanks anyway. This is our house."

Fitzroy Somerset was in his room working on some despatches and to him Julián handed a portfolio he had been carrying with him.

Half an hour later, when Alex Gordon got back to the house from headquarters, he found Fitzroy and Jimmy Doyle, who had been brought in to interpret, excited over a number of documents brought by Padre Julián.

"The reverend gentleman here," said Fitzroy, "seems to be handier with the flintlock than the rosary. In fact he presides over a band of mounted *partidas* operating out of the Sierra de Gata south of Ciudad Rodrigo."

"You mean he's another of these priest-guerrillas we've been hearing about?"

"This gentleman is no more a priest than I am, old sport. But I've promised that only you, Doyle, and the General shall know."

"I see."

"His little speciality is intercepting despatches and cutting out convoys."

"And livers and lights as well, I dare say," answered Gordon. "What's his news?"

"Nothing good. The Spanish were routed on the 19th November

at Ocaña and the Duque del Parque's forces were cut up at Alba de Tormes on the 28th and 29th. The only cheering thing is that old Cuesta has had a stroke and has retired from the conflict. What it adds up to is that the regular Spanish Army is out of the game—at least for the time being."

"Well, I don't think that is going to upset the C-in-C too much after Cuesta's lamentable show at Talavera," answered Gordon.

"I don't know," replied the other. "It means that we can't stay in Spain by ourselves with our flanks wide open."

The four men now proposed to find Lord Wellington in order to put this latest intelligence before him. In the patio, obviously waiting with some anxiety, they found Victoria. Seeing Julián she went straight to him.

"Father, if I interrupt you please excuse me, but could I speak to you for a moment? My sister told me that you were here and that perhaps you had come with some news for Lord Wellington. My husband, Jacinto Orellana, is with the army of Alburquerque and I don't know if by chance you have some news of them. It is natural to be a little anxious. . . ."

This question was difficult for Julián to answer. If he told what he knew it might cause Victoria greater anxiety.

"Doña Victoria, it is true that I have been able to bring some information to General Wellington but I have little first-hand knowledge of the general state of affairs beyond. . . ."

"But there are rumours that there have been defeats—defeats of our armies—near Aranjuez. . . ."

"At Ocaña, yes, but General Areizaga is a poor commander and not known for his personal bravery. The Duque de Alburquerque is different. He is too rich to be concerned about his reputation and too uninterested in politics to be swayed by factions. He is not perhaps a military genius but at least he has bal—I mean—that is to say, he is a man of courage."

Julián's near *faux pas* passed unnoticed.

"But has Alburquerque been engaged in battle? Where is he, Father? Do you know?"

"Yes, he is on the Tagus at El Puente de Arzobispo, but as far as I know he has not been in any major action."

"Not in action. Oh, that is a relief. Thank you, Father. But I have not heard from my husband for some time you see, so . . . ”

“Don’t worry. It means nothing. But if I find myself in contact with anyone from the staff of General Alburquerque I will make enquiries and let you know immediately.”

No sooner had the four men left to find Lord Wellington than there was another knock at the front door. Frasquita, busy in the kitchen, told Juanita to answer it. She opened to see a small, smart young man in a green uniform whose accent, rather than his appearance, declared him an Englishman.

“*Buenas tardes, señorita,*” said Harry Smith, saluting. “*Quisiera hablar con el Capitán Gordón.*”

“*Pues, lo siento pero el capitán acaba de salir. Creo que está en* ‘headquarters’. *Sabe usted donde está?*”

“*Si, gracias. No te preocúpes. Adios,*” and with a friendly wave Harry disappeared down the narrow street.

At headquarters Lord Wellington was alone with his ADC and the Military Secretary. On principle he never made his senior Commanders or staff officers privy to his counsels until the last moment before action had to be taken. This aggravated the senior officers but maintained a degree of security at a time when the French usually culled their intelligence by the simple means of reading the British newspapers. The British press usually obtained its information from the indiscretions of junior officers writing home, or from senior officers venting grievances in the form of letters to editors.

Wellington had already determined to withdraw from Spain to Portugal before Julián’s captured despatches were put before him. He only needed this confirmation of the incapability of the Spanish Central Junta in Seville and its generals in the field to implement his resolve.

“This is going to upset a lot of people in Seville, my Lord,” observed Somerset.

“A General’s duty, Fitzroy, is to gain victories. It is not his duty to lose his country’s army in prosecuting inanities at the behest of fools. Now that the Spaniards have thrown away two armies the country is wide open to the French—apart from the *guerilleros*, that is.”

“Talking of *guerilleros*, do you wish to see Julián Sanchez, my

Lord?" asked Gordon. "He is outside."

"These partisans seem to be the only fighting men in Spain who are either efficient or effective. Yes, have him come in." After Julián had been introduced, the interview, according to Jimmy Doyle acting as interpreter, went roughly as follows:

"I understand, Señor Sanchez, that you are doing capital work disrupting communications between Salamanca and Ciudad Rodrigo."

"And further afield, señor", replied Julián. "No force of less than a battalion dare move within a march of the Sierra de Gata."

"Is that so? Then how many men do you have at present under arms?"

"Just over two hundred, Señor General. We usually operate in two groups, one working from Tamamés and the other out of Hoyo in the sierra. But we can unite in five or six hours when necessary."

"That's fast. You are all mounted?"

"Well mounted, señor."

"Wish I could say the same. Lot of rubbishy stuff coming out from England these days. How do you manage for remounts?"

The Spaniard laughed. "Each time the French lose a man we gain a horse, señor."

"What about your men?"

"I am a bull-breeder," replied Julián. "All my men are bull-farmers or *charros* as the cattlemen of Salamanca are called. In our job we use a long lance—much longer than the cavalry lance. It is called a *garrocha*, and it doesn't penetrate more than about an inch, but a garrochista who knows his job can topple a three-year-old bull. I can tell you the French are careful how they pass through *garrochista* country these days."

"I dare say so," replied the General, who was clearly interested in this novel concept of cavalry tactics. "Tell me, Señor Sanchez, would you care to consider becoming incorporated into the British army? I could offer you a Major's commission. Your men would be paid and put on the army ration-strength."

Julián smiled. Possibly he was amused at the thought of being put on the ration-strength of an army known to be half-starved. "Thank you, General, but I was once a regular soldier and, if I wanted to, I could rejoin the Spanish army. No, señor. With my experience of the Spanish army I prefer to fight this war my own way."

"Most understandable," replied Lord Wellington, with a glance at his staff officers, "and I wish I had your independence and freedom of manoeuvre. Unfortunately I have to deal not only with your Junta, but also with my own Government as well. Very restricting, believe me. But you will surely have no objection if I apply for a cash advance to provide you with food and forage?"

"Who but a fool would object to the offer of a cash advance?" answered Julián, grinning. "We do not like to depend always on the country people. They are very poor and the French rob them all the time."

General Wellington got to his feet. "I would like to see your *garrochistas* at work one of these days, Señor Sanchez—herding bulls I mean."

Seeing that the interview was at an end Gordon politely interrupted to say that a Lieutenant Smith of the Rifles was outside requesting a private interview.

"Smith? Which Smith? What does he want?"

"It is concerning greyhounds, my Lord."

"Why, then send him in, Alex. Send him in."

Coming into the General's room Harry Smith was surprised to see a clergyman of the Roman persuasion about to leave it. He was even more surprised when that priest winked at him in passing. He was not surprised, though, when the General, instead of addressing him directly, turned to Somerset and demanded the latest sick-list returns. He had been warned of the Commander-in- Chief's enigmatic behaviour.

"These are Dr McGrigor's figures up to the end of the month, my Lord. Deaths from ague—328. Sick from ague—1,007. Sick from all other causes—only 96."

Wellington turned to Harry Smith. "Smith, I suppose your battalion has had its share of illness?"

"Indeed it has, my Lord. The Spaniards say it's the bad air rising from the Guadiana river. They call it *mala aire*, sir. The troops," he added laughing, "call it 'malaria'."

"Have you had it?"

"No, sir. But then I go coursing every day and get away from the river."

"I see. Well, what's your business, Smith?"

"Coursing, my Lord."

"There are some good hares at Campo Maior, I dare say."

"Plenty, my Lord. I've never had better sport anywhere."

"And you have heard, I suppose, that I have some new greyhounds out from England?"

"Yes, sir, and we—that is my friends and I—thought you might care for a bit of sport."

"You're a saucy fellow, Smith." said the General. And then after a pause, "Very good—but there is one condition."

"What's that, my Lord?"

"No wagers. Some of you young fellows gamble too much. Those of you who survive this campaign may want to enjoy life a bit; not end up in Carey Street."

"You know," said Lord Wellington to his two aides, "Smith has probably got a point about the 'malaria', as he calls it. I would have moved the army back from the Guadiana long ago but for one consideration. The Junta wanted our presence here on Spanish territory, so I have remained despite the enormous casualities from disease. But now that they have thrown away two battles and disregarded my advice on three occasions, I'm off."

"When, my Lord?"

"Tomorrow, Alex. Tomorrow. Fitzroy, you will follow with GHQ in due course. . . . Why, Alex, you look a bit pale all of a sudden. Not sickening for the ague, I hope?"

"No, no, sir. Never felt better in my life," replied Alex, and hurried off to organize an early start.

"Where actually are we going to, sir?" asked Alex Gordon, when later they made off in the direction of Santarém.

"Why, to Torres Vedras," replied his Lordship, repressing a smile at the beauty of his new secret. "Study your map, my boy, and you will see why."

The British army and the citizens of Badajoz received the news of the former's withdrawal from the Guadiana area very differently. Soldiers, with obvious exceptions, generally prefer to be on the move and the sufferers from ague, or *mala aire*, were particularly pleased to be getting away from the tainted valley. The Pazenses, on the other hand, a number of whom were profiting by the British presence, viewed the change of circumstances with dismay and many, who had reason to dread occupation by the French, felt the most morbid misgivings. Only the *afrancesados*, a small minority of liberals dedicated to the French brand of republicanism, were pleased. But they kept their feelings to themselves.

Many people, particularly those such as the De Los Dolores family who had had officers of the general staff billeted on them, missed their friendly and comforting presence. But worse was to come. A few days after the last of the British troops had crossed over the border into Portugal, a youth, who appeared to be a goat-herd judging by the esparto sling he carried, came to the De Los Dolores house and demanded to see Doña Victoria.

Frasquita, who had opened the door, looked at him with disapproval.

"You can't see her. She's not in."

"Then I'll wait here till she comes."

"What is it you want with her?"

"To give her this." And the lad showed the corner of a letter which he had in his shirt.

Victoria went inside to the study and shut the door before opening the letter. It contained a short message: 'The brigade in which Lieut Jacinto Orellana Obregón serves was transferred from Alburquerque's corps to the army of General Areizaga on 14 October. No news has been received from this unit since the battle of Ocaña.'

That night Juanita dreamed she was on the ramparts of Badajoz, bandolier slung, musket in hand, urging on the men of the Militia (including Cristóbal who was under her command) to defend their city against the French. In charge of the defence, no longer now in clerical garb but dressed in a dark-green uniform, was Don Julián Sanchez.

When she woke up she remembered her dream and wondered if she ought to make an 'act of contrition' for being in love with a priest. The question did not however, trouble her conscience for long.

CHAPTER FOUR

LIKE SO MANY brilliant concepts, Wellington's plan had the beauty of simplicity. By dint of fortifying the hilly peninsula north of Lisbon between the Atlantic and the Tagus he made an impregnable retreat behind which the Anglo-Portuguese army could hold out indefinitely, provided Britannia continued to rule the waves. This natural fortress, embellished by army engineers, took its name from a small town in the vicinity and became known as the Lines of Torres Vedras.

Where Wellington went Masséna, now commanding a huge French force, was bound to follow. And this he did until his lines of communications became extended over more than 600 miles from the Atlantic to the Pyrenees. As Masséna's lines lengthened, Wellington's inversely grew shorter. Then Wellington turned suddenly at Busaco and punched Masséna hard on the nose. While the Frenchman was recovering from the blow, the British General slipped into the lines of Torres Vedras and slammed the door shut behind him.

Such over-extended lines of communication meant that the French along the way were at the mercy of the *guerilleros*, both Spanish and Portuguese. Not a sentry mounted guard at night without starting at every shadow, expecting each moment the knife in the back or the shot in the dark. No straggler fell out along the way without the expectation of a cruel death at the hands of peasantry or *partidas*. Not even a despatch could be sent from one Commander to another without the courier being accompanied by a squadron of cavalry.

If the Spanish regular army had retired from the field the guerrillas, as it was becoming the fashion to call them, were becoming masters of it. By the middle of the year 1810 the fame of Julián Sanchez, generally known by his *nom de guerre* of 'El Charro', had spread widely and, despite various French garrisons (Ciudad

Rodrigo was now in French hands), he controlled large areas of Salamanca and Northern Extremadura between the Tagus and Douro rivers. Though rather beyond his sphere of operations, he also kept an eye on Badajoz since it continued to be the most strategically important town on the Hispano-Portuguese frontier. Apart from General Menacho, the garrison commander, his principal contact at Badajoz was the Mother Superior of the convent of Nuestra Señora de la Soledad.

Madre Soledad (she had been named after the Patroness of Badajoz) was a remarkable woman. In the first place she looked like a negress from her fuzzy hair down to her 'lark heel', though nobody actually owned to having seen either. Most people agreed that she was probably a throw-back to some Moor, a number of whom had negroid features through consanguinity with their slaves. In Spain this was nothing for anybody to be ashamed about since only a handful of families could truly claim to have *sangre azul*, or blue blood. It could hardly be otherwise in view of the fact that the Arabs had occupied large tracts of the Peninsula for eight centuries and the Jews had been there since the Diaspora.

Apart from this Madre Soledad, still in her early forties, had a severity of expression that struck awe into everyone from the junior class girls (difficult to quell at the best of times) to the Bishop of Badajoz himself. The only person with whom she seemed to have an easy relationship was General Menacho who consulted her on a wide variety of matters from pruning olive trees to the purchase and sale of real estate, both subjects in which he had an interest and she considerable expertise.

"Ay, Madre," the portly warrior invariably said at the end of one of their discussions, "the pity of it is that you ever took the veil!"

"It is just as well I did, if you ask me," she almost equally invariably replied, inferring goodness knows what. This always had the effect of making the General wheeze and splutter with delight at whatever interpretation he put on her inference.

But their relationship which was known to everyone, and likened by some to that of Saint Teresa of Avila with the then King of Spain, was a useful one. Between discussing matters of mutual concern they were freely able to exchange information about the war without causing suspicion.

"And if Soult should attack us," asked Soledad on one occasion, "would you fight, General?"

"To my last box of cigars, Madre. To my last box of cigars. And I think we shall give a good account of ourselves. The militia are coming on well. It's only the regular officers I worry about. They are all *señoritos* of the worst sort—arrogant, idle, conceited and only concerned in pirouetting about in front of women. It's the fault of the system. Our countrymen are brave and hardy fighters, but how can you expect to have a trained, disciplined army if the officers have neither training nor discipline?"

"You soldiers don't know the meaning of discipline. If you had any idea what it is like to be a novice nun. . . . "

"Ah, there you have the advantage of us. But I have always said—and many people have heard me. Oh, yes—is that what my new recruits really need is a month in the cloister under Madre Soledad."

"Soldiers would be easy, General," she replied. "Women are far more difficult to manage." To this the General, who had a wife and seven daughters, answered with feeling.

"You're right there, Madre. A division in the field is child's play compared with running a family of women—with respect of course. Have another *copita* of manzanilla."

"Thank you General, but I must go. Frankly, I tell you I pray constantly that we don't have a siege. That is something I really dread. The children can all go home, of course, and take their chance along with their families, but there's no dispersing the nuns. And then if the French do capture the town . . . "

"You say the French, but the English are much worse from all I hear."

"But at least they are our allies."

"An invading army is an invading army," said the General levering himself out of his chair in deference to his parting guest. "But do not preoccupy yourself unduly. From what—if you will forgive me—I have seen of your good ladies they will not be too much at risk." And here the tubby General broke into such a fit of laughing and coughing that he had difficulty in saying goodbye as gallantly as he would have wished.

General Menacho, who suffered from the petticoat regime at home, was fond of saying that Madre Soledad was a man's woman. Another male with whom she got on well was Julián Sanchez, alias El Charro. Their acquaintance went back to the time when she was taking a postgraduate course in theology and moral philosophy at Salamanca. They had been introduced by Dr Patrick Curtis, principal of the Irish College there, who was friendly with the Sanchez family from Santíz. That was before the war and before tragedy struck that family and Julián took to the mountains.

It was on this firm tripartite basis—Curtis, Soledad and Sanchez—that one of the most effective intelligence networks of the Peninsular War was formed. Eventually it developed many ramifications: Divinity students Burke, O'Shea, O'Grady and O'Kelly acted as couriers for Curtis to the various Commanders in the field; Doyle and Cristóbal De Los Dolores operated from Coimbra University until their roles changed with the circumstances, and the Irish College acted as a base for Wellington's personal spy, Major Colquhoun Grant. Granto El Bueno, as he was known affectionately to the Spanish, operated behind the enemy lines invariably dressed and glowing brightly in scarlet regimentals—until he was caught by the French.

But by Christmas 1810, with Salamanca and Ciudad Rodrigo in French hands, Julián had some difficulty in maintaining himself.

One day, acting on information received from Badajoz, Julián, with a detachment of his *charros*, was scouting to the south-west of Cacares to confirm the report that the French were making a reconnaissance in force in that area.

Coming down to the plain from the Sierra de San Pedro near Malpartidas, they soon found evidence of the French presence. A whistle from an outrider brought Julián over to a small olive grove. As he approached he heard the persistent whining of dogs. Then a few yards further on he saw why his scout had called him. Crucified upside down to a bifurcated olive tree was the naked body of a man—or what had recently been a man. As was all too plain to see his genitals had been hacked out, and a closer look at this revolting spectacle revealed that these organs had been stuffed into his mouth.

At that moment a shrill whistle from a leading scout brought Julián and El Fraile up forward to a position where they could see a cloud of dust in the direction of the Trujillo road. Julián took out his glass to have a better look.

"A fairly large convoy with a six-in-hand waggon."

"How many in the escort?" asked El Fraile.

"At least a squadron of dragoons, by the looks of it."

"There's only fourteen of us here. We can't tackle a whole squadron in open ground."

"How about if we could draw them off into that quarry this side of the Hermita de la Virgen, eh? The track looks innocent enough, then you're right into it. Cataplum-plim-plom! None of the horses could get out."

"But they will probably only detach one troop to chase us. The whole convoy won't follow," said the priest.

"That doesn't matter. Once we've broken them up anything could happen. It's worth a try, eh?"

"Sure. It's worth a try."

Julián gathered his men together. "Moreno and Pepe Cojo, go to the marble quarry—you know where it is?—hide your horses and take up positions on top on either side where you can cover the basin. Give a double load of powder but only use birdshot. I want to scare them without hurting the animals. Fire when I give the order. Miguel, take six men and outflank the convoy to the south, but keep your distance. Only attack if you can exploit the situation as it develops. Trail your *garrochas* as you go to kick up the dust and make your party seem bigger. Pepe Feo and Oño, you're the best mounted. Ride out and blow a few farts at the leading files. They're bound to chase you, so lead them into the quarry. Nobody can see it from the track. Once in, jump off and climb out quick. We'll get your horses along with the French ones later. The rest of you come with me. We'll close the trap if we can get them into it. *Ojala*!" And then as an afterthought he added, "Forget what you saw here. I knew the fellow. He was a *sinvergüenza*. There will be no reprisals, understand. This is a convoy. They wouldn't have done it anyway."

Julián watched the various groups move off and then, having the shortest distance to go, set off with his own party in the direction of the quarry. Once there he was able to watch the various manoeuvres as they unfolded. He could see a considerable cloud of dust to the south-east which he presumed to be El Fraile. He could also see Oño, the half-gypsy, approaching the French column at a walk. Then suddenly, just as El Fraile had predicted he saw Oño and Pepe Feo wheel about and gallop off with a troop of dragoons at their heels. And, just as Julián had planned, the two *garrochistas*, with Oño the *mestizo* keeping just a sabre's length ahead of the leading dragoon and shouting insults, came down the innocent-looking track that led into the cul-de-sac.

And then they were inside, the dragoons reining up, muddled up, wheeling about, cannoning into one another, nobody knowing where they were, what they were doing, or what orders to give. Then two loud, almost simultaneous, blasts rang out, hugely amplified in the marbled arena, causing horses to rear, saddles to empty and, before those troopers who had kept their heads as well as their seats could get out, the narrow passage was blocked by a phalanx of long lances.

"Throw down your arms and dismount," was a phrase in French which Julián had practised—and used—many times.

And to emphasize this order another volley of bird shot reverberated round the quarry peppering horses and riders but causing more chaos than casualties.

"Better to die fighting than to be butchered by these *guerilleros*," shouted a rather elderly Captain waving his sabre gallantly. To which Julián replied:

"You will be treated as prisoners of war if you have committed no crimes against the Spanish people."

The grey-whiskered Captain looked round, realized the truth of the axiom that cavalry are useless in a confined space and, with a shrug that said everything, slowly dismounted from his charger. He walked across the arena, a slight, dignified figure, and presented the handle of his sabre to Julián.

"Life is composed of a series of humiliations," said the Captain, in passable Spanish. "It is a difficult lesson to learn."

"Your name, Captain?" asked Julián.

"Guillotin. Joseph Guillotin—but please, no jokes. My father, who was a doctor, thought that he was conferring a benefit on suffering humanity. Instead he became an instrument of the Reign of Terror, and our name is dishonoured."

"A man prepared to fight his way out of this quarry need not call his name dishonoured," replied Julián. "Now, sir. What is your business? What is the purpose of your convoy?"

"That, sir," replied Captain Guillotin, "is not for me to disclose."

"Then I shall find out for myself, sir. Disarm your men. Anyone attempting to escape will be shot. I operate strictly by the rules of war."

And leaving the two men with fowling-pieces on guard, Julián with Oño, Pepe Feo and the remaining *charros* made off in the direction of the convoy and El Fraile.

The art of using the *garrocha, acosta y derribo* as it is called, is simple in theory but 'devilish difficult in practice', as the Duque of Alburquerque, an *aficionado* of the sport, once said. To test a young fighting-bull's courage the *garrochista* rides at it at an angle from behind and catches it with his lance, blunted to prevent wounding, in the hind quarters. The bull is thus knocked to the ground and, if it has the fighting spirit, it will get up again and charge the horseman. The skill lies in catching the bull off balance, which means when its near hind leg is just off the ground. To effect a successful *acosta y derribo*, therefore, requires a high degree of horsemanship and a well-trained mount. Such was the *garrochista*'s business.

A dragoon or hussar is trained to march in column and to charge in line, but neither a troop, nor a squadron, nor a regiment of cavalry can charge something that is not there. Neither could the short carbines carried by the dragoons do any harm to the *garrochistas* so long as the latter kept separate, fluid and just out of range. In any case carbine fire on the move was useless and the Commander of the convoy decided, for whatsoever reason and despite the threat of El Fraile, to keep pushing on.

This was the situation when Julián appeared to threaten the convoy's opposite flank. Distracted by this new menace, the dragoons took their eyes off Miguel for a moment and, in that moment, two of his men, their *garrochas* levelled, galloped behind the last two troopers and, before the latter knew what was happening, toppled them over, horses and all, and dumped them in the dust. The horses, not being fighting bulls, were disinclined after such rough treatment to stay on the scene and made off leaving their riders as useless as only dismounted cavalrymen can be.

"Oju! Pity General Wellington didn't see that," said Julián.

When two more *charros* galloped up for another such attack the French rear files broke ranks to evade a similar fate. These were then cut off piecemeal and easily disarmed by Julián's group.

At this point the French commanding officer, with one troop mysteriously missing and several other men *hors de combat*, decided to call a halt and to stand, as it were, at bay round their wagon.

The result of this manoeuvre brought about a stalemate. The *charros* were far too few to attack a superior force and the Frenchmen, encumbered by their heavy wagon which for some reason they were not prepared to abandon, were too slow to fight their way out to freedom. The adversaries could thus have remained making faces at each other indefinitely but for a new and unforeseen development.

Amidst shouts, shrill whistles, cracking of whips, and much waving and gesticulation, a cannon drawn by a team of mules and accompanied by a ragged gun-crew, trundled on to the field. At the head, surrounded by a villainous-looking posse variously mounted, some riding pillion, others running holding on to stirrup-leathers, was a picaresque individual wearing back to front a French General's cocked hat complete with plumes.

The wearer was instantly recognized by Julián and his men as El Oso who would have described himself as a *partida*, though the line between partisan and bandit was in his case a fine-drawn one. El Oso, The Bear, operated from the Sierra de Gredos and the captured French field-piece was his latest and most prized acquisition. This, with a great deal more shouting and cracking of whips, he now brought forward to within 500 yards of the French convoy and swiftly prepared for action.

El Oso's gunners, deserters from the artillery, turned out to be quite efficient. Bracketing professionally, their first shot fell short, the second over-reached, and the third, to the amazement of all, scored a direct hit on the French wagon and, in doing so, blew a hundred thousand pieces of golden coin into the bodies of the men and horses surrounding it and up into the air to distribute a glittering fortune far and wide across the field.

The French Commander was himself killed instantly for the price of five louis d'or which entered various parts of his body. Thus was the day won for Spain.

Luckily for some, El Oso's men were far too busy picking up the loot and gouging coins out of the dead and wounded to bother about cutting throats. El Oso himself, who had great respect for Don Julián, came to a surprisingly equitable arrangement over the gold. Both leaders likewise agreed that such a large number of prisoners would be an inconvenience since no regular army, either Spanish or British, to whom they could be handed over was near at hand. Divested of their accoutrements the Frenchmen were therefore turned loose to fend for themselves as best they could in a hostile land.

Little Captain Guillotin, taking formal leave of Julián, reiterated his view that life was just one humiliation after another, and walked off very dignified, but slightly bandy, at the head of his men.

Madre Soledad gratefully received in due course a generous, but anonymous, contribution towards the upkeep of the convent. She was only mildly curious as to why there was a blackish, tacky substance adhering to some of the gold coin.

CHAPTER FIVE

THE GOLD APPROPRIATED by Julián Sanchez and El Oso had been destined for the Prince of Essling, for such was the title Napoleon had been pleased to confer upon the soldierly but strictly non-aristocratic Marshal Masséna. As Jimmy Doyle put it, "Boney's airy dispensation of titles to all and sundry is like the act of the frog that blows itself up to frighten its enemies." The point rather escaped General Sir Brent Spencer to whom the remark was addressed, but then points usually did escape him.

"Sir Brent is an officer," Lord Wellington once said, "on whose sanity, I am sorry to say, much reliance cannot be placed."

"For whom did you say this treasure was intended?" now asked Sir Brent.

"For Marshal Masséna, sir," replied Doyle who had just received the news from one of his unofficial sources.

"Masséna? What, all of it? One feller pocketing the lot?"

"It was arrears of pay for Masséna's army, sir, so I understand."

"Oh! Oh I see, I see. Thought you . . . well anyway. . . . Damned if I know what they could have spent it on even if they'd got it. Damned if I know why soldiers want to be paid at all, come to that. Only blow it on drink—if their wives don't get their hands on it first. Money mad, most of 'em. Fellows even stop to rob a dead comrade instead of getting on with the job. Seen it happen. Seen too much of it. Wouldn't pay 'em a penny if I had my way. By the way," continued the General who, on account of his seniority, had been thrust upon a reluctant Wellington as his second-in-command, "you staff johnnies should know—what is the best way of crossing the Thames these days?"

"The Thames, General?"

"Yes, yes. Can you still get across at Santarém?"

"Oh, the Tagus you mean. I'd say the bridge is intact at Santarém all right, but unfortunately at present it is in enemy hands."

"Is it? Is it? Yes, yes, of course it is. What am I talking about? Most unfortunate, though. My man left a portmanteau of mine on the other side. Very fine river, the Thames. Inconvenient if you cannot cross it, though. Really quite inconvenient. Well, I have the honour to bid you a good morning, sir."

Sir Brent Spencer made sense about one thing: there was certainly nothing for the French of whatever rank to spend their money on, even if they had any. Wellington had seen to that. With the hesitant approval of the Portuguese government he had withdrawn all stock, crops, stores, and as many of the population as could be persuaded, back behind the lines of Torres Vedras before entering them himself and sealing them off against Masséna. The Royal Navy had taken care of the rest. A flotilla of gunboats patrolling the Tagus protected his right flank while the Atlantic ocean and the fleet looked after the left and, at the same time, permitted supplies of all kinds to enter Lisbon for the benefit of the British army.

It was now the turn of the French to go hungry and the British to pack some suet round their ribs. In order to prevent his men getting fat and short of breath, however, Lord Wellington insisted on all ranks taking exercise and suggested that games and field sports made an agreeable alternative to route marches. Colonel Sydney Beckwith took the initiative at once and organized a race-meeting which was patronized by the Commander-in-Chief and in consequence had an excellent turn-out.

Such was the success of the Rifle Brigade race-meeting that racing became a popular pastime during the winter months and the frequent fixtures were well-attended by British and Portuguese alike. Beckwith started another craze. Believing that happy soldiers made good soldiers, he organized athletics and cricket and football matches in which all ranks, both commissioned and non-commissioned, were encouraged to take part. A favourite sport with the riflemen was the greasy-pig scrimmage in which a sturdy young porker of about six months was smothered in lard or oil and at a given moment released among a specific number of contestants. The first man to retain hold of it for a slow count of ten was allowed to keep the pig. Again it was Smith's 13 Platoon, in the person of Bombproof Palmer, who showed the best form in this rewarding recreation.

Balls, picnics and parties were all the rage that winter of 1810–1811, as were musical soirées and amateur theatricals. In the latter category the 95th Rifles' production of *The Rivals* by Richard Brinsley Sheridan achieved a *succès de scandale*. The first night (which also happened to be the last) promised to be a brilliant affair with a large audience including a number of distinguished officers, some of the nobility and gentry of Lisbon, and one or two English ladies including that famous amazon, Mrs Dalbiac. The dramatis personae included Captain Patrick Uniacke as Sir Lucius O'Trigger, Mr Daniel Cadoux as Sir Anthony Absolute, and Mr Harry Smith as Mrs Malaprop.

Within the theatrical profession there is an unspoken, but generally understood (though not invariably practised), prohibition against the imbibing by actors of ardent spirits or other alcoholic beverages before a performance. The reasons for such constraint are obvious. 'First-night nerves' are faced by the thespian with the same fortitude as the enemy is faced by the soldier. This was a fact overlooked, or perhaps not fully appreciated, by the heroes of Corunna and Busaco acting in the play. Looking through chinks in the sewn-together army blankets that constituted the curtain, they found the audience far more intimidating than La Grande Armée. A little 'jumping powder', they agreed, was therefore the order of the day.

All went well in Act One with the cast warming to its work and Daniel Cadoux showing considerable histrionic talent. The applause that followed the first act curtain did much to encourage the cast and it was generally felt in the interval that another little drop of brandy, thoughtfully provided by the stage manager, wouldn't do them any harm.

At the outset of Act Two, however, Mrs Malaprop (Harry Smith) launched herself on stage only to find that Sir Anthony

Absolute (Daniel Cadoux) was standing on her skirt. The reverse was only a momentary one, however, though it did make Smith feel a little uncertain of his lines. The action proceeded nevertheless and Cadoux, feeling the audience responding to him personally, and wishing to embellish his performance with some additional 'business', took a move that had not been prescribed in rehearsal. The result was that, once again, Smith, when required to cross the stage, found Cadoux standing on his skirt. Mrs Malaprop was now clearly heard to speak a line which Mr Sheridan had certainly never written; "If you stand on my goddam skirt again, I'll black your bloody eye." There was a shocked silence, a few titters, and a shout of "Go it, guv'nor!" from the back of the auditorium. Then an audible voice from the prompt side gave the cue and the play staggered into motion once more.

Backstage during the scene-change hot words and cold looks were exchanged until the producer, one Lieutenant Orlando Felix who, having had some experience with Brasenose College Dramatic Society, calmed the fractious parties with a glass of champagne which he had been reserving for after the show. Mr Cadoux apologized handsomely to Mr Smith and the curtain went up for Act Three.

This time it was not Cadoux's fault—he was in fact several feet away—but that of a stage carpenter who had left a large nail sticking out of a heavy property screen. In executing a sort of whirling flounce (rehearsed) Smith now cannoned into the screen (unrehearsed) and caught his skirt on the nail. His next move more or less tore the garment away revealing the nether half of the actor in his small-clothes. Concerned only with his personal predicament, Smith did not heed the cries from the audience of "Heads!" and "Tally-ho!" until the huge screen, which had been teetering back and forth, finally crashed down on top of him.

It was at this moment that the man who had so often on the battlefield saved the day, now did so again. Lord Wellington got to his feet and, calling "Bravo!" in a loud voice, started to clap vigorously. Then, after a few tentative jerks, the curtain came down with a rush.

The following morning a notice was posted up outside the theatre (in fact a ruined chapel) announcing that no further performances of *The Rivals* would take place owing to the indisposition of the leading lady.

In such agreeable ways did Wellington's army within the confines of the Lines of Torres Vedras spend its leisure, while the Frenchmen starved at the gates.

But then one morning a messenger arrived at headquarters. Marshal Soult, who also went by the comic-opera title of the Duke of Dalmatia, had moved north from Andalusia and was threatening Badajoz in force.

"Hullo, Alex, are you sick?" asked the General looking at Gordon's white face as he announced the news.

"Not at all, my Lord. Why do you ask?"

"What's the matter with Alex?" asked his Lordship when Gordon had left the room. "He looks as mouldy as an old potato."

"He's said nothing to me, sir," answered Fitzroy Somerset, "but—well, it could be an affair of the heart, my Lord—that is, I think so, probably."

"Seems to be a plague of that sort of thing these days. Just heard from my brother, Mornington. Tells me one of his girls, Emily, is having fits of the vapours."

"What are you planning to do about Badajoz, my Lord?" said Fitzroy, quickly changing the subject.

"Why, nothing, Fitzroy, nothing. If I'm not mistaken Menacho is well able to look after himself."

Although there had been rumours for weeks, the first palpable sign to reach Victoria and Juanita that Soult was a reality rather than a myth came with Miguelín, the nineteen-year-old son of Miguel, the bailiff of their farm at Olivenza. From the moment of his appearance it was obvious that he brought no good news.

"The French are cutting down the olive trees," he told them; then, in response to questions, he went into detail.

"At first the ordinary soldiers came. They slept in all the outbuildings and started cutting trees for firewood. My father went to their Sergeant and said if they wanted firewood why didn't they use last year's prunings which they could have free. But they soon used that up and started again on the trees. My father went to the Sergeant again, but the Sergeant said the men had to cook and eat and what could he do about it. Well that was bad enough, but then their engineers came and started to cut the whole *olivar* for timber. My father went to the engineer officer and said he was keeping a note of the number of trees cut to apply for an indemnity. But the French officer just laughed and asked my father was he the owner of the property. My father said no and the officer laughed again and told my father not to waste his time counting trees because there was going to be no indemnity and we should count ourselves lucky that Spain had been freed in the name of liberty, equality and fraternity. My father then said that if robbing people's olive trees was liberty, equality and fraternity he could do without it *and* 'Pepe Botello' which is what we call José Bonaparte because everybody knows he's a drunk. Then the French officer hit my father across the face."

Though realizing that they were now probably ruined financially, the sisters' first concern was for Miguel and his wife and their other employees of long-standing on the farm. Victoria said she would write a letter that Miguelín could take back to his parents.

"But Señorita Victoria, I am not going back. My father has only to keep his mouth shut—he and the old one—and they will be all right. Anyway what can I do against an army by myself. No, I will join the Militia here. Don Rafael Menacho is *un hombre muy valiente*. I will find Cristóbal and he will put me in touch with him."

"I espect Don Rafael is very busy at the moment," said Juanita, "but I'm sure Cristóbal will introduce you to his *commandante*, Don Andrés Miranda."

Miguelín smiled at Juanita and looked gratified. He and Juanita had been friends since childhood. Although there was a difference in age between them, she had always been a good sport, game for anything, during those holidays which the family had been in the habit of spending on the farm. But now

Miguelín noticed a change in Juanita. She was no longer the tomboy, brown legs scratched by thistles and brambles, always the first to find the smelly nests of hoopoes and to catch the *grillos* to put in a box for her 'grasshoppers' orchestra'. In other words Juanita had grown up. She even had—yes, quite decidedly—breasts now. Miguelín looked at his former playmate in amazement and Juanita, knowing what he was thinking, blushed.

"Miguelín, go and find Frasquita. You must be hungry," she said. "When you have eaten I will take you to see Cristóbal. I have to talk to him myself."

Cristóbal and Miguelín also had an easy relationship, though the friendship diminished somewhat when the former became bookish and found a vocation. But Juanita was right: Cristóbal had changed as much as anybody. The quiet seminarist had become the friendly and extrovert volunteer who cleaned his flintlock and smoked the paper cigars which were now much in vogue. And now these two, peasant boy and landlord's son, were happy to greet each other again on the old basis.

Miguelín was careful not to stare at Juanita, but he glanced occasionally and that was enough. The grubby feet shod invariably in old cactus-fibre *alpargatas* were obviously things of the past. Her strong fine-boned ankles were now encased in silk and her feet, long and small, were in pretty shoes with an elegantly curved low heel. And her hands and wrists, he had never been aware of them before. They were so fine. But at the same time they were not the useless hands of those pampered señoritas he had seen mincing about the town who evidently never chopped onions, cleaned fish, pulled chickens, or washed the dishes.

"You've changed, Juanita."

"It's been nearly three years."

"Yes, but you've changed more than that."

"Ha, it was about time, don't you think?"

"Yes—I mean, no. I mean you look very nice now. Could we—would you walk with me in the *paseo* one evening?"

"I don't expect you'll get much time for *paseando* when you've joined the Militia. Besides if the French come I don't suppose there will be a *paseo* at all."

"But we could meet perhaps—have a chat about old times at the farm and that, couldn't we?"

"I expect Cristóbal will bring you to the house sometimes when you're off duty. Look, here he comes now."

"It's all fixed," announced Cristóbal who was carrying a bundle under his arm. "You can come with me now to the store, Miguelín, to draw arms and ammunition. You'll be attested later when Don Andrés has finished in the office. Juanita, if you're going home would you take this laundry for me. And tell Frasquita to look for missing buttons—particularly the trousers. They must be sown on with thread—cotton is no good for active service."

"Hark at you! Active service, indeed. You haven't seen a shot fired in anger yet."

Miguelín smiled happily, recognizing in Juanita the cheeky tomboy beneath the trappings of a modest young lady of quality. Cristóbal, relaxed and confident in his new manly occupation, was not as riled as perhaps he might have been before by the provocations of his younger sister.

"It won't be long now, I can tell you. Don Rafael has had all the *afrancesados* rounded up and put in the *calabozo*, and quite right too. . . . Do you care for tobacco, Miguelín?" Cristóbal added, proffering a paper cigar.

"But the French are only at Olivenza," said Juanita.

"No, I don't use tobacco," replied Miguelín. "They are at Olivenza, it is true, but they say they have cavalry and artillery west of the river."

"There, you see, Juanita. Now cut off home and let me have that laundry back as soon as possible."

The Militia of Cristóbal's company were quartered near the Puerta de la Trinidad. The walk home for Juanita, therefore, was not particularly far, but the streets, and particularly the plazas, were now full of every type of military. Moreover, the narrow streets were clogged by country people with laden mules who were either bringing in stores to provide for a siege, or seeking refuge within the city walls.

Every Spanish girl is conditioned from her earliest years to the *piropo*, the dictionary translation of which is 'an amorous compliment'.

Some girls, if they do not get *piropos* in the street, worry, lose confidence in themselves, and assume they have grown old or ugly before their time. A *piropo* may be light-hearted, good-natured and witty. It can be romantic, poetic or sincere. But the collector of *piropos* must occasionally be exposed to indelicacies, sometimes of a gross nature.

Juanita's route lay through the Plaza de Cervantes and the corner of the street leading into it was occupied by a group of oafish-looking off-duty conscripts. But Juanita was not one to make a detour when her path lay straight ahead.

"*Guapa!*" said the first soldier appreciatively as she came within range.

"*Que cara mas bonita,*" said a second politely enough.

"*Sed, sed!*" gasped another, miming the extremities of thirst as a euphemism of lust.

"*Aire, aire!*" croaked yet another soldier, fanning himself as if he were about to faint from the beauty of the vision before him. But a fifth conscript poked a long, ugly neck forward and muttered into Juanita's face an obscene reference to the bundle she was carrying under her cape. 'How different it was when those decent, well-behaved Englishmen were here,' she thought. 'I wish Captain Gordon and Lord Fitzroy Somerset were with us still.'

Struggling along with her bundle she bumped into the wife of an apothecary she knew, a little dumpling of a woman who seized her in her arms. "*Ay, hija mia*, what times! What terrible times!" she said, kissing her and looking suitably stricken. "And I hear the French have cut down all your olive trees and murdered everyone on your finca. How will you live, now, you poor orphaned things? No trees, no olives, no oil, no parents, no money. *Dio mio*, how will you live? And before Juanita had time to explain that their people had not been murdered and that it did not matter a bit about the trees so long as they—old Miguel, his family and themselves—were alive, the tubby lady had disappeared into the crowd with cries of, "Poor orphans with no money. However will Juanita find a husband? *O Dio mio!*"

"I suppose she is worrying in case we owe her husband his bill," said Juanita to herself.

"Juanita! *Hola*, Juanita!" It was school-non-friend Marie Carmen, she of the black front teeth, calling to her from the other side of Calle José Lopez Prudencio.

"I've just been to your house looking for you," said Marie Carmen hurrying up officiously. "Madre Soledad wants to see you."

"Wants to see me? What for? School is closed till further notice."

"I know, but she still wants to see you. I saw her this morning and she said so. So you'd better go. I'll come with you if you like."

"No, Marie Carmen, don't bother." And seeing the look of disappointment added, "I'll tell you what it's all about later."

When Juanita arrived at the convent she found Madre Soledad arranging into neat piles a considerable quantity of gold coin. "A little windfall, child," she replied in answer to Juanita's unspoken question. "I am glad you have come. I wanted to have a word with you about your French."

"My French, Reverend Mother?"

"General Menacho is an admirable man and a brave soldier—why do you look surprised, Juana Maria? As I say, Don Rafael is a valiant, patriotic and determined soldier. It is unfortunate that there are not more like him in the Spanish army. However, he is determined to defend this town to his utmost ability—and he will. But a man can only do as much as the material at his disposal allows him to do."

"I am not sure that I quite follow—"

"Let me go on—and I am speaking to you in confidence, Juana Maria, because I think you are a sensible and reliable girl. But I do not want my words repeated to your friends—Marie Carmen, for example, who passes on everything she hears with consummate inaccuracy. What I am saying is that the General does not have absolute confidence in all the officers and men under his command."

"But surely the Militia, Reverend Mother—"

"The Militia are different. They are our fellow-townsmen and we know where their hearts and interests lie. The same cannot always be said for others."

"But, Reverend Mother I still do not understand what—"

"Be patient, child—"

"—what this has got to do with my French," said Juanita.

"—and please do not interrupt. You are quite a pretty girl nowadays and, *in loco parentis* for your dear mother, of whom I was very fond, as well as being responsible for your spiritual welfare, I must warn you."

"Warn me, Reverend Mother?"

"Yes, I have to warn you to behave with extreme discretion at all times."

The drift of the Reverend Mother's argument still evaded Juanita completely but she decided to keep quiet and hope for a revelation. It soon came.

"In the event of the French occupying this town—and I pray to God every day, and I hope you all do too, that it may never happen—you, Juana Maria, will be in a special position. Unlike ninety-five per cent of your fellow-citizens you speak French. This has advantages and disadvantages. In the first place French soldiers will want to speak to you and they may say improper things. (No worse than the Spanish soldiers I'm sure, thought Juanita.) On the other hand—and French laxity in morals, particularly since the Revolution, is notorious—some of them, particularly their officers, in their desire for communication with the opposite sex may say indiscreet things. Do you follow me? Things relating to their army's dispositions, their future movements, the state of their commissariat, their ammunition, reinforcements, pay, lines of communication —anything. In other words if by chance you should hear anything of this sort, I want to know at once. I want any and every scrap of information that might be of use to our army, or to our allies the English, in the fight to rid our country of its godless invader. Now do you understand, child, what I meant when I said I wanted to talk to you about your French?"

After the interview Juanita stood for a moment outside the convent, her thoughts confused so that she only half-heard a distant but penetrating explosion. Then something invisible came screaming overhead to pass on, diminuendo, behind the town. Then there was another identical noise ending in a dull reverberating thud. Looking up, Juanita saw part of the castle wall collapse very slowly in a cloud of yellow dust. At once everybody came out of their houses into the street yelling, crying, pointing and gesticulating. Juanita remained quite still.

"I am about to become a spy," she said to herself. "I am about to become Juana Maria De Los Dolores De Leon, the heroine of Badajoz."

CHAPTER SIX

THE FIRST SIEGE of Badajoz began on 28 January 1811. After the initial shock of being under fire the Pazenses recovered rapidly. A mass, in which special prayers were offered to Nuestra Señora de la Soledad, was said by his Grace the Bishop who subsequently gave dispensation to all able-bodied priests to volunteer for work mending fortifications and erecting barriers in the streets of the more vulnerable parts of the town. He also lifted prohibitions on nuns in enclosed orders to enable them to work in hospitals. Victoria De Los Dolores was accepted as a nurse in the Hospital Militar and Juanita, being considered too young for service in the all-male wards, was given a job as secretary-cum-coffee-maker in General Menacho's outer office. All military, militia, religious and plain citizenry alike, rallied behind the energetic leadership of General Menacho, and morale was high in the town.

Then on 19 February a General Mendizábal, who combined in one man most of the frailties of human nature, with particular emphasis on the defects of pride, jealousy, indolence and stupidity, threw away the only Spanish force of any consequence left in Extremadura in a short and ignominious battle with Soult. Thus ended any hope of relief from a Spanish source.

Juanita could hear Menacho through the wall when he received the news. Some of the words he used to describe Mendizábal, she had never heard before.

Don Andrés Miranda was with Menacho at the time. "He's a piece of shit," said Menacho. "A *mierda*, and a big pansy. I was at school with him and I can tell you: '*Joseito mariquito*' we used to call him. Yes, and I am glad he ran from the battle to save his skin because I am going to catch him and shoot him. I am going to shoot him here, right here in the Plaze de Toros de Badajoz. And the gate-money I shall give to you Andrés, my friend, and you can buy yourself two new mistresses, or build a church, or do anything you like with it. Bah!"

At noon came a party headed by a French Colonel under a white flag stating the terms Marshal Soult was prepared to offer for the surrender of the garrison. Not only did General Menacho, with the full agreement of the town Junta under the chairmanship of Andrés Miranda, decline the offer, but he also sent back with the emissaries a dozen or so *afrancesados* being held in the town jail, thereby embarrassing the French and at the same time getting rid of superfluous mouths to feed.

One of Juanita's heroes, only slightly below Don Julián and Doña Agostina of Zaragoza, was Lord Wellington. She had seen him in the Plaza often enough and was always amused to note, when he uncovered, the sharp delineation between his red-brown face and his white forehead, a characteristic the painter Goya was to portray later.

"We've only to hold out a bit longer and Lord Wellington will drive Soult away," promised Juanita dining at home with her sister.

"I shall do no such thing," said Wellington to answer to a further enquiry by Gordon as to whether he intended to relieve Badajoz. "They have food, water, a strong fortress and a good Commander. Let them keep Soult occupied while I starve Masséna out."

Wellington was right to have confidence in Menacho. The latter saw no reason whatsoever for surrender. In fact he went into the offensive. On 25 February, the day Tom Smith, Harry's brother, was celebrating his twentieth birthday in Torres Vedras, he instigated a sortie. Throwing out a strong bridgehead of the Militia in order to give them a bit of battle experience, he pushed through two squadrons of cavalry who galloped out, sabred a crowd of siege-engineers and some unsuspecting gunners, and returned without losing a man. The French quickly counter-attacked, however, and Cristóbal with the Militia got his first shot at a Frenchman—and missed him. It became a hot little action which General Menacho watched with professional attention from the battlements. But as he was lighting a fresh cigar a French round-shot pushed it through his face. Thus died a gallant soldier.

Unaware of the death of his chief, the cavalry Colonel who had led the sortie was delighted with his achievement.

"Not only did we not lose a man—we gained one," he said, pointing to a swarthy fellow with slicked-back black hair like Brunswick leather. "What do they call you, friend?"

"My name is Antonio, but they call me Oño," said the man grinning and revealing several gold teeth. "And I have here a letter from Don Julián Sanchez for General Menacho."

"Then I will take you to the General myself as it is probable that he will wish to felicitate me after this affair."

The moment chosen by the Colonel and Oño to visit headquarters could not have been more inopportune. They coincided precisely with the arrival of stretcher-bearers bringing in the tubby—and being now headless, grotesquely short—body of their erstwhile chief. Such was the commotion at the Town Hall that Oño, despite impeccable credentials, had great difficulty in finding anybody to pay attention to him. Beyond wondering briefly what a rather villainous gypsy was doing there nobody gave him another glance nor a second thought. Eventually deciding that Don Andrés Miranda was the sanest-looking person present, Oño seized him by the wrist and slapped the packet into his hand.

"Read that, caballero," he said "and mark it well, for it comes from the hand of Don Julián Sanchez."

Despite the general hubbub the name of Julián Sanchez registered with Don Andrés sufficiently for him to break away from the vociferous crowd and to open the letter. Dismissing Oño with a brief word of thanks and a handshake, he started to read but had hardly got through the rather flowery preliminaries when he was surrounded once again by members of the Junta and several senior officers disputing loudly and simultaneously the claims of various candidates to succeed to the command. By right of seniority the job went to a staff General called Imaz who was a master of logistics but whose knowledge and experience of arms were as minimal as his stomach for fighting. Those, including Andrés Miranda, who were aware of the infirmity of purpose and pusillanimity of this man, opposed his appointment hotly. But a vote taken by the Junta went in favour of the 'safe' man; Imaz was appointed Governor, and the meeting broke up in a flurry of recriminations and Don Julián's letter was forgotten.

By this time Oño had already left the building. Furious that he had risked his life only to be received with so little consideration, he only briefly recorded the piquant face of a girl seated at a desk who seemed so fascinated by all that was going on about her.

When everybody had gone Juanita started to tidy up. Lying open on the table where Don Andrés had left it was the letter that Oño had cleverly brought into the town by joining the sortie from the enemy lines, an act that required the timing and nerve of a bull-fighter.

Juanita had never had much of a conscience about reading other people's correspondence, nor had any such embargo been put upon her with regard to papers in the office. The document was signed by one who called himself El Charro. Its message was to the effect that Masséna was at the end of his tether—the tether being his almost non-existent lines of communication—that his army was starving and that, in consequence, he was bound soon to retreat. The exhortation to General Menacho, to whom the letter was addressed, was that Badajoz should hold out at all costs in the knowledge that the retreat of Masséna would necessitate the withdrawal of Soult. In short, relief was only a question of time. All this Juanita related to Victoria at home that evening.

"But who is El Charro?" asked Victoria.

"I haven't the slightest idea."

Presently Cristóbal arrived who, having just smelt powder for the first time, had become intoxicated with its heady aroma.

"Hullo everybody. Have you heard about today?"

"Of course we have, Tobi. What a tragedy. Poor Don Rafael. What shall we do without him?" responded the sisters antiphonally. This was not quite the reaction that Cristóbal had hoped for.

"Ah, yes. Poor man. A soldier's fate. He that lives by the sword. . . . We are burying him with full military honours tomorrow. Did you hear about the sortie?"

"Yes," answered Victoria. "I believe Colonel Gómez led a very gallant charge."

"Yes, but it was the Militia that made the bridgehead for them and covered their withdrawal against a strong counter-attack."

"Was Miguelín there?" asked Juanita innocently.

"I suppose he was. I was there, too, in case you're interested."

"Did you shoot anybody, Tobi?" asked Juanita.

"Uh, it's very hard to tell in that sort of scrimmage," lied Cristóbal. "Somebody seemed to go down when I fired. We had two fellows wounded very close to me."

"Oh, that's right," said Victoria. "Two militiamen came into hospital. One had quite a nasty sprained ankle and the other had cut himself on his own bayonet. By the way, who's El Charro?

"Don't tell me you've never heard of El Charro. He's one of the most famous *guerilleros* in the country. Why do you ask?"

"Apparently somebody brought an important despatch from him through the French lines today."

"I can't believe you've never heard of him. Why, only recently he ambushed an enemy pay convoy. The waggon with the money blew up and all the escort were riddled with louis d'or. They said it took hours digging the coins out of the bodies."

"Oh, my God!"

The sudden exclamation escaped Juanita before she could suppress it. She had just remembered the neat piles of gold coins on Madre Soledad's table.

Some 200 miles away, near Torres Vedras, a military exercise of a more frivolous nature was taking place. Ever since the Green Jacket race-meeting, when certain riflemen had been 'on to a good thing', Sniper Jackman had coveted Pongo Prickett's donkey. Prickett himself was not unwilling to negotiate but he considered any offers Jackman had so far come up with to be derisory. The non-negotiations had been going on for weeks and the frustration was driving Jackman mad.

"I'll tell you what we'll do," said Jackman suddenly one day. "We'll shoot it out."

"What d'you mean shoot it out?" replied the corpulent Corporal.

"Why like we done before. You hold a target in your hand at two hundred and fifty yards and I shoot, then arsy-versa."

"I don't hold no target not at two-fifty I don't. No, mate, sorry. Not for old Nosey hisself."

"All right then, two hundred."

"And what do I get if I win?"

This made Jackman bare his black and broken teeth in some sort of inward pain. He knew there was only one thing Prickett wanted. It was a hunting rifle, made in Lexington, Virginia, in 1775, and captured in the American War of Independence. It was very long but it had been made with loving care by a master craftsman and was the most accurate weapon that Jackman or any other rifleman had ever handled. Prickett wanted it. Jackman treasured it, but he wanted Prickett's donkey with its earning potential even more.

"All right, then," he said, "I'll put up the Lexington."

"You're on," said the other.

It did not take five minutes for the news to get round that a shooting match was about to take place between two of the best marksmen in the battalion and, by the time a one-foot square target had been drawn and cut out, quite a crowd had assembled on a piece of flat ground behind the camp. The distance was paced out by Sergeant Brotherwood who was appointed umpire. Brotherwood flipped a coin, Jackman called "heads" and won the toss. Prickett accordingly waddled off, pigeon-toed, to the two-hundred-yard mark and held out the target at arm's length.

Jackman now adopted his favourite shooting posture, lying on his back, the sling looped behind his elbow, and the muzzle of his rifle resting between his toes.

He took a long time taking aim but Prickett's arm never wavered. Then his shot rang out, Prickett shouted 'magpie' and when this was confirmed by Brotherwood, encouraging shouts and catcalls went up from the Jackman supporters. The two men then changed places.

Prickett, being a man of minimal agility, adopted the kneeling position. He licked his thumb, rubbed it over the foresight, took quick aim and fired. There was silence while Brotherwood crossed over to Jackman. After a moment's hesitation Brotherwood shouted 'bull' and a roar went up from the crowd. But Jackman appeared unconvinced and held the target up to the sky the better to see the hole.

From his slothful and untidy appearance it seemed impossible that Prickett could ever move fast, but on very rare occasions he did. This was one of them.

In a second he was on his feet and in thirty seconds he had reloaded. Jackman, still examining the target held above his head, was aware of nothing until a second shot, again hitting the hand-held target, nearly 'gullied him shitless', as Prickett afterwards put it.

"Ha, ha! You'll not get my burro, Jackman," shouted Prickett, and the crowd went wild.

Jackman was demented. Shaking the target at Prickett in his rage he threw it on the ground and attempted to trample on it. But Prickett had already reloaded and, taking a standing shot, hit the target a third time almost knocking it from under Jackman's feet.

By this time the crowd was in a frenzy, individuals rolling on the ground, thumping each other on the back, throwing their caps in the air, chi-iking and cat-calling like the inmates of Bedlam at the full moon.

Jackman was now beyond anything and started to run like the devil to where he'd left his own rifle—possibly with homicidal intentions. It was well, therefore, that Harry Smith appeared at this moment.

"Sergeant Brotherwood, what the devil's going on here?"

"Well, sir, like as you might say—"

"Don't tell me. Fall in the platoon. We're on half an hour's notice to move."

At his headquarters not far away Lord Wellington was finishing a letter to his bootmaker, Mr Hoby:

> ' . . . and have the goodness to make them round, that is to say flat, at the top, not in the Hessian style. Further they should be easy fitting from ankle to calf that they may be put on and pulled off without difficulty in wet weather.'

As he was appending his signature Alex Gordon came in to report the return of a patrol of the 14th Light Dragoons from Santarém.

"Lieutenant O'Malley, my Lord," announced Gordon, showing in the patrol Commander.

"O'Malley? Are you not the damn feller who was taking side-bets with young Smith during that coursing-meeting at Campo Maior?"

"Bets, my Lord? Why, I—er—might have ventured a trifling sum, though I can't call to mind—er—"

"Hmm. . . . So Masséna's gone, eh?"

"Cleared out bag and baggage, my Lord. Not a sinner in sight."

"I thought he would break cover pretty soon."

"There's neither hide nor hair of him to be seen in Santarém, sir."

"You are one of the Galway O'Malleys, I dare say."

"I am indeed, my Lord."

"Ever get a day's hunting at Tuam or Loughrea?"

"Any time you are out that way, my Lord, we'd be happy to give you a day with the Blazers."

"I should like that. Meanwhile we have another fox to hunt. . . . Alex, I want to see Generals Craufurd and Stapleton Cotton right away."

CHAPTER SEVEN

JULIÁN SANCHEZ's prediction had been correct. Masséna, with the Light Division on his tail, began his retreat on 3 March. Not that this had the slightest effect on Badajoz. General Imaz and his play-it-safe faction were in command and Andrés Miranda and the other advocates of an aggressive policy were disregarded. In consequence morale that had been so high under 'Fighting Menacho' now took a plunge; the soldiers went about dirty and disgruntled, a clandestine black market of foodstuffs and other commodities came into being, and civilians started to talk about the advisability of surrender in order to avoid the sacking of the town. Only the Militia under the command of Andrés Miranda tried to hold their heads high, but it required a conscious effort. Imaz himself was perpetually unavailable, closeted with the Junta which had lately been rigged with his own cronies including a suspect *afrancesado*. He, the Commander-in-Chief, never appeared to his troops, nor was he ever seen on the battlements.

Soult for his part played a soldierly game. Knowing that the best way to help Masséna was to get inside Badajoz and stay there, he kept the pressure up on the town. Then on 9 March he ordered an assault in sufficient strength to look serious. The main attack came against the Militia at the Puerta de la Trinidad. The militiamen beat off the first wave, but then, just before dark, the French came on again. Miguelín, who was beside Cristóbal at the time, saw the latter fall over backwards.

"What's the matter with you, Cristóbal?"

"I don't know. Feels like something hit me."

"What d'you mean hit you? Get up, they're coming again."

But Cristóbal could not get up. He looked down at his chest and was surprised to see blood coming through his tunic.

"Oh, God, I'm bleeding. Help me, Miguelín." But Miguelín was too busy firing and reloading his musket.

"Get up, Tobi, get up," he kept repeating. "Get up and shoot, man."

At the Hospital Militar the wounded were coming in fast and soon there was a line of stretchers right down the main passage bearing men waiting for the surgeon. Victoria expected to be there all night.

Elsewhere in the town old Frasquita, who had been queueing for bread, got caught by the bombardment and took refuge in a cellar next door to the baker. Juanita was therefore alone in the house. She wanted to go out and see if she could find Cristóbal. She wanted to be up there on the battlements as an inspiration to the men, like—but she had promised Victoria not to leave the house. Presently the firing seemed to quieten down, and all of a sudden Juanita got a feeling of unease, of something bad about to happen. Then they came pounding on the door. Miguelín and two other young fellows whom Juanita vaguely knew struggled in carrying Cristóbal.

"Sorry, Juanita," said Miguelín. "Where shall we put him?"

"*O Dios mio!* Quickly, put him there on the sofa."

When they had laid Cristóbal down they stood for a moment awkwardly. Then one of them, nudging Miguelín, said "Come on" in a low voice.

"I'm sorry," said Miguelín whose right cheek, Juanita noticed, was bruised and blackened from his flintlock. "We've got to get back. We're not really allowed—"

The young men were embarrassed and got out of the house with clumsy haste. When they were gone Juanita turned to Tobi. His face was very pale under his olive skin. His hands, where they were not covered in dried blood, had gone a yellowish colour. They lay covering the wet bloody patch on his tunic; at the same time his eyes anxiously sought those of his sister as if wishing to explain the whereabouts and nature of his wound.

Juanita sat down beside him and, cradling his head in her arm, began to pray for the intercession of Our Lady. She said a decade of the Rosary and said private prayers to Our Lady of Solitude. But Tobi did not speak, nor did he move. He just kept staring at his sister as if he wanted to explain something to her.

After a while, Juanita became aware that he had not blinked for some time. She then realized that he was dead. She could no longer feel her arm that had been supporting him. With difficulty she pulled it out and laid him down.

When the pins and needles in her arm had ceased she set about doing those things that she knew should be done. Juanita closed Tobi's eyes and kissed him. She washed his bloody hands that had been clutching his wound and placed a crucifix between them. She closed the curtains of the room and lit two candles which she placed either side of his head. After that she knelt beside the sofa and said all the prayers she knew by heart. In all this time Juanita did not cry. It was only Frasquita, when she came in with her noisy grief, that forced the tears out of her.

Marshal Soult's attack had been more of a threat than a full-scale operation. On the 10th once again, but in more peremptory terms, he demanded the surrender of the town. Imaz spent most of the day in irresolute conference. Then at six o'clock in the evening, accepting abject terms, he capitulated. The following morning, 11 March 1811, the French army took possession of Badajoz.

Whenever an army remains static for any length of time it collects baggage. Despite Wellington's efforts to keep his troops on their toes during their winter of peace and plenty, he somehow failed to prevent them equipping themselves with a great many 'comforts' such as feather beds, immense candlesticks (church property?) and a great assortment of livestock.

Jenny Cochrane, the wife of Rifleman Cochrane, though it would be quite wrong to class her as baggage, was a case in point. A true daughter of Cathleen ni Houlihan, and as lovely to look at as An Roisin Dubh, she could be seen riding up the valley of the river Zezere, her fine legs (she never wore shoes) hanging over the flank of a sturdy donkey to which was attached, in addition to blankets, pans, kettles and other domestic appurtenances, a number of trussed and disaffected hens. A strong young pig, which Jenny held by a rope tied to a hind leg, and a free-running lurcher made up just one fighting-man's equipage on the march.

In the same context could be classed certain bachelor elements of 13 Platoon who had clubbed together to invest in a small herd of goats, together with attendant Portuguese goat-boy, which, while providing them with milk and, occasionally, meat on the march, did nothing to keep the roads clear for essential traffic.

Dissatisfied with progress in the pursuit of Masséna, whose lean and hungry troops were making good speed towards Spain and fresh sources of revictualment, Wellington decided for once to observe the rear, rather than the forward, echelons of his army. Surrounded by a larger staff than usual (his intentions being administrative rather than combative) he rode to the top of a hill which commanded a good view of the general axis of advance.

After expressing amazement at the numbers of camp followers and the quantity of baggage his eye was caught—as was everybody else's—by the rhythmical flashing of something persistently catching the sun.

"How far away would you say that was, Fitzroy?" asked his Lordship of the Military Secretary.

"About five miles, my Lord."

"Well it's actually near seven if my map is correct. Who is it do you suppose?"

"Should be the tail of the Light Division," volunteered Colonel Murray, the Quartermaster-General.

"Send a galloper, Fitzroy, to find out who and what is causing that remarkable flashing. . . . Does it not strike you, Ned," went on the Commander-in-Chief addressing the Adjutant-General, who happened to be his brother-in-law, Colonel the Hon. Edward Pakenham, "that in a sunny country like this a far-reaching reflection might be a useful means of making signals? Look into it, Ned, won't you."

It took the Dragoon galloper three-quarters of an hour to trace the source of the intermittent flash. When he came upon it in the baggage-train of the Green Jackets it turned out to be a full-length gilt mirror loaded on a mule. The rifleman leading the mule explained that the huge looking-glass was "The property of my officer, Mr Cardo. He likes it for dressing up. He's very particular about his clothes, yes. You should see him sometimes. If I don't have a smoothing-iron at the ready when he is preparing to go out I don't half catch it, I can tell you."

Before the dragoon had had time to make his report to headquarters Alex Gordon came galloping up to the Commander-in-Chief. He looked unhappy.

"Hello, Alex," said the General. "You look as if you have brought me bad news."

"Very bad, sir, I'm afraid. General Menacho has been killed and his successor surrendered Badajoz more or less unconditionally on the 11th."

Wellington remained thoughtful for a few moments. "Today is the 14th, is it not, Ned? If we had been using light instead of flags for signals we should have had this news the same day—not that it would have made a damn bit of difference."

The Commander-in-Chief remained silent as they resumed the march. Then he turned to Pakenham and Murray: "I wish all Commanders to be informed that they are to reduce their baggage-trains by half. From now on if the roads are blocked to essential services for even one minute I will reduce them even further." There was a pause, then: "The fall of Badajoz will have to be paid for in British lives, you know."

Later, when he found himself riding more or less alone with Somerset, he said, "You know, Fitzroy, I miscalculated about one thing."

"What was that, my Lord?"

"It never occurred to me that Menacho would get himself killed."

"No sir. It did not occur to me either."

"Tell me, Fitzroy. Why do you think Alex was looking so shook just now?"

"Well, sir, as I mentioned before, I think he left his heart in Badajoz."

"Oh, in Badajoz, is it? I had no idea. Would it be indiscreet to enquire—?"

"A married lady, my Lord."

"Oh dear. I hope he will do nothing rash."

"You know Alex, my Lord."

"Matrimonial entanglements, Fitzroy. Extra-matrimonial entanglements. They can bring down the best of 'em."

"True, my Lord."

"Take Lord Uxbridge, Fitzroy."

"Indeed, my Lord."

"And my brother, Wellesley."

"A very salutary lesson to all of us, if I may say so."

"Mark it well, Fitzroy."

Harry Smith had been given permission by Colonel Beckwith to go forward with Charles O'Malley on a reconnaissance in depth in the direction of Sabugal and the upper reaches of the Coa river. For Harry this was a welcome relief from the tedium of route-marching and for O'Malley, apart from the companionship, it was a help since Harry spoke Spanish. To mark the occasion of going on patrol with the Light Dragoons Harry rode a new acquisition, a very small but strong thoroughbred Andaluz called Chiquito. Rifleman West came too, riding Paddy. The weather was fine, the country beautiful and it occurred to Harry that perhaps God might be in his Heaven after all.

The banks of the Coa were conspicuous for enormous granite boulders, round in shape, and some at least twenty feet high. Between these grew scrub-oak and tamarisk to the water's edge. Among the rock and scrub sang and flew a variety of birds. Harry, attracted by a rich contralto fluting, was lucky enough to glimpse a pair of golden orioles, the cock-bird flamboyant in his yellow and black uniform. Beyond, and in contrast to the elegant oriole, on a boulder perched a rare blue rock thrush, solitary in its gunmetal plumage. Then Harry's eye was caught by a flash of sapphire streaking downstream.

"Did you see the kingfisher, Charley?" he called out to his friend.

"I bloody well did not. I'm keeping me eye on that cool-looking customer on the bridge there. He's no ordinary bog-trotter I'm telling you."

Harry focused on a raffish-looking character sitting on a bridge quietly observing them through the smoke of a cigar which he held between his teeth.

"*Oiga, amigo*," called out Harry. "*Ingleses.*"

"*Es muy evidente*," replied the other.

"*Los Franceses, donde están?*"

For an answer the fellow, without getting up from his seat, made a dismissive gesture with his cigar indicating that the French were far enough away to be of no consequence.

When Harry finally arrived at the bridge the man rose in a leisurely manner to his feet, threw away his cigar and extended a hand.

"We have been waiting for you, *amigo*. Where have you been?" he said and smiled, revealing a number of gold teeth. "The French passed through here two days ago. We expected you to be treading on their coat-tails."

"And who's 'we', might I ask?" said Harry, nettled at the suggestion that either Lord Wellington or the Greenjackets, or even the 14th Light Dragoons, might be backward in the chase. The man, clearly delighted with the effect of his remarks, laughed loudly and slapped Harry on the shoulder which did nothing to improve the latter's temper.

"They call me Oño," he said. "I am the special man of Don Julián Sanchez, he who has much fame and is known also as El Charro."

"Isn't that the guerrilla chappie?" put in Charles O'Malley who had been waiting for some elucidation of the conversation.

"My chief, Don Julián, is a friend of General Belinton. He wants to see you now."

"And I'd like to see him," replied Harry with asperity.

Harry had long been intrigued by the idea of the *guerilleros* and badly wanted to see what the famous El Charro was really like. Charles O'Malley, rather untypically, counselled caution, at which Harry laughed and replied that he presumed El Charro could wipe out their whole patrol if he cared to do so, so why not go and meet him man to man and face to face. Finally it was agreed that Harry, with Rifleman West, should go with Oño and that the dragoons should continue with their legitimate patrol.

Oño left the main road taking a mule-track leading in a north-westerly direction which soon started to ascend into pine woods. The gypsy, as Harry assumed him to be, had an annoying habit (as Harry felt) of turning round in his saddle and staring at them. Even the usually imperturbable West finally became irritated. "Got your eyeful, mate, have you?" he said in English.

West and Oño then entered into the sort of nonsensical exchange—it could hardly be called a conversation—that is typical the world over between soldiers of different nationality and tongue. Harry, enjoying a moment of peace and freedom from responsibility, let Chiquito's rein slacken and dropped behind. His thoughts ranged over all the things that had—or more specifically had not—happened to him since the approach march to Talavera on his second Peninsular campaign. A sense of non-achievement was beginning to spoil his holiday mood when he was brought sharply back to thc present by a shrill whistle, quickly followed by another answering one. Oño and West were out of sight, but now Harry noticed that the bridle-path was heavily marked with fresh hoof-prints. He gave Chiquito a slight nudge and the little horse, with a happy shake of his Arab head, broke into a canter and quickly covered the ground which separated him from his stable companion.

Harry found Oño, with West, talking to two armed men whom he rightly took to be sentries. Unlike Oño, who wore a round velvet Rondeño cap over a brightly coloured head-scarf in the Andaluz style, these men were all in black with wide-brimmed hats in the matter of the *garrochistas*, or *charros*, of Salamanca.

The sentries stared with fascination at Harry and would have liked to have examined his horse and all his accoutrements had not Oño led the party on.

The country now opened up into a sandy plateau shaded by well-grown umbrella-pines. Harry's idea of a *guerillero* hide-out had been conditioned by adventure stories about bandits and smugglers' caves. He was not at all prepared for what he saw when he came to it. Instead of a scene of dissipation and squalor he saw a camp that would have done credit to a British cavalry regiment. Under the trees were properly laid out horse-lines and, at them, were men at 'stables' grooming their mounts in a thorough and diligent fashion. In a sandy open space in the centre, fire-arms were piled in neat rows ready for instant use. At the far end of this open 'square', or plaza, again under the umbrella-pines, were a number of *chozas*—huts made of cane and roofed with chestnut branches. A little way off to the right was a cook-house area where a number of men were busy stoking wood fires and cutting vegetables into several huge earthenware casseroles from which ascended a delicious aroma of stewing mutton flavoured with mountain herbs. And nearby there was even a mud bread-oven that had obviously been in use that very morning.

Everywhere in the camp there was activity. Behind the horse-lines two farriers worked at an anvil, and near them stood a number of horses, slack-hocked over their own shiny green droppings, waiting to be shod. Those not occupied with horses were cleaning flint-locks, sorting ammunition, mending saddles or spoke-shaving staves for *garrochas*. Only a few men, those who had come off sentry-go or who had just returned from a patrol, Harry presumed, were sleeping comfortably under the pine trees.

Dismounting and leaving the horses with West, Harry followed Oño to one of the huts which was open on the side facing the square. In it were two men at a table who broke off their discussion to rise when Harry entered. One was a big bearded fellow and the other—Harry for years kept a very clear memory of this first impression—looked, apart from his charro costume, as much like a Rifle Brigade officer as anybody he knew in the regiment. In fact, so strong was this sensation that Harry felt that he must know him, while at the same time discounting this as being a sheer impossibility.

This man, who now came forward to greet Harry, appeared to be a little more than thirty years old. His hair was light-brown, just beginning to show signs of grey. He was tall for a Spaniard—considerably taller than Harry—and well built. He had a clean-shaven red-bronzed face with the usual white forehead above the cap line. A longish high-bridged nose ended at a friendly mouth that had a deep cleft in the upper lip. This lip was made slightly asymmetrical by an inch of white scar-tissue in the corner of it. This had the effect of making him seem always to be smiling slightly. His only Latin characteristic, Harry thought, was a pair of very large dark eyes. Once again Harry felt confused, searching his memory (in all the wrong places like the Mess at Shorncliffe) for a name to the face that he felt he ought to know.

"I am Julián Sanchez," the man said, shaking hands.

"And I am Harry Smith."

"*Hari Esmeet de los Rifleros, verdad? Encantado,*" he said and indicated a chair.

"You know," said Harry, "I could have sworn we had met before."

Julián laughed. "Everybody mistakes me for Pedro Romero the great torero, but I'm not so famous."

"I'm not so sure about that. You are already very well known."

"But the difference is this, they know Pedro Romero by sight but they only know me by name. Would you like a cigar?"

Harry declined and Julián, having dismissed Oño with orders to look after Rifleman West and the horses, lost no time in getting down to business.

"We had been expecting you before this but I think you had trouble getting unstuck from Lisbon, eh?"

Harry did not care for this insinuation, but in honesty he felt bound to agree.

"But I am glad you have come. It is necessary for me to talk to someone from the English before they engage with Masséna," Sanchez continued. "It is lucky for me that you speak Castellano. Perhaps your General does not know that the French have now received reserves of food and warlike stores and ammunition that had been intended for Rodrigo. So now they may stand and fight, maybe near here on the Spanish frontier, if not, further back at Ciudad Rodrigo. But my guess is that it will be here at Fuentes de Oñoro. But Masséna, he will fight now that he has got food and ammunition, that is sure. What I want your *ilustrissimo* General Belinton to know is that I can put three hundred horsemen in the field at an hour's notice. That could be a help. Now I have infantry too, but they would not be of use in a pitched battle because that is not their way. They know only our guerrilla tactics. But my *garrochistas* are trained to fight like any other cavalry. You understand?"

Harry, always at home with countrymen, particularly horsemen, was beginning to like this no-nonsense guerrilla leader.

"I understand," he answered, "and I will tell General Headquarters. Masséna must be feeling a different man now that Soult has taken Badajoz."

"Taken Badajoz? He didn't take Badajoz. He bought it. Soult bought Imaz. . . . You look surprised?"

"Well, it is a bit outside my experience, buying and selling of fortresses."

"You mean you have no traitors in your country?"

Harry felt pricked by this remark but his growing respect for the Spaniard curbed his instinct to make a sharp riposte.

"Who knows. Our country has not been overrun by the French."

"Right, my friend. And nobody can tell how people will behave until they have experienced it."

Harry changed the subject or, rather, returned to the original one. "Badajoz is clearly the key to this campaign."

"Without Soult inside the Badajoz fortress Masséna would have had to go all the way back to Salamanca or beyond. Now he can turn here and give you a *puñatazo*—how do you say?"

"A bloody nose."

"Yes, and I say he will do it here at Fuentes de Oñoro because from Fuentes he can also support his fortress at Alameda. That garrison is still in your path."

"You seem to have made a very thorough appreciation of the situation, Don Julián."

Julián's normally agreeable expression changed. His mouth with the white scar ceased to smile. He leant forward across the table.

"Why are you fighting here, Señor Esmeet? Why?"

Harry, never averse to defending himself, was again taken aback by the suddenness and seeming ferocity of the question but, for the second time in their conversation, he kept his temper. He even managed a smile. "Why? Well the first good reason I can think of is that I'm paid for it. I've taken the King's shilling. I hold the King's Commission. I am bound to fight wherever it is required of me."

"Good. I too was once a regular soldier, but that's not why I am fighting now."

"Why are you?"

Julián Sanchez suddenly reached down and grabbed a handful of the sandy soil from the ground at his feet and kissed the hand that held it. "Because this is mine," he said, raising the hand, "and no French bastard of the Gran Puta is going to take it from me," and he let the earth slowly trickle down through his fingers.

When night came and the business of the day was done, Julián took Harry round the camp. Later they found a good fire burning in front of Julián's hut and a table, supervised by the man Harry had been introduced to as 'El Fraile', being laid for supper. Soon a steaming casserole of stew was brought on together with a large fresh loaf of wholemeal bread and a two-litre jug of wine. While 'El Fraile' was dishing out the *puchero* Julián cut the bread, holding the loaf to his chest and drawing the huge blade of his clasp-knife towards him. When all were served some instinct made Harry remain standing. His instinct was right. The two Spaniards crossed themselves and the big man with a beard said Grace before sitting down to eat. This was not how Harry had imagined life with a guerrilla chief.

"Miguel is a priest," laughed Julián. "Dedicated to God and the kitchen."

Harry had never been a man who thought much about food, but the steaming aromatic dish that was set down before him was indeed food for thought. The thick reddish stew seemed to have a basis of *garbanzos* or chickpeas, in which were embedded pieces of succulent mutton and slices of red spicy *chorizo*. This ragout had clearly absorbed quantities of onion, garlic and red peppers and the whole had been flavoured, he noted, with bay leaves, oregano and thyme. Sharp set, Harry realized he was having a new experience.

The wine jug passed frequently and in the course of conversation Julián and Harry satisfied each other's curiosity as to their different ways of making war. El Fraile, who went at his victuals with the intensity of an expert, did not take much part in the talk. When, at the finish of the meal the other two discovered a mutual passion for horses, he made his excuses and went off to bed.

When he had gone Julián laughed. "Poor Miguel! He hates horses and loves sleep. He gets too much of the one and not enough of the other. Brandy?"

Harry accepted the brandy and noted that it was French, not Spanish.

"What, I wonder, makes an educated, perhaps town-bred man like your friend turn *guerillero*?" asked Harry.

"You mean that, as a patriot, why does he not serve his country through his vocation? That is an interesting point. I have never asked Miguel that question. Probably I never shall. Let me try to explain. If I were to say to you Miguel loves his country so much that—how can I say it. It is not enough that he does his best for it in his own walk of life, you understand? He feels he has to do something more to prove his love—something quite contrary to his nature. He feels that he has to *fight* which is something quite opposed to his calling. Now do you understand?"

Before answering Harry thought for a moment: a moment in which Julián filled Harry's glass and his own.

"You like the brandy?" Julián asked, laughing. "Fine champagne de Cognac. It belonged to the French Governor of Ciudad Rodrigo. He is a great gourmet—or was. We captured him *and* his brandy."

"The brandy has a subtle flavour," said Harry, putting the glass to his nose. "So has your argument. Yes, I understand you right enough but, coming from that little island of ours, I cannot pretend to feel as you and Miguel feel. We English have never been invaded—at least not in modern times. All the same, if we were I'm sure—I know—that many Englishmen who never even dreamed of becoming soldiers, men who would in any case be quite unsuitable for the job, would fight to the death to defend their country. So perhaps we are not so different after all."

Julián looked at Harry hard for a moment, then nodded. "Hari, you are a soldier, you like good horses. You like to drink wine and you eat our country *puchero* as if it were more than just food. These things are the essence of all that is good from the land—from this Extremadura land of ours. Let me tell you something. My father was *mayoral* of a bull-farm near Salamanca. You know what is *mayoral*? The man in charge. His whole life was horses and bulls and that was my life, too, until I grew up. Then I got bored as any young man gets bored, and I thought: 'I'm fed up with doing out horses' docks and looking up bulls' arses. I'll join the army.' My parents did not want me to go. They knew there would be war and they would have preferred me to stay home. But they did not make a fuss. I think my father thought joining the army might teach me a bit of sense, and he was right."

"How did you get on?" Harry was genuinely interested.

"Quite well. In two years I was a Sergeant. I might have got a commission in time but for the change in circumstances."

"What happened?"

"What happened? Napoleon invaded Spain. That's what happened. My regiment was in Andalucía at the time, doing nothing. I asked for leave to go home as Salamanca was in the direct line of Junot's advance. My Major was a decent fellow—one of a very few—and he persuaded the Colonel to let me go. That permission changed my whole life."

He paused for a moment and Harry saw that Julián's eyes were glistening as he stared into the fire. Emptying his brandy glass he turned towards Harry.

"My mother and father and one unmarried sister were at home when the French arrived. They were a party of dragoons out foraging. They wanted fodder but my father wouldn't give them any. He had hidden the grain in an old dry well and covered it with soil. They threatened him but he was stubborn, my father, so they tied them all up: my mother, my father and my sister, Rosario, and they said they would find the fodder for themselves. They didn't find it but they found the wine bodega. Of course they helped themselves and got a bit drunk. Then they came back again to make my father tell them where the grain was. He wouldn't tell them."

All the time Julián was staring into the fire with the same fierce look that he had seen earlier.

"So these bastards had a great idea. They untied my sister and tore all her clothes off. Then they raped her—six of them—right in front of my mother and father."

Harry found Julián's eyes unbearable to look at. He turned away.

"Miguel says it is God's will. It is difficult to imagine sometimes what is this grand plan God has for us all. . . . You may wonder how I know all this. There was one witness, a little girl of fourteen, a neighbour's daughter, who used to come in to help my mother in the house. When the Frenchmen came she was terrified and ran upstairs to the loft to hide. Ours is an old house and there are plenty of chinks in the old timbers. She saw everything that happened below. Another neighbour, a man who had been lying low some distance from the house, also heard shots and saw the six dragoons come out of the house and ride away. When he had got up enough courage he ran over to the house and saw what they had done. My father and mother had been shot dead and my sister had been clubbed to death where she lay naked on the floor. It was the very next day that I arrived home on leave."

There was silence when Julián had finished. Then with a sudden, almost violent, movement he sat back in his chair.

"There! I have told you. Now you know why people like Miguel and myself are fighting as partisans. I never bothered to go back to my regiment. They were no good. Well, the men were all right. But, except for my Major, the officers were useless—just conceited *señoritos* and *neñatos*. Some had courage but no sense. Most had neither guts nor gonads. None had any serious professional qualifications to be leaders of fighting men. You, Hari, were surprised that I had such a good grasp of the strategical situation here. Well, I have made it my business. I am fighting the war my way now. And though we are still small in numbers we, the *partidas*, are fighting it more successfully than any single regular Spanish unit in the Peninsula."

Julián laughed and gave Harry a friendly thump on the shoulder as he got up.

"Now we must go to bed. We have work tomorrow."

Harry, lying by the embers of the fire, stayed awake for some time, his mind full of all that Julián had said to him. Lying there, he was half aware of a certain restrained merriment (Julián did not permit late nights on operations) at a neighbouring fire. Someone was playing a guitar. Then he heard the voice—a sweet and gentle voice—of Oño singing a sad *soleá*, a gypsy song from the canon of cante flamenco, which came in quavering quarter-tones across the fire-lit night.

Esta serenía perra	In these accursed mountains
Me está jasienda pasa	I am fated to pass
Er purgatorio en la tierra.	My purgatory on earth.

It was first light when West woke him with a cup of scalding coffee.

When the time came for Harry to say goodbye to Julián, the latter offered Oño as a guide back to the Coa, but Harry declined saying that he and West could find their own way.

A roseate sun was up and glinting through the pines as Harry and West started down the mountainside. From time to time, when they came to a clearing in the trees, they could see below them the valleys hung with pockets of pink mist. The sharp air was spiked with the scent of thyme and rue.

Harry took a deep breath. Suddenly he felt purged of his earlier discontent. Being quite a religious young man, he now did what he had not done since boyhood: he thanked God for the life he had been given.

CHAPTER EIGHT

WHEN HARRY SMITH eventually found advanced Headquarters they were well forward at a village called Covilha at the foot of the Estrela Mountains.

"Hullo, Smith, where have you sprung from?" said Gordon who was himself dismounting when Harry rode up.

"From a visit to the *partidas*," replied the latter. "I've been the guest of El Charro—very interesting."

"Really? Are they in contact?"

"I can't produce any severed heads, but I've been drinking good French brandy."

"Well, hold hard a minute and I'll see if the General wants to hear about it."

"Oh, but I don't need to. . . . "

"Hold on," and the ADC disappeared inside a small and unassuming house which, never being one to advertise his presence with the pomp of a numerous and pluméd staff, Lord Wellington had chosen as his tactical headquarters.

"Which Smith? That saucy fellow in the Rifles?" said his Lordship at the mention of Harry's name. "Wants to sell me a greyhound, I suppose."

"Not that I'm aware of, my Lord," answered Gordon, smiling, and went on to explain Harry's recent contact with the guerrilla leader.

"Well, send him in for five minutes."

No sooner had Harry gone into Lord Wellington's room than Sir Brent Spencer arrived. Omitting the normal civilities he demanded an immediate interview with the Commander-in-Chief.

"His Lordship will see you in five minutes, sir."

"Five minutes? Why five minutes? Who's in there?"

"An officer of the Rifles, sir."

"Rifles? Rifles? Every Jack-a-dandy seems to get himself up in a green jacket these days. Green jacket? Green jacket? What's the matter with a red coat, that's what I want to know. A red coat's been good enough for me these last thirty years and look at me: I'm a General. I suppose they're frightened somebody might take a pot-shot at 'em." And muttering about the relative merits of Red-Coats and Green Jackets the irritable old General got out some very crumpled maps and tried to orientate himself.

"What's this place called, young man? Coventry?"

"Covilha, sir. This village is Covilha."

"Ah, yes. Here we are, Coventry."

While Sir Brent Spencer was struggling with his map and Harry Smith was giving Lord Wellington Julián Sanchez's appreciation of the situation, Rifleman West was giving his own version of the adventure to a group of grooms and orderlies minding the horses outside headquarters.

"Grub," he said, "Stacks of it! Mutton, any amount. But then they go and spoil it all. Muck it all up. Why mess up good butcher's meat with a lot of garlic and grease and stuff? One thing I can't abide is nasty messed-about foreign food."

The grooms and orderlies were inclined to agree with him though one of them, who was burnishing a glossy chestnut horse with a wisp of straw, stated a strong preference for beef as opposed to mutton.

"All very well and good," replied West, "and I wouldn't argue with you in the normal way, but certain things have to be taken into consideration—like quality now. You can take a lamb or hogget off of any hillside you like to name in any country in the world and the meat will taste sweet. But you can't do that with beef. You've got to *know* your beef. Your beef has to be *fed*. And you've got to *kill* your beef and you've got to *hang* it. It's no good knocking off your cattle any old how and expect sweet tender meat. That's why I say when it's campaigning, stick to mutton."

The groom with the chestnut did not seem altogether convinced by Rifleman West's argument.

"You can't beat good beef," he said, straightening out the saddle-cloth and pulling at a stirrup-leather.

"*Good* beef, yes. I'd be more than inclined to agree with you if you're talking about *good* beef," answered West. "But tell me where you can get good beef in *this* country."

With this conclusive comment West considered his point made and now began to turn his critical attention to the horse-flesh about him.

"Nice-looking horse, that," he said with barely perceptible condescension to the groom.

"Ought to be. Belongs to the Commander-in-Chief," replied the other. "Old Nosey's favourite," he went on, quite unnecessarily adjusting the animal's curb-chain by way of showing who was in command of the Commander's horse.

"Oh, yes?" said West, trying not to seem impressed. "Got a bit of Arab in him, I wouldn't be surprised."

"Yes, he's got a bit of Arab—by John Bull out of Lady Catherine," stated the groom. "He's called Copenhagen."

"Thought as much," said West, gratified to have been proved right. "Silly name for a horse though, Copenhagen."

Lord Wellington, having heard Harry's message, pronounced himself quite in agreement with El Charro's views, but with certain qualifications.

"I don't expect much from the Spaniards," he said. "They cry 'Viva!' a good deal and are very fond of us but they are the nation most incapable of exertion I have ever known."

"I think you would find a very different spirit with Sanchez's *guerilleros*, my Lord," answered Harry.

"Aye, the partisans I own fight monstrous well when circumstances force them to overcome their national inertia. But their regular army is a disaster."

"El Charro would agree with you there, sir."

"Depend upon it, Smith, there is no country in Europe in the affairs of which foreigners can interfere with so little advantage as in Spain. They love us but hate us; they need us but do not want us. And of course their Generals deeply resent us. And they are sublimely inefficient. It was the sheer whimsical perversity of General Cuesta that nearly lost us Talavera. . . . Ah, I hear the dulcet tones of General Spencer. I fear we shall have to terminate this interesting conversation, Smith."

"Very good, my Lord, but may I ask you one question?"

"Do I wish to buy a greyhound?"

"No, sir. Who in your opinion is the greatest soldier of all time?"

"Why, without hesitation—Hannibal."

"And of the French Generals, my Lord?"

"I don't very well know which, after Boney, is the best General but I always find Masséna just where I don't want him to be."

Walking out of Lord Wellington's room Harry found himself in the focus of Sir Brent Spencer's malevolent glare.

"Whole damn army seems dressed up as grasshoppers these days," the latter muttered ungratefully as Harry picked up one of the maps the old gentleman had dropped on the floor.

"Bloody old curmudgeon," said Harry when Sir Brent had gone inside.

"Friends in Whitehall," answered the ADC, "or he'd have been on the first frigate home."

"Well, I must be going home too—to Uncle Sydney Beckwith."

"Goodbye then, Smith, and if I can be of service any time. . . ."

Back in Badajoz Juanita, once having got over the shock of Cristobál's death, was not finding life too intolerable. Since the French occupation things had improved slightly. The cold and hungry winter was behind them, food supplies were adequate, and school had not yet reopened. Juanita herself was doing a responsible job which she enjoyed and which she could not have hoped to have held but for her language qualification. Moreover, most of the young French officers on the staff were amusing and mildly flirtatious without being a nuisance as (thought Juanita) Spaniards might have been in similar circumstances. She particularly liked Captain Soula who was an ADC to General Phillipon, the French Military Governor.

Jean-Pierre Soula was a rather older man with the sort of blunt, humorous French face that is not uncommon among the Gascons. He joked with Juanita but never flirted with her—not, she thought, because he found her unattractive, but because, she intuitively felt, it would have been undignified for a man of his age who admitted to being proud of his wife and four-year-old son. Their jobs brought them into almost daily contact and Captain Soula became Juanita's best single source of information. The fragments of news which he innocently dropped in course of their being interpreted were diligently passed on by Juanita to Madre Soledad.

In fact it was through information passed by Juanita that the quondam French Governor of Ciudad Rodrigo, together with about two hundred men and his precious stock of claret and cognac, fell into the hands of El Charro's *guerilleros*. Juanita did not, of course, know this. Nor indeed did she know except by repute who El Charro was. Still less did she know that a certain Lieutenant Harry Smith, whom she had inadvertently spoken to on her own doorstep two years previously, had recently been in El Charro's camp and had been the bearer of the latter's very accurate military appreciation to Lord Wellington. In fact Juanita De Los Dolores was not aware of the existence of Lieutenant Harry Smith.

Harry Smith met Julián again sooner than he expected. It happened when the 95th were starting to pull back in order to strengthen the threatened right flank at Fuentes. Sanchez was at the village of Nave de Haver and had paraded, possibly for reasons of pride, his full force including infantry and a pair of light field-guns. The two men had no time to do more than clasp each other by the hand before Harry had to move on with his battalion. This was, of course, before Harry was wounded.

The Rifles played a very active part in the battle of Fuentes de Oñoro. Their most effective action took the form of a difficult manoeuvre in which, while yet closely engaged with the advancing enemy, they had to swing at right angles from a position facing west to one facing south. During this operation Colonel Beckwith was nicked by a ball through his cap just above the left temple. The wound bled profusely but he paid little attention to it beyond taking off his headdress and sticking a handkerchief inside it. What was bothering his head most was that the men should realize that they were being asked to change position, not to withdraw. So he called out in his loud but calm voice: "Now my lads, we'll just go back a little if you please. No, no," as some of the men began to run, "I don't mean that—we're in no hurry—we'll just walk quietly back and you can give them a shot as you go along." And then, when he was satisfied that they were in their proper position, he spoke again: "Now, my lads, this will do—let us show our teeth again." And the riflemen started banging away as hot and strong as ever.

There had been a lot of grape-shot earlier and it was this that had wounded Colonel Beckwith as well as his horse which had been hit in the shoulder. But the artillery fire presently ceased in order to allow a cloud of *voltigeurs* to advance. Riflemen Costello and Cochrane, both Irishmen, were side by side behind some large boulders from which they were doing considerable damage to the enemy. It was midday and the sun was strong even though it was still only May.

"Oh Jasus, Ned, this is thirsty work," said Cochrane, and laying his rifle carefully against the rock he unslung his calabash and, tilting back his head, raised it to his lips. At that moment Costello saw his companion's whole face, neck and hand spattered most unnaturally with wine.

"Bad luck about you, Pat," said Costello laughing. "Hit a Scotsman in his pocket and an Irishman in his drink!" Then to his surprise Cochrane, who had been kneeling, slowly keeled over sideways. He now saw that the shot that had shattered his calabash had also gone through his head. Costello, looking quickly to his front, was in time to see about fifty yards away a *voltigeur* ducking down behind a bit of broken stone wall in order to reload. His own rifle being primed and cocked he waited, aiming at the spot where the Frenchman had dodged out of sight. Twenty, thirty, forty seconds, forty-five seconds, forty-six—then up came the black-shakoed head. Costello fired.

"There's one for Patsy's widow!" he shouted and, not knowing why he did so, in seconds he was across those fifty yards and behind the wall where the Frenchman had fallen. The bullet had entered the man's cranium but his eyes were still wide open and stared accusingly at his killer. Costello stood there for a moment looking down at the man whose eyelids now fluttered violently for a second or two before closing for ever.

Standing thus, breathing hard after his run and hearing nothing of the tirade of shots both coming and going, he was startled by a groan coming from very close at hand. Turning, he was surprised to see another Frenchman, a wounded Sergeant, watching him with tears pouring down his sunburnt face.

"*Hélas!* said the Sergeant, a big heavy man, pointing a blood-spattered hand at the other whose life Costello had just taken. "*Vous avez tué mon pauvre frère!*"

The rifleman looked from one to the other in horror.

"My brother. He could have been alive," Costello understood the man to say, "if he had not stayed to protect me." And the Frenchman carefully peeled away fragments of torn trousers to show his thigh which had been shattered by a ball.

"Can't you see?" the Sergeant went on. "Our men have withdrawn." And, sure enough, Costello now noticed that the firing on their immediate front had more or less died out.

"What's on you, Costello?" came the voice of Corporal Corrigan from some way back. "Come on out of that!" There was a pause while Costello tried to pull himself together.

"Costello!" This time it was Captain Uniacke, the Company Commander. "What in the name of God are you doing? Get back here. We're moving on."

With one last glance at the two brothers, one dead, one severely wounded, Costello dumped his calabash on the living man's chest and ran back to his own lines.

"Did you get him?" asked Captain Uniacke, who was not quite sure what was going on.

"Yes, sir," answered Costello, but without any of his usual brio. "I got the man that got Patsy Cochrane, if there is any merit in that."

Towards evening, when failing light precluded further battle, the contestants drew apart to rescue wounded, bury dead, light fires, cook food and do all the other things that men find necessary to do when they are not actively employed in killing each other. Finding himself only half a mile from where he had left the wounded Frenchman, with the excuse of going to look for his calabash, Costello got unofficial permission to leave the lines.

He found the Sergeant quite easily. He was still in the same place. But he was quite naked—and dead from several bayonet wounds. The Portuguese *caçadores* had passed that way and they never took prisoners on their own soil.

*

Fuentes de Oñoro is a muddle of grey granite cottages and stone walls which look more akin to County Galway than to the Iberian Peninsula.

The actual frontier between Portugal and Spain at Fuente de Oñoro runs along the line of a stream which, after heavy spring rains, is entitled to be called a river.

The river Dos Casas, as it is called, was at this time in flood, thus making effective crossing by troops only possible at an antique bridge consisting of half a dozen granite piles on which rested massive slabs of stone. In fact the whole structure looked as if it had been put there by Stone-Age man. It was also the pivot-point where modern man in the shape of Captain Jonathan Leach and "I" Company of the 95th were ordered to stay and hold until the whole of Colonel Beckwith's manoeuvre had been completed.

To deny the bridge to the enemy was the logical thing to do, and the logical way to do it was to take up a position on the outskirts of the village on the far side of the Dos Casas. The logical plan from the French point of view was for them to take the bridge as soon as possible in order to open the road to their fortress at Almeida. The inevitable fight that ensued can most succinctly be summed up in the words of the famous author and military commander, Julius Caesar: *pugnatum acriter utrimque partes*—hard fought it was on both sides.

In the early stages of the battle some French hussars in their bearskin caps and smart pelisses got in amongst George Simmons' platoon and succeeded in sabring some of his men; whereupon the rest quickly took cover behind stone walls where they could not be got at. However, in the mêlée, Simmons himself got separated from the others and at one moment was surrounded by three or four hussars who were all trying to cut him down at once. Fortunately they each got in one another's way. But for a minute or two they had the portly George hopping, skipping and jumping about to avoid the vicious swipes they were taking at him. This caused a good deal of nervous laughter from Harry Smith's platoon who had been ordered not to fire for fear of hitting Simmons.

Had the hussars any sense one of them could easily have ridden Simmons down and thus polished him off. But, no, they were equipped with, and trained to use, the *arme blanche* and they had to sink its cutting edge into flesh at all costs. Likewise Simmons, between ducking and dodging, felt that he had to use that obsolescent weapon and was aiming airy blows at his attackers like someone trying to swat butterflies with a cricket bat.

Then, just when it looked as if he must soon be sliced up, he heard an Irish voice shout, "Over here, Green man," and at the same time a volley rang out which knocked one of the hussars out of his saddle. This disconcerted the other horsemen and, seeing his opportunity as well as a line of red-coats out of the corner of his eye, Simmons ran towards them with more agility than most people would have given him credit for. In a moment he was across about a hundred yards of ground where a line of friendly red-coats parted to let him through.

"That was a close shave, Green feller," said Captain Declan Doyle of the 43rd, "and a fine dance you gave us."

It was just after George Simmons had got back to his own Company, congratulating himself on having beaten off a cavalry attack single-handed, that he got a bullet right through his thigh just below the left buttock.

This was the beginning of the main French infantry attack. Lead by boy-drummers sounding the dread *pas de charge*, and officers shouting and cavorting about like monkeys, waving their hats on the end of their swords, the Frenchmen came on in such numbers that no small detachment, not even a company of the Rifles backed up by the gallant 43rd, could stand in their way without being annihilated. To be annihilated was not the Light-Bobs' role. Instead, the 95th and the 43rd together fought a well-judged rearguard action and withdrew, taking a toll of the enemy out of all proportions to their numbers.

It was during this *pugnatum acriter* phase of the action that Harry Smith found himself all alone on the wrong side of the river with a bullet lodged in his ankle. Lying there, working out the odds against being shot dead, bayoneted, or made prisoner, Harry was surprised to see Peter O'Hare, coming from goodness knows where, mounted on his horse. "Quick. I'll give you a leg up," said O'Hare, jumping off.

"You'll do nothing of the sort," replied Harry ungraciously.

"It's your bloody horse."

"Yes, and I'm your bloody senior officer. Now get up."

"What will you do, then?"

"I've got two legs, haven't I? Now for God's sake get up before they do for the two of us." And, one running and one riding, the two men got safely back across the river.

And that was the end of the battle of Fuentes de Oñoro for Harry Smith. It was also the end of the battle for Tom Smith who had his thigh flenched to the bone by a shell fragment. The two brothers met at the Field Dressing Station. It was the end of the battle for Pongo Prickett who lost two fingers when his rifle accidentally went off when he had his hand over the muzzle. ("I've still got my courting-finger," he announced happily to anyone who had time to listen to him.)

It was the end of the battle and campaign for Sydney Beckwith who became delirious from ague that night and had to be evacuated with the wounded. Failing to recover in Lisbon, he was invalided home to England and never returned to the Peninsula again. Had he not been succeeded by one Andrew Barnard, who had many of the same qualities, his loss to the regiment would have been immeasurable. As it was, 'Uncle Sydney' was missed by all, from the most junior rifleman to Black Bob Craufurd himself.

Fuentes de Oñoro, too, was the end for the *mestizo*, Oño. Riding right up to the French lines in order to shout insults he was mistaken for a Frenchman by a private of the Coldstream Guards who shot him dead. This clumsy accident made Julián Sanchez so angry that he swore he would never fight in alliance with the English again. But Wellington eventually won him round and offered him the job of going north to Gallegos to anticipate a French convoy destined for Almeida, thus to menace Masséna's communications with Ciudad Rodrigo. This was altogether a more suitable role for the Charros than taking part in a pitched battle.

It was the end also for Harry's friend Rutu Stewart who was knocked off his horse by a ball, but was actually killed by hitting his head in falling on a jagged stone. He was buried near the little church at Poco Velha.

It was the end, indeed, of some 1,500 killed and wounded on the

Allied side alone. The French losses were higher. But in war no one has time to grieve for long over fallen comrades and, for those alive on the British side of the Dos Casas, the night was a cheerful one, for everyone thought they had won the battle whether they had or not.

The next morning pickets reported that the French had withdrawn in the night.

"Well, here we are, Fitzroy," said Lord Wellington, eating a cold chicken leg for breakfast, "still in the same spot, and the French have gone away. So I think that constitutes a victory, wouldn't you say?"

"I suppose so, my Lord."

"Aye, well write me up a victory then. . . . You know, Fitzroy," he added as an afterthought, "that young fellow Smith has made me reflect: Soult, I have often felt, has never quite understood a field of battle. I am much inclined now to think that the best General after Boney is definitely Masséna."

"Well, my Lord," replied the other smiling, "you've just defeated him. I'll go and write that up."

At which remark Wellington had one of his infrequent outbreaks of hearty laughter. It reminded Lord Fitzroy of someone having a fit of the whooping-cough.

CHAPTER NINE

ONE WARM SUNNY day, soon after the battle of Fuentes, Juanita was just leaving the *Ayuntamiento* to go home for lunch when she ran into Captain Soula who was about to do the same thing.

"Hola Juanita," he said. "Where are you going?" And without waiting for her answer he went on, "I'm just going to my billet to look at my horse. Come with me and see him. It is only round the corner."

Juanita knew where the Captain lived and a slight detour home would, she decided, make a pleasant change to her daily routine. She was annoyed, though, as the two of them were walking along, to pass the apothecary's fat wife gossiping with another woman on a street corner. Juanita smiled politely but as soon as she and Captain Soula had passed by she felt that the two women were discussing her and would be sure to report that Juanita De Los Dolores was seen *paseando* with a French officer.

Soula was billeted in a fairly typical large town house. Its main claim to originality was a cobbled path which cut a swathe from the big front door, through the tiled front hall, continuing on and out of the back of the house, along an outdoor passage adorned with geraniums, amaryllis and many flowery pots and urns of variegated greenery. Finally, turning left, it ended quite unexpectedly in a small yard overhung by a vine. In this yard was a stable.

No one unfamiliar with Spanish domestic architecture would have dreamt of a stable being there unless they had been sharp enough to have taken the cobbled pathway as a clue. The half-door of a loose-box was open but, in the warm subfusc within, Juanita could at first see nothing. Then, in response to what was obviously a familiar noise from Soula, the inhabitant raised its head and she could see a white star between two very large bright eyes.

"He is all black except for the white star. A big horse—sixteen and a half hands, as the English say."

Making soothing French noises the Captain opened the stable door.

"Come, come," said Soula to Juanita. "You have a farm. You must be used to horses."

"We only had mules on our *finca*."

"Then come and see something a little less *rustique*."

Juanita entered the warm dark stable and smelt horse and hay and manure. She found it pleasant. Though she had never ridden, she liked these big, strong, gentle animals. The horse turned his head and, extending his nostrils, breathed at her noisily, testing her unfamiliar smell. She put her hand on his glossy black neck and the horse turned his head away, fidgeting slightly on his feet. Soula, to calm him, also put his hand on the animal's neck and Juanita saw their two hands side by side, her small whitish one and his large and brown, with blunt white fingernails.

"What is his name?" asked Juanita, at a loss for something to say.

"He has not got a name that I know of," answered Soula, "because I got him in Spain from a Spanish dealer in a hurry and I don't know if he is Spanish, French or English—and," he added laughing, "he has never let me into the secret."

Juanita laughed too. "But you must call him something," she said.

"Oh yes. I call him Monsieur Barsac. Barsac is my home town on the banks of the Garonne where they make a sweet white wine, and where my father has a little vineyard. It is a good name for a horse, don't you think?"

But Juanita did not answer. Instead she was wondering what it was like at Barsac on the banks of the Garonne and what did Jean-Pierre Soula look like when he was at home among the vineyards and not dressed up as a soldier.

And then she imagined him with a pretty wife and a noisy little boy with a flat-nosed, humorous face, perhaps a bit like his father. And still she did not take her hand from the black horse's neck, nor did Soula cease to massage the same neck with his strong brown hand. And she wondered how she would feel if perchance his hand were to touch hers. And now she felt that she could not remove her hand without seeming rude, or stand-offish, or prudish and because it would put an end to this moment. Then suddenly her heart began to pound and she felt quite a new sensation: a sort of tingling all over her body because Captain Soula had just then taken her hand in his.

"Come, my little cabbage," he said. "You must go to have your lunch now and I must have mine or I shall get a scolding from my landlady." And he led her out of the stable.

But Juanita could not eat any lunch and made the excuse that she had to get back to the office, and left despite Frasquita's angry protestations. Passing the *Ayuntamiento*, she left a message to say that she was going to the convent and would be available if needed. She then walked fast down to the convent and obtained admittance to Madre Soledad.

The Mother Superior was an intelligent woman and had not been a school headmistress without learning a good deal about the workings of the hearts, minds and bodies of young girls coming into flower. She saw at once Juanita was upset and decided that, in Juanita's case, an abrasive treatment was most likely to have the best effect.

"Now, Juana Maria, what have you for me today?" Juanita, who was normally cheerful and composed, looked embarrassed and awkward. Eventually, under her Superior's stern interrogative eye, she spoke.

"Reverend Mother, I have fallen into temptation," she said, feeling her face and neck going blotchily red.

"What sort of temptation, child?" replied the other calmly. Juanita paused, searching for the right euphemism.

"Carnal temptation," she eventually managed to come out with.

"Oh that! Is that all? Everybody suffers from that from time to time. It's all rubbish. If you've got anything serious you need to confess, tell it to Padre Antonio or whoever you go to. Priests are expert on that sort of thing. But don't bother me with it."

"Yes, Reverend Mother," replied Juanita, already much relieved and inwardly laughing at the Reverend Mother's little joke because Padre Antonio looked as if he could never have had a carnal thought in his life.

"Now child, what I want to know is what news you have for me."

"Only that Captain Soula lives at Barsac in the vineyards by the river Garonne, near Bordeaux." Madre Soledad quickly noted that Captain Soula was obviously the source of Juanita's problem of conscience.

"Well, unless he can produce a case or two of good Bordeaux wine that information is not going to help us much, is it, child?"

And Juanita laughed happily at Madre Soledad's light dismissal of the subject and felt altogether much better.

The nun then told Juanita about the heavy fighting at Fuentes and explained that the French had retired to Ciudad Rodrigo without being really defeated. She said that now everything depended on Lord Wellington and conjured Juanita to pray hard for him and the British army.

"Oh, but I always do, Reverend Mother, and especially for—"

"Do not worry, we do not forget your friends the Captains Gordón and Esomerset—and of course your dear brother Cristóbal. Now run along, child, and don't let your conscience overwork itself unnecessarily."

And Madre Soledad kissed Juanita, which was a thing she seldom did, and sent her on her way.

Another person suffering the prickings of conscience was Acting-Corporal Costello, who had recently been given a stripe. After the battle at Fuentes de Oñoro the regimental wives assembled, as was the custom, to hear the roll called. Among them was the lovely Jenny Cochrane. When Rifleman Cochrane failed to answer to his name for the second time she let out a terrible scream and threw herself to the ground and would perhaps have done herself a mischief had not two or three other Irish wives rushed to lay hold of her. Captain Uniacke, accustomed to these painful scenes, called out for Costello.

"See what you can do to comfort Mrs Cochrane, Corporal," he said. "Fall out now and go and talk to her."

As much as he sympathized with the pretty widow, it was the last thing he wanted or felt able to do, but an order was an order. However, as he approached the group of Irishwomen the bereaved

Jenny Cochrane started to wail, and first one, and then another began to keen in the way the Irish do for their dead. There was nothing Costello could do, therefore, but make himself scarce and this he did. The keening went on till late in the night and when they were done the women lay down together a little way off from the men and, like the soldiers, went to sleep under the canopy of Heaven.

The next day Jenny Cochrane approached Corporal Costello and asked him if he would take her to the spot where they had buried her husband Patsy. He agreed, though with some misgivings since he feared that the two French brothers might still be lying there unburied. When they reached the spot Jenny took out her Missal and read the prayer for the dead. Then, having shed a few tears, she told Costello that she was worried that her Pat had not been buried on Holy ground and therefore might never get to Heaven.

"Don't mind that, Missis," he said. "Sure, you can go to Heaven from anywhere."

"Please God so," she replied. "But what about the unburied dead?"

"Sure there's thousands of brave lads scattered all over the place and isn't this a Catholic country? And aren't they covered by the sky and God over them?" And as he was saying these words which he hoped would please Jenny, he was all the time worrying about the Frenchmen who were probably lying there unburied behind the wall.

"Please God so," Jenny said again. "You're a great comfort to me Mr Costello and I'm grateful."

"I don't remember the time anybody ever called me Mister. Please call me Ted."

"I will so, and you may call me Jenny. You were a good friend to my Padraic and I'm grateful for that. If there are any of his things that would be of use to you, sure he would be glad for you to have them."

Ted Costello thanked Jenny and together they made their way back to camp.

The regiment was soon on the move again and Jenny followed Captain Uniacke's company on her donkey. The regiment was a home, as much for the wives as for the men—and for the widows too. Where else could they go? For Jenny it was the only home she had.

And from that time on Ted Costello took to seeing Jenny every day, or as often as duties allowed, and a warm friendship grew up between them.

In Wellington's army there was no general organization for the removal of wounded from a battlefield. This task of mercy was left to the same men in whose hands lay the administering of corporal punishment—the regimental bandsmen. Playing fife and drum, wielding cat-o'-nine-tails or bearing stretchers were all part of the day's work to them. It was left to Napoleon's doctor, the Baron Jean Dominique Larrey, to devise an ambulance service, but this took time to recommend itself to the old gentlemen at the Horse Guards.

So, for a badly wounded soldier, his chance of being taken to a surgeon at a dressing station, or indeed to a hospital, was largely a matter of luck. He might be found by a group of bandsmen (who could have been instrumental in flogging him the week before) or he could be left to die of wounds, thirst or starvation because no one had found him, and because his own comrades, who were not in any case allowed to help the wounded during the course of an action, had moved on elsewhere.

Harry and Tom Smith and George Simmons experienced days of misery in getting themselves back from the Spanish border at Fuentes to Lisbon. Their sufferings were to some extent mitigated by the fact that they had each other for company, that as officers they were able to exert some slight authority here and there, and that they had more money than the average private soldier to buy whatever was available in the way of food, transport or shelter.

At Lisbon Tom Smith's wound was considered sufficiently serious for him to be ordered immediately aboard a transport for England. The brothers said goodbye and the normally ebullient Tom, feeling very low, was put on a bullock wagon to be taken with other wounded to Belem docks.

The next day Harry and George Simmons found themselves before the doctors under the direction of the celebrated Staff

Surgeon Morell. The nature of Harry's wound was that a musket ball had lodged in the joint of the heel having partially severed the Achilles tendon. The problem was whether to operate or not. The wound had so far shown no signs of sloughing, or 'going bad'. But surgery would inevitably increase the chances of a slough, in which case the only remedy would be amputation.

"It is up to you, Smith," said Morell. "We will do the best we can, but there are no guarantees."

"Well, I'm quite useless as it is. I can scarcely ride, let alone walk."

"Then I would advise you to consider yourself as a man with a wooden leg," said another surgeon called Higgins. "But at least it is your own leg and not one chopped out of a tree."

"All very well but a wooden leg wouldn't hurt me all the time, would it?" answered Harry. "I'm all for taking a chance with the knife."

"As I say," said Morell, "it is up to you. In my experience washing a wound very well before section seems to diminish the danger of sloughing. I also make it a practice to wash my hands and my instruments thoroughly before an operation."

"Well, if it were my leg," said a third surgeon called Brownrigg, "out should come the ball."

"Hurrah, Brownrigg, you're the man for me," said Harry.

"Very well," said Staff Surgeon Morell, "if it is your desire we will do it directly."

"Right away it is then," said Harry, his resolution cooling somewhat. But after a scarcely discernible pause he cocked up his leg.

"There it is, gentlemen. Slash away."

"We are not a regiment of dragoons, Smith," said Morell. "Give us leave to make a few preparations."

It was during the preparations that Harry began to wonder whether Higgins' advice about the wooden leg might not have been the wiser after all. But before he had screwed himself up to the point of asking for a stay of execution four burly orderlies seized him and pinioned him to a table.

"Good luck, Harry," said George Simmons who was present and waiting his turn.

"I don't want luck," snapped Harry. "I want skilled surgical attention."

Whether the three surgeons overheard this last remark or not will never be known, but there followed five minutes of the most excruciating torture Harry could ever remember.

"There appear to be certain adhesions of fibrous tissue to the projectile," muttered Surgeon Morell to his colleagues.

"Yes," replied Brownrigg, "you can see that the ball is jagged. Probably became distorted on coming in contact with the tarsus."

"Presumably," answered the senior medico, continuing to probe away.

"Holy Moses! What the devil are you doing now?" roared Harry.

"I'm going to have to make an incision here Brownrigg," went on Morell, paying no attention to the patient or his outburst, "to avoid the tendon Achilles. It is partially severed there, look."

"What is partially severed?" asked Harry tetchily.

"Why, the big tendon attached to the heel, of course. Don't worry, it will heal up once we get the foreign body out. . . . Damn! The forceps have broken, can you get at it Higgins?"

"Not sure if I can quite. . . . " hissed Higgins through clenched teeth, dodging his head this way and that.

"It's all right, I've got the ball now, if you could just . . . Morell."

"What the hell's going on down there?" roared Harry.

"All right, Brownrigg," said Morell, still paying no notice to Harry. "When I make my second section you pull. All right, Higgins?"

"Very well," replied Higgins.

"Ready," said Brownrigg.

"Here we go then," announced Morell.

"AARRGH!" roared Harry.

"Got it! There you are Smith," said Morell addressing Harry with great civility and presenting him with a small piece of lead. "A keepsake to show your grandchildren."

"If I'm still capable of having any!"

"I need linen," said Brownrigg, looking about him.

"None left I'm afraid," said Higgins. "Used it all on that amputation."

"I've got a spare shirt," said Harry, turning to George Simmons who was sitting bolt upright, all attention, "in my haversack there. Tear it up, will you, George."

"But that's far too good a shirt to tear up for a bandage," replied Simmons with Yorkshire circumspection.

"Damn your eyes, George, I said tear it."

Harry, who was sweating profusely, now struggled out of the relaxed grip of the orderlies, flicked the perspiration off his forehead and sat up. Two minutes more, and bandaged in his own shirt, he managed with help to hop off the operating table.

"I strongly recommend sea-bathing, Smith," said Surgeon Morell. "Who's next? Simmons is it? Over here, Simmons. . . . Smith, if you care to sit over there while we deal with your friend. . . ."

Harry, with the relief of one whose ordeal is over, was able to watch with clinical interest how the surgeons dealt with George. He was only mildly put out to note that when Surgeon Morell probed the thigh wound and extracted a small fragment of bone George Simmons did not utter a single sound.

CHAPTER TEN

IT WAS NOT until the end of the year that Harry Smith, convalescing by the sea at Cascaes, was passed fit to return to duty. Arriving back at the regiment, which was at that time at El Bodón a few miles from Ciudad Rodrigo, the first person he saw was Pongo Prickett now with Sergeant's chevrons on his sleeve.

A regiment, like a family, while its component parts continually change, remains the same regiment (or family) for year after year, or indeed, generation after generation. After six months' absence Harry was at first surprised to find certain superficial changes in the battalion. For one thing it had a new Colonel. Andrew Barnard was a completely different human being from Sydney Beckwith, yet he was the same in that he was a kindly man, a surrogate father to all, and quintessentially a Rifleman. As to other differences in the regiment, some men, killed or wounded, had departed and others had replaced them; some had grown fatter and others thinner; this man limped, that man had a new scar; one man had been promoted, another had been flogged; and so on—a hundred minor variations on the same theme amounting to nothing at all. In five minutes Harry felt completely at home again.

He had hardly finished greeting old friends, and submitting to the usual good-natured jokes and leg-pulls, when a summons came demanding his presence at Battalion headquarters.

Although he knew what to expect, it was, nevertheless, a slight shock to find the fair, fresh-faced Colonel Barnard in the place of Uncle Sydney.

"Harry Smith," said Andrew Barnard "I've both good and less than good news for you. First your promotion has come through and you are now a substantive Captain as from the first of the month. Congratulations! Secondly the rumour has apparently got about that you have the makings of a good staff officer. At any rate you are to report to the Brigadier, Colonel Drummond, where you have been posted as Brigade Major. So it is goodbye to regimental soldiering for a while. But I fancy you will find Colonel Drummond perfectly congenial."

Harry thanked Colonel Barnard and, having spent some time in saying hail and farewell to a number of friends, he collected Rifleman West, his horse Chiquito and another, Portuguese horse, a baggage-mule, the greyhound Moro and a couple of other long-dogs, and made off to report to the 'congenial' Colonel Drummond.

Arriving at 2nd Light Brigade HQ Harry could not find Colonel Drummond at all. Neither did anybody seem to have any idea as to where, congenial or otherwise, he could be found. Entering the house that served as headquarters Harry waited around for a while wishing to report for duty. Eventually, guided by pangs of hunger, Harry followed his nose to the kitchen from which came appetizing smells. There he saw a portly old man in an apron cooking up what promised to be a savoury meal.

"That smells good," said Harry cocking his leg over a chair and watching the culinary operation with interest. "I feel I haven't had a square meal for a fortnight."

"Then, sir, if you care to join me," said the old man carefully adjusting the seasoning to his dish, "I see no reason why you should not dine very presently—that is if you care for saddle of hare done in the French manner with red wine, glazed onions and sauté potatoes." Then, looking up for the first time, the cook stared hard at Harry. "Are you by any chance my new Brigade Major?" he said.

Harry took his leg off the chair so quickly that he knocked it over and had to pick it up again before he could stand to attention, salute and report himself.

"Smith, 95th Rifles, reporting for duty, sir."

"And I am Drummond of the Foot Guards at present commanding 2nd Light Brigade—though how I got the job I do not know. However, it suits me very well and they are a capital lot of fellows and seem to know what they are doing. Now, Smith, it will give me great pleasure to have your company for dinner."

At dinner, which was the best Harry had eaten since the night in the camp of Julián Sanchez, Colonel Drummond explained that he had just retired from the service and was looking forward to a bit of hunting, shooting and fishing at his country place near Ross-on-Wye when he was recalled to the Colours.

"Frankly, my dear fellow, having been a Guardsman all my life I have not the foggiest idea about Light Infantry work and I shall have to lean very heavily upon you. It will be your duty to run the Brigade, therefore, and mine to have a damn good dinner ready for you every day."

Harry, amazed and delighted at this extraordinary prospect, began to ask questions about the present situation of which he was necessarily ignorant.

"Pass the port and I'll put you in the picture," said Colonel Drummond, when they had polished off the *râble de lièvre*. "Of course the Commander-in-Chief plays his cards very close to his chest, don't ye know, but there's a very decent fellow on his staff called Fitzroy Somerset—knew his father, the old Duke of Beaufort. He seems to think—I'm talking about young Fitzroy—that we will never shift Johnny Frenchman until we've winkled him out of Badajoz. Now, we can never get him out of Badajoz without winkling him out of Ciudad Rodrigo first—all a question of lines of communication, axes of advance and that sort of how-de-do. So it looks to me as if we'll be having a crack at Rodrigo pretty soon. . . . Oh, by the way, my dear boy, a fellow who calls himself Colonel Sanchez was round here asking for you—give the port a favouring breeze, if you'll be so good. Seems a very decent sort of chap," continued this amiable old gentleman, filling up both glasses, "but I'm no good at the lingo so couldn't make heard or tail of what he had to say. Seems to have an independent brigade—very queer uniform! But he runs a good show, they say—though it wouldn't do for St James's, if you know what I mean."

One day in Badajoz Juanita noticed more than usual activity at General Phillipon's headquarters. There was much coming and going of adjutants and aides-de-camp and, in the streets when she went out for coffee, she saw French soldiers everywhere bringing materials for strengthening and arming the fortifications. That day her services as interpreter were not needed by Captain Soula who was busy all morning with the General, and she did not see him until late in the evening when she was about to go home.

"I will accompany you to your door," the Captain said.

"What does it all mean?" Juanita asked when they were clear of the town hall, "All this coming and going?"

"Ah, Juanita *ma petite*, it is a funny thing about soldiers, they are always coming and going. One day one army wins a battle and moves forward, and the next day the other army wins and the army that has won the day before moves back."

"And who has won this time, *mon capitaine*?"

"You will know sooner or later so I might as well tell you, though it pains me to do so. The British have taken Ciudad Rodrigo."

It was getting dark when they reached Juanita's door. Captain Soula stopped and, taking Juanita's shoulders in his two hands, tried to see the expression in her eyes but could not. He was only able to feel her slightly apprehensive presence.

"You know, Juanita, we cannot expect to be here for ever. One day sooner or later, I shall be gone, we shall all be gone. I am not talking about death. I do not think of the possibility of being killed because no one knows what fate has in store in that respect. But I only know that soon we must go. When that day comes I hope that you will think kindly of Jean-Pierre Soula." And he felt her go tense as he bent forward to kiss her on the forehead.

As soon as Soula had gone Juanita begged Frasquita to come with her to the convent, since at this time no young woman went out alone after dark.

Leaving Frasquita in the chapel to light a candle and say a few prayers, Juanita made her way to Madre Soledad's room where she found Sister Rosario with the Mother Superior. Sister Rosario immediately began to blink back tears of joy at the sight of her favourite pupil.

"I've got some good news for you, child," said the Reverend Mother.

"And I for you, Madre," blurted out Juanita. "Ciudad Rodrigo's fallen to the English!"

"Oh, so you have heard already!"

"You mean to say you know?" answered Juanita, disappointed not to be the first with the intelligence.

"I have just been informed of the fact, which is why I say I have some good news for you . . . Sister," she said turning to Rosario, "would you kindly go to the refectory and bring in the messenger if he has finished his meal."

When the gentle, lachrymose nun had gone on her errand Juanita turned with a questioning look to Madre Soledad, but the Mother Superior gave nothing away and began to talk about the situation in general. Presently they heard the door being opened and both turned. And there, being ushered in by Sister Rosario, was a smiling young man in leather gaiters whose spurs clanked as he advanced a little awkwardly into the room.

Juanita stood absolutely still for several seconds before screaming, "MIGUELÍN!" And she hurled herself at the young man.

"It is rather a long story," said Madre Soledad, "and our young friend has not very much time to tell it as he has to leave while there are still people about. He must not attract attention from the sentries. Take him into the visitors' room—but a quarter of an hour is all I can allow."

"Yes, Reverend Mother, thank you," said Juanita. "Come, Miguelín."

The story as told by Miguelín to Juanita and Frasquita (frequently interrupted by cries of "Ay-ay-ay!", and "*Bendito sea Dios!*" from Frasquita) was in fact a simple one. Escaping from a prisoner-of-war camp near Salamanca, Miguelín tried to make his way back to Badajoz walking only at night. In the mountains near Sequeros, nearly exhausted from fatigue and hunger, he was picked up by a patrol of *garrochistas* and taken to their chief. On being questioned by El Charro he revealed that he and his father were employees of the De Los Dolores family. The guerrilla leader immediately took him on the strength and finding him a handy and resolute lad made him his personal assistant. So pleased was Julián with Miguelín's progress in the ways of guerrilla warfare (there was no false modesty about Miguelín) that he began sending him on special missions. This was his first attempt at getting through the French lines and it had been his privilege to bring the news of the British victory at Ciudad Rodrigo.

In January 1812 Ciudad Rodrigo was a charming little fortified town on the banks of the river Agueda. It had a fifteenth-century castle, a cathedral, various palaces and monasteries, a Renaissance town-hall and a bull-ring. The approach from the west was across a fine Roman bridge. The town itself stood on a slight eminence and dominated a vast undulating plain on which there grew not a single tree. There was only one thing wrong with Rodrigo so far as Wellington's men could see: it was full of well-armed veterans of the Imperial Army.

Before Lord Wellington could lay siege to the town, which he did on 8 January 1812, Julián Sanchez carried out a highly successful raid with his *garrochistas* and drove off 200 head of cattle that had been grazing on the glacis of the ramparts, thus depriving the French of their *biftek* for some time to come.

The night after the cattle raid the captured steers broke loose and stampeded through 2nd Light Brigade HQ camp. A nervous sentry, newly out from England, shouted 'cavalry' and a general panic ensued. It so happened that General Craufurd was passing at the time and he had the pleasure of seeing one of his Brigadiers, Colonel Drummond, who had been asleep in his camp-bed, shinning up a cork-tree in a short nightshirt. Harry Smith said to Johnny Kincaid the next day that it was the first time he had ever seen Black Bob laugh.

But the laugh turned sour two days later when Colonel Drummond had a sudden heart attack and died in Harry Smith's arms. The old gentleman, being addicted to the pleasures of the table, was overweight, and not up to the rigours of campaigning. The brigade was taken over by a cavalryman called Colonel Vandeleur, an Irishman from Queen's County, who turned out to be a good 'Light-Bob' as well as a good fellow.

As the January days dragged on frost set in and life became quite miserable for the besiegers of Ciudad Rodrigo who frequently had to wade the Agueda river in order to work on, and defend, the fortifications being set up facing the north side of the town. Having reached their positions they then had to dig the frozen ground in their wet clothes to prepare trenches, gabions and breastworks. Then once relieved (every fourth day) they had to ford the icy river once more. The only advantage to be gained from these distressful circumstances was that the men were so miserable that they longed for the day when the breaches of the walls would be declared practicable for an assault.

Meanwhile plans were drawn up for the attack and volunteers were called for to man the 'Forlorn Hope'—an almost suicidal assault group whose job it was to be the first into the breach and there to hold a small bridgehead for the storming party.

"What did you want to go and volunteer for?" said Billy Doubleday when Sergeant Prickett casually mentioned that he had just done that very thing. "You must be barmy!"

"Why, I just thought I would, that's all. It's so bleedin' cold here I kind of fancied a place where it would be a bit hotter."

"Oh yes. You'll be in the hot place soon enough volunteering for the Forlorn Hope. You'll be roasting for all eternity."

"Very poetic. But I'll be in good company, won't I?"

"What you mean?" said Doubleday, sharply suspicious.

"Why," said Prickett, relishing the moment, "I volunteered for you as well, didn't I?"

"You WHAT?" yelled Doubleday in a shrill falsetto, leaping to his feet. "You volunteered for ME? Nobody can't volunteer for nobody else. It's a private matter. It can't be done. I've not volunteered never in my bleeding life—not for nothing, I haven't."

On 19 January Colonel Sturgeon of the Royal Artillery pronounced the breaches practicable and Lord Wellington ordered the attack to go in at eight o'clock the same night.

Harry Smith also volunteered for the Forlorn Hope but was turned down by General Craufurd on the grounds that he was already too senior (and, it was hinted, too valuable as a Brigade Major). A subaltern called Willie Johnstone from "A" Company got the job, together with Gurwood and Kincaid. They were given three equal detachments from the 52nd, 43rd and the 95th Rifles. The rifle contingent included Corporal Costello, Sergeant Prickett and Rifleman Doubleday, who now took it quite as a matter of course that he should go along too.

The storming of a fortress, or indeed any set-piece attack, can not easily be described by one person even if he be an eye-witness. True, the Commander-in-Chief has some sort of overall view, but he is too deeply concerned with moment-to-moment issues: conflicting reports from messengers and ADCs, conflicting advice from his staff or Divisional Commanders, demands for reserves, for artillery, for cavalry, and so on and so forth. Even in his hind-sighted despatches, therefore, (and even if he is an honest man) his picture can never be quite a true one.

So the picture of a battle or set-piece attack can only be a pointilliste canvas, a patchwork quilt, made up of minuscule incidents. For example, shortly before the hour for the attack on Rodrigo Ted Costello was standing thinking tenderly about Jenny Cochrane when he overheard a brief exchange in the dark.

"Why the hell did you bring these short ladders?" General Craufurd's voice had no kindness in it.

"Because I was ordered to do so by the Engineer, General," came Lieutenant Simmons' reply, offendedly self-righteous.

"Go back, sir, and get others. I am astonished at such stupidity," retorted the General, angry and dismissive.

And Costello, his heart softened by thoughts of Jenny Cochrane, felt sorry for Lieutenant Simmons.

Costello, together with the Forlorn Hope and storming party were soon afterwards assembled and addressed by General Craufurd as follows:

"Soldiers, the eyes of your country are upon you. Be steady, be cool. Be firm in the assault. The town *must* be yours this night. Once masters of the wall, let your first duty be to clear the ramparts, and in doing this keep together."

Then Craufurd shouted out, "Now lads, for the breach!" and led the way himself. They were his last recorded words.

Up to this point there had been comparative silence and perfect order. But, from the moment that a gun shot gave the signal for the attack, pandemonium reigned and chaos became lord of all.

Doubleday, first up one of the ladders, caught a Frenchman just as he was reloading and lunged at him with his sword. The point, instead of penetrating soft flesh, hit a human rib and gave Doubleday a nasty jolt in the right wrist. Perplexed by this, he was just wondering what to do next when he received a swingeing blow on the side of the face from a musket butt which knocked him back on top of Sergeant Prickett just as he was getting off the ladder. This stopped Prickett in his tracks as well as the queue of men behind him.

"For fuck's sake get on unless you want a bayonet up your jacksey," came a voice from a lower rung. Prickett needed no such encouragement and, pulling Doubleday to his feet by the collar, pushed on to where he could see the tall figure of Lieutenant Kincaid silhouetted in the light of a flare.

On a ladder to the left Costello reached the top only to see the ladder next to him with about fourteen or fifteen fellows on it being pushed over backwards by a burly Frenchman. Forgetting his sword, or perhaps because he instinctively could not bring himself to use it, he swung his rifle butt and caught the fellow a sort of rabbit-punch on the back of the neck which sent him hurtling down on top of the men he had just pushed over. Rushing on he suddenly saw Captain Smith who was not, as far as he knew, supposed to be there. Smith was having a furious argument with Captain Doyle of the 43rd.

"For God's sake, Doyle, get your men over there to the right. You can enfilade those fellows stopping the 95th getting up."

"The hell I will, Smith, my orders are to work round the rampart to the left."

"Don't be a bloody fool. This is a chance in a million. Get them over."

"Don't you be giving me orders, Smith. I'm a senior to you."

"Bugger you Doyle! I'm giving you orders in the name of the Brigadier. Come on the 43rd! Follow me!"

And the 43rd did follow Harry Smith, and so did Costello who joined up with them and they doubled across to a point where they were able to enfilade the French, causing the latter to abandon the rampart. But Doyle was not satisfied.

"I'll be calling on you after this show, Smith," he said, panting with the recent exertion.

"It will be a pleasure to meet you, Doyle," replied Harry, quite forgetting that the odds were heavily against either of them remaining alive long enough for them to fight a duel. Harry, rushing on with a mixed bag of 43rd, 52nd, a handful of riflemen, ran straight into Paddy Uniacke at the head of "C" Company.

"Come on, Harry! This way!" shouted Uniacke.

"Which way?" answered Harry.

"Round to the right. The General's there. Come on, 'C' Company!" And Paddy Uniacke ran on before Harry could turn his men round.

Uniacke had not gone more than a few yards when there was an explosion which made the ordinary din of battle sound like silence. Harry felt the hot pressure of it tear at the left side of his tunic, forcing him back on the man behind. Recovering, Harry ran on and rounding the next ravelin saw a vast smoking hole and apparently not a living man in sight.

"My God!" said Harry and, out of decency more than hope, shouted "Paddy" two or three times. But no human voice replied. Nor as far as anyone could see were there any signs of bodies — only dismembered fragments of them. At Harry's feet something was moving. Looking closer Harry saw that it was a human diaphragm—all that was left of a man whose lungs were still violently working.

Suddenly there was a wild shout and down the scarp and up the opposite *fausse braye* rushed a company of Connaught Rangers. The leading man, an enormous grenadier, seeing Harry's dark uniform assumed him to be a Frenchman and before Harry could divine his intentions, the grenadier seized Harry by the neck and lifted him off his feet. Harry was unable to utter a sound and in another second his brains must have been dashed out against the wall of the ravelin had not Sergeant Prickett appeared.

"Put my bleedin' officer down, you stupid bog-trotter!" commanded Prickett. Whereupon the Irishman dropped Harry like a sack of potatoes and, with a solicitous "Beg your pardon, sorr", rushed off to find someone else to strangle.

But in another minute came a great, brutal, ugly, unmistakably British roar from the main breach which signified beyond any doubt to anyone that the town had been taken.

The actual assault had only taken a matter of minutes but in that time the devastation had been considerable.

General Craufurd had been mortally wounded at the outset. Colonel Vandeleur who took over from him was badly wounded, as was Colonel Colborne of the 52nd. Among many junior officers Paddy Uniacke had been killed. Two out of the three officers of the Forlorn Hope had miraculously been unhurt, only Gurwood sustaining a minor head wound. Harry Smith had lost the left side of his tunic which had been blown off in the blast of the magazine explosion (the right side had been protected by the ravelin) and his shoulder and arm were full of tiny particles of stone. Billy Doubleday was unrecognizable owing to the swelling on one side of his face.

"Bloody vampire!" commented Prickett. "Got his gollup of blood today all right." The only sign of blood on Prickett was on the end of his sword-bayonet which he proceeded to wipe on the tail of Doubleday's shirt which was hanging out.

Two days later General Sir Robert Craufurd was buried at the foot of the little breach and given full military honours by the Light Division that he had created, and by whom at one time he had been so much hated.

On return to their cantonments the Division was led by 13 Platoon, "I" Company of the 1st Battalion, the 95th Rifles. On the road there was a deep crater which, owing to rain and an overnight thaw, had now become full of water. The road at this point was just about wide enough for the column to split and go round the crater, but this was exactly what the men, as if of one mind, decided they would not do.

"This one's for old Craufurd," said Sergeant Prickett and he waddled into the crater up to his knees. And so followed the rest of 95th, then the 52nd, and after them the 43rd, not one man saving his feet from the icy water.

When the Division eventually stopped for its midday halt the talk around the camp-fires was not so much about Ciudad Rodrigo, but what a fine fellow Bob Craufurd had been.

CHAPTER ELEVEN

By March 1812, Napoleon was at Dresden and had turned his vainglorious face towards Moscow. He was about to launch himself into yet another war, thus committing himself fatally to two distinct fronts. Spain was, therefore, temporarily forgotten by the Emperor and this in some imperceptible way must have communicated itself to his army in the Peninsula. It certainly communicated itself to its senior Commander, Marshal Marmont, who then held the beautiful, if ephemeral, title of the Duke of Ragusa. As a result of this, and as a result of the capture of Ciudad Rodrigo, the initiative passed to Wellington and the latter wasted no time in doing what had to be done. As George Simmons noted in his diary:

> March 17th, 1812. Marched to the camp before Badajoz. . . . Some time after dark broke ground before Fort Picurina. . . . March 25th. About twelve o'clock noon our first battery opened and played handsomely on Fort Picurina.

And, although their home was some distance away, Juanita and Victoria could hear, like everybody else in the town, the British guns 'playing handsomely' on Fort Picurina. Indeed they listened to it with mixed feelings, remembering the previous siege when it was the French who were outside the walls. Now, with the British banging at the gates, the Pazenses were once again subjected to the hardships of food and fuel rationing, on top of which General Phillipon had imposed a dusk-to-dawn curfew.

There was an additional cause for disquiet which the sisters felt but which was only put into words by old Frasquita.

"Do you think the French mean to defend the town?" she asked when she brought in the soup on the first day of the siege. "Or do you think they will give in like General Imaz?"

Victoria looked at Juanita, deferring to her younger sister in matters of military concern.

"There is no doubt that General Phillipon intends to defend the town," answered Juanita. "Look at all the arrangements he has made. They have been weeks and weeks making *chevaux-de-frises* and digging trenches with sharp spikes in the bottom and all sorts of horrible things."

"*O Dio mio!*" said Frasquita. "Then that's a terrible bad thing for us."

"Why do you say that?" asked Victoria, knowing instinctively the answer.

"Because they say that the harder they have to fight the more savage the English become. They also say that the English will sack the town because of all the *afrancesados* in it."

"Who is 'they' who say all these stupid things?" replied Victoria.

"Why the women in the market, of course. And they're always right." And Victoria and Juanita in their hearts believed the market gossip to be true.

"Do you think the English will sack the town, Madre?" Juanita asked Madre Soledad on her next visit to the convent.

"If it is God's will that they sack the town, then they will sack it and we must offer it up to God as a penance for our sins. Meanwhile console yourselves with the fact that Milor Belington was well content with Badajoz when he made his headquarters here. Also remember that you have two good friends on his staff."

"*Los capitanos Gordón y Esomerset.* Yes, they must be quite close to us now, this very minute. Oh, if only we could get a message to them."

"You know that is impossible now, child."

"Madre, what will you do if—if—"

"If the British sack the town? What else can I do but pray?" answered Madre Soledad, smiling. "Nothing that English soldiers could do to me could be worse than what the Roman soldiers did to Our Lord Jesus Christ. Besides, what have I got to fear—an ugly old *negra* like me?"

"But you are not ugly, Madre, particularly when you smile," said Juanita looking at the nun's beautiful black eyes.

"Then I must keep smiling—and so must you. Go in peace now, child and pray to Our Lady to make you as brave as she was. Kiss me." And Juanita kissed her and turned away quickly because she felt tears coming into her eyes.

6 April 1812. In the morning of this day the breaches of Badajoz were declared practicable and the whole process of Forlorn Hopes, storming parties, laddermen, men with fascines and grass-bags, were once more assembled according to a plan long prepared in advance.

The storming of Badajoz was not a particularly big affair in terms of scale, nor were the casualties so very great (though per capita of men involved they were colossal), but it probably was one of the most savage battles ever fought between Europeans in modern times. Let therefore those who took part in it tell the story in their own words. What follows is history.

MAJOR WILLIAM NAPIER, 43rd Light Infantry
Dry but clouded was the night, the air thick with watery exhalations from the rivers, the ramparts and trenches unusually still; yet a low murmur pervaded the latter, and in the former lights were seen to flit here and there while the deep voices of the sentinels at times proclaimed that all was well in Badajoz. The French, confiding in Phillipon's direful skill, watched from their lofty station the approach of enemies whom they hoped to drive blasted and ruined from the walls. The British, standing in deep columns, were as eager to meet that fiery destruction as the others were to pour it down, and both were alike terrible for their strength, their discipline, and the passions awakened in their resolute hearts.

CORPORAL EDWARD COSTELLO, 95th Rifles
For the second time I volunteered for the Forlorn Hope. After having received a double ration of grog, we fell in about eight o'clock in the evening. I happened to be on the right of the front section when my old Captain, Major O'Hare, came up with Captain Jones of the 52nd regiment, both in command of the storming party. A pair of uglier men never walked together, but

a brace of better soldiers never stood before the muzzle of a Frenchman's gun.

"Well O'Hare," said the Captain, "What do you think of to-night's work?"

"I don't know," replied the Major who seemed, as I thought, in rather low spirits. "To-night I think will be my last."

"Tut-tut, man! I have the same sort of feeling but I keep it down with a drop of the *cratur*," answered the Captain as he handed his calabash to the Major.

Lieutenant John Kincaid, 95th Rifles
The enemy seemed aware of our intentions. The fire of artillery and musketry, which for three weeks before had been incessant, had now entirely ceased as if by mutual consent, and a death-like silence of nearly an hour preceded the awful scene of carnage.

Captain Jonathan Leach, 95th Rifles
Soon after dark the columns moved out of the trenches to the different points allotted to them to attack. Major Peter O'Hare commanded the storming party which headed the Light Division, and some companies of our corps lined the glacis to keep down the fire of the enemy from the ramparts.

Captain Harry Smith, 95th Rifles
Old Alister Cameron came up to Barnard and said, "Now my men are ready. Shall I begin?" "No, certainly not," says Barnard. The breach and the works were full of the enemy looking quietly at us, although not firing a shot. So soon as our ladders were all ready posted and the column in the very act to move Barnard called out, "*Now*, Cameron!" and the first shot from us brought down such a hail of fire as I shall never forget, nor ever saw before or since. We flew at the ladders and rushed at the breach, but we were broken and carried no weight with us though every soldier was a hero.

Corporal Costello
Three of the men carrying the ladders with us were shot dead in a breath, and its weight falling upon me, I fell backwards with

the grass-bag on my breast. The remainder of the stormers rushed up, regardless of my cries or those of the wounded around me, for by this time our men were falling fast. Many in passing were shot and fell upon me so that I was actually drenched in blood. At length, by a strong effort, I managed to extricate myself, in doing which I left my rifle behind me, and, drawing my sword, rushed towards the breach.

MAJOR NAPIER
Now a multitude bounded up the great breach as if driven by a whirlwind, but across the top glittered a range of sword-blades, sharp-pointed, keen-edged on both sides and firmly fixed in ponderous beams chained together and set deep in the ruins; and for ten feet in front the ascent was studded with loose planks studded with sharp iron points, on which feet being set the planks moved and the unhappy soldiers falling forward on the spikes rolled down on the ranks behind.

CAPTAIN SMITH
A Rifleman stood among the sword-blades on the top of one of the *chevaux-de-frises*. We made a glorious rush to follow but, alas, in vain. He was knocked over. My old captain, O'Hare, who commanded the storming party, was killed. All were awfully wounded except, I do believe, myself and little Freer of the 43rd.

LIEUTENANT GEORGE SIMMONS, 95th Rifles
The ditch now, from the place where we now entered to near the top of the breaches, was covered with dead and dying soldiers. If a man fell wounded, ten to one that he ever rose again, for the volleys of musketry and grape-shot that were incessantly poured among us made our situation too horrible for description. I had seen some fighting, but nothing like this.

QUARTERMASTER WILLIAM SURTEES, 95th Rifles
All sorts of arms were playing at once, guns, mortars, musketry, grenades and shells thrown down from the walls, while every few minutes explosions from mines were taking

place. This continued without a moment's cessation, or without any apparent advantage being gained by our struggling but awfully circumstanced comrades. Lord Wellington had also taken his stance upon this hill, and appeared quite uneasy at the troops seeming to make no progress, and often asked, or repeated to himself, "What can be the matter?"

Lieutenant Simmons

I saw my poor friend Major O'Hare lying dead upon the breach. Two or three musket balls had passed through his breast. I called to remembrance poor O'Hare's last words just before he marched off to lead the advance. He shook me by the hand saying, "A Lieutenant-Colonel or cold meat in a few hours."

Major Napier

Officers of all ranks, followed more or less numerously by the men, were seen to start out as if struck by sudden madness and rush into the breach, which yawning and glittering with steel seemed like the mouth of a huge dragon belching forth smoke and flame. Yet there was no want of gallant leaders or desperate followers until two hours passed in these vain efforts had convinced the troops the breach of the Trinidad was impregnable.

Quartermaster Surtees

Still our people at the breaches did not get forward, although we distinctly heard with emotion the bugles of our division sounding the advance. His Lordship seemed now to lose all patience and aides-de-camp were sent to ascertain the cause of the delay. They flew like lightning, while the whole rampart round the town seemed enveloped in one flame of fire. Our brave but unsuccessful comrades were heard cheering every now and then, but still the fire at the breaches did not slacken. At length a despatch arrived from General Picton stating that he had established himself in the castle. This was cheering news to his lordship who expressed very strongly the gratitude he felt for that gallant General.

Corporal Costello

After the horrible scene of carnage had lasted some time, I heard a cheering which I knew to proceed from within the town, and shortly afterwards a cry of "Blood and 'ounds! Where's the Light Division? The town's our own—Hurrah!" This proceeded no doubt from some of the Third Division. I now attempted to rise but, from a wound which I had received at what time I know not, found myself unable to stand. At the moment of this discovery I saw two or three men moving towards me who I was glad to see belonged to the Rifles. One of them named O'Brien immediately exclaimed, "What! Is that you, Ned? We thought you laddermen all done for."

Captain Smith

Now comes a scene of horror I would willingly bury in oblivion. The atrocities committed by our soldiers on the poor, innocent and defenceless inhabitants of the city, no words suffice to depict.

Major Napier

Yet who shall do justice to the bravery of the British soldiers? Who shall measure out the glory of Ridge, of MacLeod, of Nicholas, of O'Hare of the 95th who perished on the breach at the head of the stormers and with him nearly all the volunteers for that desperate service? Who shall describe the springing valour of that Portuguese grenadier who was killed the foremost man at the Santa Maria? Or the martial fury of that desperate rifleman who, in his resolution to win, thrust himself beneath the chained sword-blades and there suffered the enemy to dash his head to pieces with the ends of their muskets?

Corporal Costello

Supported by O'Brien we proceeded in the direction of the market- place. It was a dark night and the confusion and uproar that prevailed in the town may be better imagined than described. The shouts and oaths of drunken soldiers in quest of more liquor, the reports of fire-arms and crashing in of doors, together with the appalling shrieks of hapless women, might have induced anyone to have believed himself in the regions of the damned. The scenes of wickedness that soldiers are guilty of on capturing a town are ten times truly diabolical. We entered a house that was occupied by a number of men of the Third Division. One of them, on perceiving me wounded, struck the neck off a bottle of wine and presented it to me, which relieved me for the time from the weakness I had felt. Unhappily they discovered the two daughters of the old padrone who had concealed themselves upstairs. They were both young and very pretty. The mother, too, was shortly afterwards dragged from her hiding-place. I will not dwell on the frightful scene that followed, but it is to be considered that the men who besiege a town in the face of such dangers, once they get a footing within its walls, flushed by victory and maddened by drink, they stop at nothing.

LIEUTENANT SIMMONS
I went into a genteel house. The Spaniard told me the French Quartermaster-General had lived with him. I found a bottle of wine and two glasses on the table. I sat down and drank the bottle of wine and got some eggs and bacon fried.

CAPTAIN SMITH
Civilized man, when let loose and the bonds of morality relaxed, is a far greater beast than the savage, more refined in his cruelty, and more fiend-like in every act; and oh, too truly did our heretofore noble soldiers disgrace themselves, though the officers exerted themselves to the utmost to repress it; many who had escaped the enemy being wounded in their merciful attempts. Yet this scene of debauchery, however cruel to many, to me has been the solace and whole happiness of my life.

CHAPTER TWELVE

7 APRIL 1812 was the watershed in Harry Smith's life. It was never to be the same again.

In the early hours before the break of day, when the taking of Badajoz was fast changing its character from an assault to a saturnalia (in one narrow street a drunken fusilier was sitting on top of a barrel of brandy forcing everybody, including officers, to drink at musket-point), Harry decided to give up the impossible task of trying to control the soldiery. Perhaps, had he known then that some of the more brutal elements of his old 13 Platoon, inflamed with drink, had broken into the convent of Nuestra Señora de la Soledad, he would certainly have tried to intervene. But Harry was no longer the Commander of 13 Platoon; nor was he even aware of the existence of that convent.

Harry's body ached all over. When first light came he sat on a bastion and undressed himself. He found on his ribs and left thigh two severe contusions but came to the surprised conclusion that he was not otherwise wounded. He took off his shako and noticed with amusement that it had not one, but two, bullet-holes in it. He then rubbed his short curly hair vigorously with the finger-tips of both hands and set the cap back straight on his head. Dressed again, he emptied a handful of grit out of one of his tunic pockets, re-tied his sash, checked the priming of his pistol, and set off towards the Trinidad breach.

Early in the night he had seen Peter O'Hare go down. Peter had probably saved his life at Fuentes. If Peter was only wounded there was just a chance that he might now be able to do something for him. In any case, he decided, he could be more effective helping to organize the evacuation of the wounded, or at least to alleviate their sufferings a bit, than attempt the impossible in the town. As he knew from recent experience, it was not until the 'hangover' period had set in that authority could hope to deal with armed professional killers maddened with alcohol. The cliché 'brutal and licentious soldiery', much in vogue in London at the time, was a matter of harsh reality to Wellington's officers.

The first person Harry saw as day dawned was Bill Surtees, the regimental Quartermaster, who was obviously intent on the same purpose as himself. Between them they cajoled and cudgelled those less intoxicated soldiers, some of whom were now drifting back with their loot, to drop everything and pick up the wounded. Many of the latter, who had gone into the fight with such gallantry, were now unable to extract themselves from under the piles of dead and dying, and were crying out for help and being ignored by their erstwhile mates staggering by with their booty.

"Look, here he is! Here's poor old Peter!" called out Surtees. Harry knelt down beside a body whose bright red hair contrasted grotesquely with the deathly whiteness of his ugly face. Surtees put a hand to him, "He's cold already," he said. "Cary and Croudace are dead too," he went on. "I dined with the two of them last night. They were expecting it. And now here's O'Hare and Allen—and Sergeant Fleming over there beside Peter. Somebody said Charlie Beckwith had been hit."

"No, I don't think so. But what about Johnny Kincaid?" Harry asked.

Johnny had in fact got away without a scratch and entered the town via the breach soon after the Castle had fallen to Picton's division. He had been going down a narrow street when he was almost knocked down by a French officer who, running like the devil, was being chased at bayonet-point by some Connaught Rangers. The Irishmen, being as yet only mildly inebriated, were easily prevailed upon by Kincaid to desist, greatly to the relief of the Frenchman who had no wish for sudden death in hot blood and cold steel.

The French officer, who described himself as an aide-de-camp to General Phillipon, now insisted on staying close to the tall rifleman lest worse befell him.

"Listen, monsieur," said the Frenchman, "you have saved my life, for which I am grateful. Now I am a prisoner of war, but there is one thing I can do for you in return. If you please, you follow me." And the officer led Johnny to a large door near the Plaza de

España and took him by a cobbled path through a house, down an outdoor passage to where, somewhat to Johnny's surprise, there was a stable. "There!" said the Frenchman with a theatrical gesture, pointing into the blackness. "It is for you. It is yours." Kincaid looked in, saw nothing, smelt horse. "*Cheval?*" said Kincaid, whose French was minimal.

"*Mais un cheval superbe!*" replied the officer.

"Oh, good!" said Kincaid. "That is the only thing that British officers are really allowed to loot, you know. *Merci beaucoup*."

An hour or so later, having left his prisoner in the comparative safety of a room in the castle where a good many other enemy officers had been assembled, Johnny Kincaid was back in camp, having ridden there on his new black horse whose name, as Johnny had been careful to find out, was Monsieur Barsac.

Too over-tired and over-excited to sleep, he sat down outside his tent to have a cup of tea and to swap adventures with Charlie Eeles. In the course of describing some vivid experience, the latter, whose head was bound with a rather romantic-looking bandage, but who otherwise appeared to be in perfect health, turned to glance back at the town.

"Look! Those stupid buggers have set the place alight," said Eeles pointing to where smoke from several fires could be seen rising brownish against a background of pale sunlight. The town was nearly a mile away but they could still hear shouts and an occasional shot on the still morning air. "What old Nosey wants to do is to string two or three of those drunken bastards up."

"I saw him this morning," replied Kincaid. "Some fool was trying to force him to have a drink, calling him 'old fellow', if you please."

"What did he do? Did he take one?"

"Not a bit of it. He just raised his forefinger to his hat and rode on as if he was going to breakfast at Boodle's."

"More tea, Mr Kincaid?" asked Rifleman Rutherford, Kincaid's servant, appearing with a kettle. "Hullo—'ullo! What's this?" he said suddenly, straightening up. Heedless of his officer's outstretched mug, he looked in the direction of the town. "Two señoritas—coming this way by the looks of it. I can tell you didn't waste much time last night, Mr Kincaid."

Ignoring Rutherford's pleasantry, Eeles and Kincaid turned and saw two young women who certainly seemed to be making towards their tent. The elder and taller had her arm round the other's shoulder, while the younger clutched her companion round the waist. Though somewhat dishevelled they both appeared to be good-looking and well- though not smartly-dressed.

"You are British officers," said the elder.

"We are ma'am, yes," said Kincaid saluting. Then in a mixture of French, Spanish and English the elder of the two girls tried to explain their situation.

"I am Victoria De Los Dolores," she began, "and this is my sister, Juana Maria. I wish to speak, please, to Capitán Gordón or Milor Esomerset."

"I think the lady must mean the C-in-C's aides," said Eeles to his friend. "Lord Fitzroy Somerset?" he went on turning to the two young ladies.

"*Exactamente!* He who lived in my house."

"Oh, I see," said Kincaid. "They were billeted on you, were they?"

"What is it, billeted? *No entiendo.*"

"Captain Gordon and Lord Fitzroy are known to you and you want to see them. Of course. But—um—that could be rather difficult just now. I mean, I have no idea where they might be. . . . Ah, there's Harry Smith—a friend of ours who speaks Spanish. I'll get him over." And Johnny called out to Harry Smith who was passing through the lines on his way back to Brigade headquarters.

Harry and Bill Surtees, together with little Freer of the 43rd, had spent nearly three hours struggling to get together enough men to take care of the wounded. They had pulled out and tried to make comfortable a good many men themselves, but it was an exhausting and almost impossible task since there were no bandages, little water and no food to give them. Harry particularly, who had taken part in the assault (as indeed had little Freer), was very tired, and he certainly did not look his usual regimental self. Apart from two holes in his cap, his face was grey from gunpowder, his tunic was torn in several places and, despite the fact that he had washed his hands in a puddle, his sleeves and trousers were stained with blood.

When Kincaid had explained the situation Harry greeted the sisters in Spanish and offered to do what he could to help. Victoria spoke again.

"You will be surprised that we come to your camp. This is not what Spanish women do—except for women of a certain sort. But we have no alternative. Yesterday we had a house, we had clothes, we had food. Now today we have nothing—nothing! The French destroyed our farm at Olivenza and the English have now destroyed our house and everything we have left." And here her eyes betrayed a flash of anger. "Look what your soldiers have done!"

Victoria drew back her sister's and her own mantilla to reveal their ears. The blood was still drying on their necks where their earrings had been torn out by drunken looters. "They could not even wait for us to take them off and give them."

Though the three subalterns had within hours seen every bloody sight a battlefield could offer, they were horrified anew at this defilement of the young women.

"They are worse than brutes when they get hold of the drink," said Johnny Kincaid, looking at Eeles for confirmation. Charlie Eeles nodded vigorously but it was Rifleman Rutherford, taking the liberty of an intimate servant, who decided to voice an opinion.

"It's not right," he said. "It's the drink what does it. Them Frenchies don't drink, not like what our lads do. But it's not right, is it?" And he assumed a self-righteous expression and deliberately evaded a silencing glare from his officer.

Up to this moment Harry Smith, concentrating on what Victoria was saying, had not noticed the younger sister. But when her mantilla had been drawn back to display the injury to her ears it was not the blood on the torn flesh that he saw, but the exquisite ear itself. And this led him to note the set of a brown head on so slender a neck, the russet glow of health on such sweet cheeks, and the look of courage and complete absence of self-pity in the largest brown eyes he had ever seen. And he continued looking at Juana Maria long after his look had turned into an impolite stare.

"You are British officers," Victoria was saying, "and therefore honourable men. It is for that reason I am coming now to you. I am a married woman and my husband is also an officer in the army of General Alburquerque, but I have no news of him for two years and it is possible that he may be dead. For myself I am not preoccupied, but for him and my sister who is only fourteen—"

Harry felt himself in a daze, a sort of sweet dream in which all sorts of improbable things kept happening. He felt that at any minute he would be able to levitate and fly off into the air. He tried to reason with himself and tell himself that he was suffering from hallucinations induced by lack of sleep. He wondered if in fact he had been blown up in the breach and had not yet come down again. He tried to pay polite attention to what Victoria was saying and to stop staring at Juana Maria, but he could do neither of these things. Juana Maria! Is that what they said her name was? And Juana Maria was fourteen. Fourteen? But she was already a woman. A precise and perfect woman. An exquisite woman of fourteen. And her name was Juana Maria De Los something — something rather beautiful, but what?

"Juanita was still in the convent when the French came," he heard Victoria say. "Since then she has been with me at home. But now we have no home and I must go to find my husband. I must find out if he is alive or dead. But first I must find protection for my sister, so if I can speak to El Capitán Gordón—"

"You need look no further for your sister's protection," said Harry Smith who prided himself on taking quick decisions. "My friends and I will guarantee her safety".

Eeles and Kincaid, who sensed the drift of what was being said, looked at each other questioningly.

Victoria paused for a moment and looked at Harry. She saw a spare man of middle height who looked more Spanish than English, though his manner was all English. She also saw, above and beyond his tattered appearance and dirty face, a look of authority and integrity.

"But there is no woman to be with her, and I must take my servant with me. I cannot travel alone," she protested.

"There are women belonging to this regiment who could be found to take care of her," answered Harry. "She could be given a tent to herself. There are empty tents enough—after last night." And Harry turned to his friends to explain what he had in mind.

"Pretty irregular, Harry," said Eeles, "but all the same—"

"Tricky, yes," said Kincaid, "but damsel in distress and that sort of thing. I don't see what else one can do!"

"What else? I know what else *I* can do," said Harry. Again he addressed himself to Victoria.

"Even among British officers there are men who would take advantage of a young woman if opportunity presented itself—if for example duty prevented any of the three of us from being there to protect her. Therefore there would seem to be only one way to guarantee your sister's safety and honour."

"Yes?" said Victoria. "There is a way?"

"Yes, there is a way," said Harry. "She must marry a British officer as soon as possible." Harry turned to Juanita.

"My name is Harry George Wakelyn Smith. I am a Captain in the Rifle Corps. I would consider it an honour if you would consent to be my wife. If you wish we shall be married immediately."

To Harry's joyous astonishment the answer came back with a forthrightness and aplomb that he had not thought to expect.

"My name is Juana Maria De Los Dolores de Leon. I can sew and I can cook and I speak good French. I am grateful for your offer of marriage which, with my sister's permission, I accept." And Juanita looked at the spare young man whose dark eyes looked resolutely at her; and she saw the bullet-holes in his cap, and his tattered tunic and his dirty face. She let her heart say what it had to say.

"I will be a good and true wife to you as long as I live," she said.

CHAPTER THIRTEEN

THE FACT THAT Harry had suffered what the French call a *coup de foudre* made him impervious to all other obtrusions: exhaustion, shock of battle and even—for a while—grief for fallen comrades. If, however, he was confident that he had found a neat solution to a delicate problem, then he was—at least in part—mistaken.

In the first place not one but two men had fallen in love with Juanita at first sight. The other was Harry's best friend, Johnny Kincaid. Johnny now reminded him that the Smith family were devout Anglicans whereas Juanita was a convent-educated 'cradle' Catholic. He also pointed out that the town of Badajoz, the provincial capital, had just fallen after a fierce and bloody siege and there was, in consequence, no civil administration whatsoever, and so on. Harry listened, or pretended to listen, to Johnny's strictures, then deliberately ignored them and set about making his own dispositions.

Colonel Barnard was now commanding the brigade in the absence of Vandeleur who had been wounded at Ciudad Rodrigo. But it could hardly be said that he had much of a brigade to command since about half the strength had fallen in the assault, and the remaining half had then fallen to Bacchus. The Colonel was therefore at Harry's disposal.

"Harry," he said, "I have not had the pleasure of knowing you very long, but Sydney Beckwith had a high opinion of you and I will therefore do my best to put myself in his position—not an easy thing to do, by the way. His standards were very high. . . . What, I wonder, would he have said? You tell me that the young lady comes from a good family. Very well, but apparently she is only fourteen. That is very young, surely? Another thing, I know one should not be prejudiced about marrying someone from another country but have you considered how, as your wife, this young person would fare in Cambridgeshire—isn't that where you live? And how would she get on with your family? Then there is the question of religion. . . ."

Harry listened politely. "Colonel," he said when the latter had finished, "I appreciate all that you have pointed out to me, but please let me say this. I don't wish to sound smug, but all my adult life to date I have lived for the regiment and for my job as a soldier. At home in Cambridgeshire I was always more interested in the hunting-field than in the ballroom, and I have certainly never even thought of marriage. But suddenly—this very morning a totally new, and marvellous—miraculous, it seems to me—dimension has come into my life and I am determined to have this girl for my wife."

There was a pause while the two men looked thoughtfully at each other. Then Colonel Barnard spoke again. "Then, Harry, there is no more to be said. Please know that I was only being the devil's advocate and in no way was I trying to oppose you. As earnest of my good intentions let me offer—I take it that the young lady has no male relative available? No?—let me offer then to give away the bride at your wedding."

But a wedding, for all the goodwill of Colonel Barnard and the earnest intentions of the bridal pair—and one consideration was that Victoria was now more than ever anxious to find out whether she had a living husband or not—was far from easy to achieve.

Charlie Eeles and Sergeant Mayberry, having been despatched into the town on various errands, came back with Frasquita, the De Los Dolores' cook, but no priest. The only one they could find had locked himself in the crypt of the cathedral with an ancient lady called the Marquesa de Hinojosa, and his reverence would not come out for love or money; least of all to perform something as frivolous as a marriage ceremony. But he was prepared to discuss the matter from his side of an iron grille. His excuse, probably a legitimate one, was that he could not marry a Catholic to a Protestant without the permission of his Bishop.

"And where is the Bishop?" asked Harry.

"In the monastery of Guadalupe—about a hundred miles away," said Eeles.

"Then how the hell does one get married in this country?" asked Harry angrily, lack of sleep having done little to improve his temper.

"I suppose Parson Parker would do the job," suggested Johnny.

"Yes, but Juanita is a Catholic and I don't suppose Parson Parker's 'job', as you call it, would serve in Spain."

"Does anybody know what the Spanish law is on mixed marriages?" asked Charlie.

"General Álava. That's it. Miguel de Álava, the C-in-C's Spanish liaison officer. He might know. I think I'll get over to GHQ and see if I can talk to him."

"At the same time you could inform Alex Gordon and the Boy from Badminton that their erstwhile landladies are here," Johnny said.

Harry did not respond to this suggestion. He felt a disinclination to get involved with GHQ staff in a matter of private business. On the other hand he did not know how he could get to General Álava except through Gordon.

"Perhaps we should consult the ladies first," said Charlie.

Rutherford and West, in the early hours of this novel situation—they already had some ideas as to what was afoot—had appointed themselves unofficial guards over 'Mr Smith's fiarncy' and had posted themselves in front of the entrance to the ladies' tent which had been pitched at a discreet distance from the company lines. There they made a fire and sat down to peel potatoes into a camp-kettle.

"Yes," said Harry, "we should talk it over with the ladies." And as he said so Rifleman Rutherford appeared like a genie out of a bottle to announce that 'the ladies was restin'—and that the old 'un—beg pardon, what's-er-name, Mrs Frasqueeta—was properly done up an' carryin' on like she had bin rummaged by a squadron of dragoons—some hope!" he added, clicking his tongue and rolling his eyeballs skywards.

"I'll go over and see how things are," Harry said and crossed with Rutherford to where West was sitting outside the tent. West's attitude towards Harry was always half-regimental and half-avuncular. Today he looked at Harry like a family doctor whose patient was in need of special care and attention.

"West," said Harry, "just see if the young señorita is available to have a word with me, would you."

Hardly had he done so than Juanita came out smiling, looking so sweet and fresh and happy that Harry's heart turned over for the second time in one day. She was wearing no mantilla this time and he could see that her hair was dark-brown, slightly wavy, and that one or two wayward curls seemed to fall naturally forward over her brow. She wore a shawl crossed over her bosom, accentuating a full, firm, trim figure, a beautiful ankle and a small foot.

Chivalry has nothing to do with this, Harry said to himself. He was right, he knew he was right, to marry this girl and nothing, he swore to himself, nothing saving Acts of God or the King's enemies was going to prevent him from doing so.

"Juana Maria," he said.

"Juanita," she replied smiling.

"Juanita," he began again, then looked at West who backed off discreetly to join Rutherford at the camp-kettle, which last now had a bright and aromatic fire burning under it.

"Juanita," said Harry, I think we should talk a little."

"I should like that very much," answered Juanita. "What is your name again?"

Harry gave a bark of genuine laughter. "That is a very good question to ask your novio. My Christian name is Harry—Enrique in Spanish."

"Then I will call you 'Enrique'. And your surname?"

"Smith."

"Then I shall be called Juana Maria De Los Dolores de Esmeet, no?"

"Just Mrs Smith will do."

"Meesis Esmeet?"

West approached with two ammunition boxes. "Would you and the young lady care to sit down by the fire, sir? Rutherford and I have a few jobs to do so you'll have it to yourselves."

"Thanks very much, West."

"Every modern convenience, Miss," said West placing an ammunition box for Juanita who rewarded him with a bright smile.

"*Muchas gracias.*"

"*De nada, señorita,*" answered West, pleased with his Spanish.

"Listen to me, Juanita," said Harry as soon as West had gone, "it was not for *caballería*—chivalry—that I asked you to marry me."

"I know that, Enrique. And it was not for my own safety that I accepted. I would not marry just for that."

"I wish—I wish I could kiss you, Juanita."

"I too would like that—very much. Soon, when we are married."

"That is another thing we have to talk about." And Harry explained the immediate problem of finding a priest and the other attendant complications, including his doubts as to the value in Spain of Parson Parker's ministrations.

"But, what does it matter?" said Juanita. "If we are both Christians we would be married in the sight of God. It is the intention that counts." Then suddenly Juanita remembered Padre Julián. "Yes, of course," she exclaimed happily. "I know a priest who would marry us. Padre Julián. Then we could have your Parsomparquer as well and we would be doubly married."

"Where can we find your priest?" asked Harry.

"I think," replied Juanita, "if you can find El Capitán Gordón he will know where Padre Julián is."

"Then I will go and look for him immediately." And, getting up, Harry took hold of Juanita's hand and, as he did so, he felt such a current of love pass from him to her—and back again to a point infinitely recurring—that he could scarce let her go.

Arriving rather light-headed at General Headquarters Harry found Alex Gordon wrapped in his boat-cloak taking a nap outside the Commander-in-Chief's door. He woke up when Harry came in.

"Hullo, Smith," he said, yawning and turning on to one elbow. "Had a rough night?"

"I don't think I've slept since about the day before yesterday. . . . Listen, Gordon, there is something you could do for me."

"Yes?"

"Introduce me to General Álava."

"Not possible, I'm afraid," said the ADC yawning again. "He has gone down south to report last night's proceedings to the Central Junta and to try to get some sense out of them about future operations."

"Oh?" said Harry, feeling baulked.

"Good chap, Álava. The C-in-C thinks the world of him. Says Miguel is so English he makes him feel like a foreigner."

Harry, thinking of his own problem, missed the point. "Look here, Gordon," he said, "there is something else. . . ."

"What's that?"

"Can you put me in touch with a Spaniard—I'm told you know him—a priest called Don Julián."

"Padre Julián! What the hell do you want *him* for?" asked Gordon loking considerably more alert.

"It's rather a long story."

"Well, I'm sorry but I can't tell you where he is."

"But you do know him, don't you?" he asked.

"Yes and no. That is a long story, too. But what in the world do you want to get in touch with *that* fellow for?"

Harry paused for a minute, feeling dashed by the note of disparagement in Gordon's voice.

"All right then, Gordon. I'll tell you—but I would be glad if you would keep this to yourself for the time being. I am going to—that is, I want to get married."

"Do you, by Jove! What, *now*?"

"As soon as possible."

"Then, my dear fellow, I suppose I must congratulate you. Pray, who is the lady?"

As Harry told his story Alex started to pace up and down again, his fingers fidgeting with his chin. "It has been a terrible business, Badajoz," he said finally. "A terrible business for everybody. As the General himself put it, 'the next greatest misfortune to losing a battle is to gain such a victory as this'."

At that moment they both heard the voice of Lord Wellington calling for his ADC.

"Coming, my Lord," answered Alex, and turning to Harry Smith, "I'm sorry, my dear fellow, but I'm not in a position to be of much help at present. I will try to get over tomorrow. Failing that, if there is anything I can do, come and see me here."

After leaving Gordon, Harry, feeling disconsolate, turned his horse's head and proceeded at a walking-pace towards the Light Division camp. Having reached the Albuera road he noticed some horses tethered outside a tavern and recognized the bucket-stirrups and saddles with high pommel and cantle used by the *garrochistas*.

Harry suddenly felt sure that the one man who could help him out would be Julián. He dismounted and walked into the bar.

There at the far end of the room, at a table with El Fraile and various others whose faces he knew, was Julián Sanchez.

If Harry's business at GHQ had not exactly been crowned with success, it had not been roses all the way for Juanita either. Whether it was due to tiredness, or to a reaction setting in after the multifarious happenings of the past twenty-four hours, the toughness she had acquired throughout the sieges of her home town seemed now to have evaporated. Having committed herself totally to Harry Smith, and having fallen completely in love with him, she felt more vulnerable than ever before. And when a party of French officers were marched as prisoners-of-war through the Rifle Corps lines, and when she saw Jean-Pierre Soula among them—and worse, when she thought he had spotted her happy there among the riflemen—she went inside and cried at the pity of it all.

Harry, for his part, when he entered the bar in the hope of seeing Julián, was feeling equally depressed. He knew that this was largely due to lack of sleep—he had felt this way before, especially after La Coruña—but the knowledge did not make it any better. It was not until he had received something like a hero's welcome from the *garrochistas*, who immediately insisted on him taking wine with them, that he began to perk up a bit.

Julián, his anonymity being no longer relevant, had ridden into the town that morning accompanied by Miguelín. Their first visit had been to the house of Victoria and Juanita which they had found, like many others, to be a total wreck. Drunken vandals had blown in locked doors, female garments had been strewn all over the house, a fire had been made out of the furniture in the salon, and food and wine mingled with excreta and vomit covered the patio.

Julián next went to the convent in the hope of seeing Madre Soledad. He found her in the chapel with her sleeves rolled up, wearing an apron and wielding a mop like a professional. Seeing Julián, the first friendly face since the ghastly events of the night before, she broke down and wept.

But she did not give in to her tears for long. Pulling herself together, she made Julián sit down and told him the whole story then and there. The defecations on the altar steps did not defile God's House, she explained. It was those who perpetrated the outrage who were defiled. And, after all, it was a salutary act of humility to clean up the filthy mess. As to the numerous acts of rape committed on the younger nuns in the convent, apart from the shock to their bodies and minds, it was only what had happened to thousands of religious since the beginning of the Christian era. It was something that all who took the veil were prepared to suffer in Christ's name.

"But what," she asked, "am I to do if any of the Sisters get pregnant?"

"Madre," Julián replied, "contrary to what some people still think, I am not a priest and cannot answer your question. What I *can* do is to ensure that you and your people will not be molested again." And he forthwith sent Miguelín to bring over a detachment of *charros* to mount guard on the convent.

"Madre," he said when Miguelín had gone, "I have been to the De Los Dolores' house. It is wrecked. There is no one there. Do you know anything?"

"No, Julián. I know nothing. But I have been praying to God and Our Lady that they have not suffered the same fate as ourselves. . . . Little Juanita—if—" and her lip trembled and Julián was witness once again to the fearful ugliness of this good woman crying.

It being totally impossible to search the town effectively while the soldiers were still rioting—such women who had escaped them would obviously continue to remain in hiding—Julián, having comforted Soledad, returned to camp. It was, however, with rather mixed feelings that he did so.

His feelings towards the British for what they had done—and were still doing—to his fellow-countrymen and women in the town were at odds with his admiration as a soldier for the incredible feat of arms they had performed.

Now the sight of Harry Smith, who had obviously been in the thick of the fight and had survived, helped to cheer him up.

After a few '*Vivas!*' for the English, a few '*Vivas!*' for the Spanish, and a few glasses of wine to go with both, Harry managed to separate his friend from the rest so that they could talk privately.

Julián was astonished when Harry announced his intention of getting married, doubly so—the Spaniards being accustomed to long engagements—when he said he needed to get married at once. To a Spanish mind there could only be one reason for that. But when he had been reassured by Harry on this score, and when he had been told that the bride-to-be was Spanish, he was delighted.

"You couldn't do better," said Julián sincerely. "You are a man who would appreciate a Spanish woman just as you appreciate our country, its language and its customs. We must drink to that."

"Just a minute," said Harry, "there is something I want to ask you. We are having trouble in finding a priest—there are complications—but my *novia* has a friend who she says will marry us, a Padre Julián. Do you know of him?"

El Charro's reaction was a slow one.

"Padre Julián, did you say?"

He paused for so long that Harry began to feel uneasy, even irritated. A curious sensation came over him that he had dreamed this situation, or that it had all happened before. He began to feel that he was falling into a trap of his own making. He even began to think that he knew the answer to this long-standing conundrum of identity.

"Hari," said Julián, looking serious, "May I ask you how she is called, your *novia?*"

"Certainly," said Harry, only too pleased to speak the beloved name. "She is called Juana Maria De Los—"

"Dolores de Leon," finished the other.

And suddenly Harry saw it all. Now at last he knew the answer. Here was the priest who had winked at him coming out of Lord Wellington's office. His anger drained away like the colour from a turkey's wattle.

"You see," Julián explained, "the French are very anti-clerical and there are plenty of Spaniards who feel the same way. Therefore no one would choose to look like a priest if it was not his vocation. At the same time no one would think it strange to see a priest travelling about which was something I needed to do. It was perhaps vain of me to have called myself by my real name, but it all began more or less as a joke. . . . But—much more important—tell me," he went on, "where is my little friend Juanita? This morning I went to their house and—"

"Your little friend Juanita," said Harry, his temper improving with every moment, "is very well and is with her sister and their old *muchacha* in our camp, but—"

"*Hombre! No mi diga!* You couldn't have given me better news. Now we must have a drink to celebrate."

"Yes, but look here, Julián. I still have no priest to marry us."

"Of course you have a priest! Do you think I would fail you? . . . *Oyé*, Miguel!" he called over to the bearded friar who looked up, glass in hand, and started over towards them.

"El Fraile!" said Harry. "Somehow I had always thought that 'El Fraile' was a nickname."

"Like I am known as El Charro he is known as El Fraile," answered Julián. "But I assure you he is as much a priest as I am a *charro*. And Miguel will marry you, won't you Miguel?" went on Julián, reaching out to give the big cleric's hairy cheek a pinch.

"Are you a Catholic, Hari?" he asked.

"No."

"And your *novia?*"

"Of course she is," interrupted Julián. "She is our Juanita, our little heroine of Badajoz."

"Good. But, Hari, I have to ask you, are you a practising Christian?" went on Miguel.

"Yes, I am."

"Then if you are prepared to be married according to the rites of the Holy Catholic and Apostolic Church I will marry you any time you like—right now, if you wish. Otherwise the best I can give you is a blessing."

"I just want to be married and the sooner the better. Can you do that?"

"I can do it. When?"

"Tomorrow."

"Very good," said Julián. "So it shall be. You and Juanita come here tomorrow at twelve o'clock with your friends and you can leave the rest to us. Now we will have that drink."

An hour or so later Harry was on his way back to camp feeling happy, tipsy and sleepy. All he wanted was to see his beloved for a moment and then fall into bed.

But bedtime for Harry was not quite yet. As soon as he arrived back Juanita popped out of her tent with a half-happy, half-anxious expression on her face. In answer to the query in her eyes Harry said, "Everything is arranged and I've got a big surprise for you, Juanita," and he used the familiar second person singular for the first time.

"And for you too I've a surprise," replied Juanita also using the familiar '*tu*' and blushing happily at the intimacy.

"What is it?"

"Shut your eyes."

"Oh, must I?"

"Yes, promise—till I tell you."

And Harry, having drunk enough not to feel inhibited, stood there with eyes shut hoping he would not fall asleep standing up. After rather a long moment Juanita said "Open" and he did so and saw, grinning in front of him, his brother Tom.

"You missed Talavera by one day and I missed Badajoz by one day. That makes us quits, old boy."

"Tom," said Harry, "you've arrived just in time to put me to bed. Now I'm going to say good-night to Juanita, even if its only four o'clock in the afternoon, and you can take me to my tent. You'll be my Best Man in the morning."

And that, so far as Harry was concerned, was the end of the longest day in his life.

Only in the small hours did he wake briefly to worry as to whether or not he had told Juanita that she was to be married in the morning. Then almost at once he was asleep again, but this time to be enmeshed in terrible muddled dreams in which he was at the breach on top of a ladder which was slowly being pushed over backwards, or he was in the streets of Badajoz powerless to stop drunken troops violating the poor people of the town, or, worst of all, he was struggling, struggling with all his might, struggling helplessly to prevent unmentionable things being done to Juanita by members of his old platoon.

It was a great relief to Harry when Rifleman West woke him with a cup of tea and reminded him that it was his wedding day.

CHAPTER FOURTEEN

On that day, Harry and Juanita's wedding day, the Commander-in-Chief, Lord Wellington, caused a gallows to be erected in the main plaza of Badajoz.

"It is curious how men, who think nothing of powder and ball and who would stand up to Boney's cavalry as they might watch a knuckle-fight, tremble marvellously when they are faced with a gallows," he said. "I have no doubt it is a congenital matter," he concluded.

To make assurance doubly sure, however, his Lordship sent in a Portuguese brigade under General Power with orders to clear every British man-jack out of the town, at bayonet-point if necessary.

The withdrawal of the last debauchees from Badajoz was not a pretty sight. Drunks were supporting drunks, many wore women's clothes, some more the canonicals of priests while others had got themselves up in the habits of nuns. Every sort of booty was carried out of the town from feather-beds to hams and cuts of meat impaled on bayonets. And soon there arrived families of gypsies and peasants from the surrounding countryside to trade livestock and foodstuffs for articles of loot, and in no time the cantonments outside the town began to resemble a vast fair or market rather than an army camp.

The news, conveyed by West, that the wedding was scheduled for twelve noon at the headquarters of El Charro put the cat among the pigeons in the ladies' tent.

"*Bendii-ito sea Dios!*" wailed Frasquita. "Whatever will you wear? Well, there is no other remedy. I shall have to go and see the gypsies."

"But we haven't got any money," said Victoria.

"Don't you worry, *hija*, Frasquita will take care of that." And she lifted up several petticoats and tapped a pocket that gave out chink of coin in an area where no man in his senses would go looking for it.

Not half a mile away West was brushing Harry's best (and now his only) uniform and buffing up his Hessians, while the two Smith brothers, in between washing, shaving and exchanging news, were planning the business of the day.

"What have you done about a ring?" asked Tom.

"My God, I'd never even thought of it."

"It is customary, old boy."

"Yes, but how—I mean, where—"

"Excuse me, sir," interrupted West in the quietly officious voice (he had others) of the family physician, "but when I've dagged up your boots I'll just dodge over to 'I' Company and I wouldn't be surprised—well, just let me see what I can do."

"About a ring?" said Harry, genuinely surprised.

"Yes, sir, a wedding ring."

"Well, how would 'I' Company—"

"No names, no pack-drill, sir."

"But how would they know about the size?"

"Like I said, sir, just let me see what I can do."

Twenty minutes later West was back with a plain gold ring which he presented to Harry with the urbanity of a Bond Street jeweller.

"But, West—I really don't—I mean to say—"

"A perfect fit, sir. We've tried it on Madam."

"We?"

"Doubleday and myself, sir."

"Oh no! . . . Well, I suppose there's nothing for it. How much do I owe you?"

"Doubleday says a penny—just for luck. It's with the compliments of 13 Platoon."

"Oh, God! . . . Well, thanks West. No names, no pack-drill and all that, I suppose. Tell 13 Platoon they're invited to the wedding. How are things over at the ladies' tent?"

"Terrible, sir. There's a pile of gypsy women in there all shouting and screaming at once. Poor Miss Juanita—I don't know."

"What d'you mean you don't know?"

"Well they're all sticking pins and needles into her and pulling her about and sewing things on to her. You know how it is with them didecais, one's company, two's a crowd and three's an open rebellion. And then there's Mrs Frasqueeta—"

"Oh my God! Tom, can't you do something?"

"What can I do?"

"Well, try and sort things out a bit. . . . What's the time? Heaven's above! We've only got two hours."

"Now don't panic, Harry—"

"I'm not panicking. I'm just being realistic. Poor little Juanita, I hope they're not upsetting her. Who's got the ring? Oh, I've got it."

"Give it to me, Harry, and keep calm or you'll cut yourself with that razor."

West came into the tent again.

"Beg pardon, sir, there's a galloper from GHQ with a letter, sir."

Harry, who was still shaving, opened the letter and looked at the signature. It was from Alex Gordon.

"Read it out, Tom," he said handing over the letter.

"Dear Smith,

By the time you get this I shall be on my way to Lisbon for passage to England. The Commander-in-Chief has done me the signal honour of entrusting to me his despatches concerning the capture of Badajoz for conveyance to H.M. the King, and thither I am presently bound. It is my great regret, therefore, that I shall not have an opportunity of congratulating you on your wedding day and that I shall not have the pleasure of paying my respects to your bride and her sister, Doña Victoria. Please have the goodness to give them my kindest regards.

"With all good wishes for your future,
yr humble servant,
Alexander Gordon,
Capt., 3rd Foot Guards"

"Do you think I'm mad, Tom?"

"Mad? How do you mean mad?"

"Mad to get married."

"Harry, you are quite sane. Juanita's no five-furlong filly. She'll go a mile and half any day. You're on a winner."

"I'm greatly relieved to hear you say so. What's the time?"

"Excuse me, sir," said Rifleman West putting his head round the tent flap, "Corporal Costello says can he have a word with you?"

"Corporal Costello. What does he want?"

"Couldn't tell you sir," and here West dropped his voice until it was almost inaudible with discretion, "but there's a lady with him."

"Oh? Well, tell him I'll be out in a minute."

"Very well, sir. Can the galloper go, sir?"

"I thought he'd gone. Yes, there's no reply. . . . Oh, Tom, did I tell you, Andrew Barnard is lending us his chaise to take the ladies to the taverna."

"Yes, old boy, you told me three times. The chaise will be here at a quarter-to."

When eventually Harry went outside he saw the little corporal from Mountmellick standing there with the help of a pair of makeshift crutches, his cap balanced precariously on top of a bandaged head. Behind him, looking very smart in a new outfit including stockings and shoes (from Badajoz?), was the pretty Mrs Cochrane.

"Won't try a salute, sir, if you don't mind," said Costello grinning, "or me cap might come off."

"Glad to see you standing up, Corporal. Weren't you with the Forlorn Hope?"

"Yes, sir."

"Well, are you bad?"

"I thought I was at the time, sir, but Surgeon Bowker patched me up. One ball passed through the calf of the leg—no damage done, and another nicked me cap and no damage in that department either, thank God."

"Good. So, what can I do for you, Costello?"

"Well, sir," said Costello looking round at Jenny Cochrane, "as you can guess, the news has gone all round about your getting married, sir, and I was wondering if—being an old mate of Rifleman Cochrane—this is Mrs Cochrane—"

"Good morning, ma'am. Yes, I know Mrs Cochrane." Mrs Cochrane smiled and bobbed a curtsey.

"You lost your husband at about the same time as Captain Uniacke was killed, isn't that so?"

"No, sorr, my Padraic was taken at Fuentes. That was before Captain Uniacke, but if I may say so, your honour, two better men never wore a green jacket."

"True enough, true enough," added Costello. "Well, sir, we were thinking, that is to say I had the idea, that may be your lady would be needing someone to look after her—a lady's maid, like as you might say. Jenny Cochrane would be a great one for the job, sir, if you take kindly to the suggestion."

"Jenny," said Harry making one of his quick decisions, "the job is yours. Can you talk Spanish?"

"Though I say it myself, sorr, I manage well enough. The way it is, if they don't understand me in English I give them the Spanish, and if they don't like my Spanish then I give them the Irish, and between hopping and trotting we get on grand. And aren't the Spaniards only Irish anyway a bit to the south?"

"Have you a tent, Jenny?"

"I have me bivvy and a donkey and a goat—"

"Well, get your kit over here as soon as you like and report to Rifleman West. We'll arrange everything else tomorrow. Now you and Corporal Costello are invited to the wedding. How will you get there?"

"Don't worry about that, sorr," answered Jenny Cochrane. "I'll get him there on Garryowen—that's the donkey."

"Tom," said Harry re-entering the tent, "I need a drink. The brandy's in the corner there."

"Much better not, old boy."

"Just a stirrup-cup?"

"Just a stirrup-cup, then."

Just as the two brothers had their elbows raised, they heard: "Stand-to-Your-Front!"

"Good morning. Stand easy, if you please."

A familiar voice came from outside the tent, followed hard upon by the entry of Colonel Barnard.

"Good morning, Harry—Tom," he said, affecting not to notice

the embarrassment of the Smiths caught in the act. "I have come to say, Harry, that I have just met your bride and she is enchanting. I shall be proud to give her away. See you at the church. Good luck!"

Julián Sanchez had been every bit as good as his word and the arrangements he had made were admirable. There were *charros* standing by to take care of horses as the wedding guests arrived and others to indicate the way to the 'chapel'. The whole tavern had been converted overnight by the innkeeper, his family, and Julián's men. One room had been prepared by Miguel, 'El Fraile', with an altar and its appurtenances, while the main room had been laid out to seat a hundred people to the wedding breakfast.

When Harry arrived (his last visitor having been Quartermaster Surtees with the gift of a new shako) his stage-fright was intensified by the sight of this elaborate setting for a play in which he was to play a leading part. He remembered Torres Vedras.

The first time Harry looked at his watch it was twenty minutes past. The fourth time, or was it the fifth? it was twenty-five to.

"Do you think after all she has decided to back out?" Harry asked Tom in a whisper.

"Not the slightest chance," answered Tom. "Don't forget, the Colonel is there."

Harry looked across to where Julián was nonchalantly leaning, his hand against the wall, chatting to the innkeeper. He envied the Spanish their gravitas, their ability to look calm, even indifferent, under almost any circumstances. But those who knew Julián better than Harry could tell that, despite his indolent attitude, he had a sharp eye out and that he was only as calm as a bull-fighter watching a new bull come into the ring.

"Here they come now," said Tom. "We had better get inside." And in the distance they could see the chaise with the three women in it, two in black and one all in white, escorted by a number of green-jacketed horsemen.

By now a considerable crowd, gypsies, country-people, soldiers not directly connected with the Light Division, as well as a good many riflemen and *charros*, had collected outside the taverna, so that when the chaise eventually drew up there was an involuntary murmur of admiration at the sight of the sweet young bride. And when the good Colonel Barnard handed her down from the carriage there were audible exclamations of delight from the peasant and gypsy women present, particularly from the latter, some of whom had sold the lace for the veil.

For Juanita, by a miracle of skilful improvization mainly due to Frasquita, was as pretty a bride as ever walked down any aisle—even if the aisle in this case was the stone-flagged floor of a wayside inn. Her veil draped over a high comb, was a long piece of cream lace which, covering her face, fell to finger-tip length in front, but at the back almost touched her ankle-length hem-line. Below it she wore a long-sleeved bodice of white muslin, the collar of which was made from a broad band of ivory silk which crossed over the bosom to tie with a bow at the back of the waist, thence falling to the hem as a sash. The skirt, again of white muslin, flouncing stiffly out over several petticoats, was trimmed with three bands of ivory satin ribbon. On her strong little feet she wore white satin shoes with paste buckles (these last a present from a gypsy) and in her hand she carried a bouquet of winter jasmine by courtesy of the innkeeper who was very satisfied with the lavish plans made for the wedding breakfast.

Behind Juanita, as Colonel Barnard tucked her arm in his, came Frasquita fiddling with the bridal veil and behind her, looking spectacular in black relieved by a collar of the same cream-coloured lace, came Victoria.

There was only one anxious moment for Harry, and that was at the altar when Juanita, expecting Padre Julián, started visibly at the sight of the bearded Fray Miguel, huge and impressive in alb, stole and chasuble. But Harry gave her hand a reassuring squeeze and the bad moment passed.

Parson Parker began by giving them his "Dearly-beloved-brethren-we-are-here-gathered-together-" down to, "I now pronounce you man and wife." Then it was the turn of Fray Miguel. 'El Fraile' then proceeded to steal the scene. Having given the Latin Service in an orotund baritone, and having blessed the bride and groom from "*Dominus Deus omnipotens. . . .* " down to "*Per Christum Dominum nostrum amen,*" he then blessed all those present irrespective of race or creed (including Parson Parker) and told them that they might go in peace.

"Well, we should all be the better for that, wouldn't you say, Tom?" said Colonel Barnard as they mixed with the crowd filing out towards the dining room.

"Where you have one wedding, you could have two," said Ted Costello to Jenny Cochrane. But the remark seemed to escape Jenny who was savouring in her mind's eye the details of the new Mrs Smith's wedding dress.

Julián Sanchez had made himself as inconspicuous as possible during the marriage ceremonies. But the first thing Harry did, having taken his place with Juanita, Victoria and the Colonel to receive the guests, was to ask where Julián was. Then, almost immediately, he caught sight of him near the door and called him over.

"Juanita", said Harry, "I want you to meet my friend Don Julián Sanchez. He may be better known to you as El Charro." And the look of disbelief on Juanita's face as Julián kissed her hand was everything that could have been hoped for.

"But," said Juanita, "you are Padre Julián!"

"No," replied the other smiling. "the good father has long since ceased to exist. Later I will explain, but now—" and he looked at the queue growing behind him—"you have other guests to greet."

If the landlord of the inn had made a good profit from his catering for the wedding breakfast, his wife and three daughters had certainly worked for it. They had been up since five in the morning cutting and cleaning and chopping and slicing, frying, roasting and boiling. Now, sweaty and smiling, they proudly produced the results of their labours.

These appeared in a rich relay of dishes to the various tables. There was *bacalao al Pil-Pil*—salt cod cooked with garlic and chillies. There was smoked ham, there were *chorizos, butifarras* and *morcillas.* There were potatoes in *allioli* and stuffed artichokes. There was tripe and pig's cheek with saffron and hot peppers; there were quails cooked in white wine, and duck roasted with black olives. And finally, to crown the feast, there were *lechazos* —larded baby lambs stewed in wine from Almendralejo and garnished with mountain herbs. With all, and served in large pitchers, was wine from Medallín and Zafra, red and white, rough and ready, and very strong. At the end came quince cheese, *turrón* and other sweetmeats made of almond and honey, as well as *polverones* which reminded Johnny Kincaid, with a sort of guilty start, of the nunlets in the convent at Abrantes.

To the men who had made the now legendary march from Lisbon to Talavera on all but empty stomachs this was indeed a banquet, and even Rifleman West, tucking into a whole leg of baby lamb, scarcely uttered about messed-about-foreign-food.

As voices rose, so did the colour in convivial cheeks. Then suddenly half a dozen gypsies burst on the scene, hands clapping like firecrackers.

The flamencos came on without any musical instruments other than the palms of their hands with which, for the next twenty minutes or so, they beat out a variety of intricate rhythms to which they both danced and sang. They danced and sang till their voices were hoarse and the sweat was shining on them. And still their palms beat out the complicated, syncopated rhythms, sharp as gunshots. And only when they were quite exhausted did they leave the centre of the room to refresh themselves and to recoil to jump again.

When the gypsies had left the floor two guitarists took their place and started to play *fandangos de Huelva* and *sevillanas*. With the first *sevillana* a smart young fellow, slim as a sword-blade, himself a Sevillano (a deserter who had joined El Charro), went boldly up to the top table and, bowing to the bride and groom, asked Harry's permission to dance with his lady.

Juanita blushing with pleasure, looked quickly at Harry to reassure herself that permission was really granted. As soon as the music started it was clear, even to the British, that as dancers these two were star performers.

"*Debajo de un pino verde,*" sang the singer.

Debajo de un pino verde	Under a green pine tree
tiendo mi manta en la arena	I lay my blanket on the sand
cojo la guitarra y canto	pick up the guitar and sing
pa que al escucharme	so that when you hear me you
vengas.	will come.

"Can Juanita ride?" asked the Colonel.

"I don't think so," answered Harry.

"Well, you teach her to ride and let her teach you to dance and you will be an invincible couple."

Vente a la manta	Come to my blanket
donde por tu cariño	where for love of you
mi corazon canta y canta	my heart sings and sings
vente a la manta conmigo	come with me to my blanket
morena que me hace falta.	my dark girl for it is you that I crave

After the *sevillanas* two of the innkeeper's daughters made up a foursome with two *charros* to dance the local version of a *jota*, and a very pretty sight the girls made with their red skirts and coloured stockings dancing with the slim horsemen in black.

When Juanita, her sister, and their partners had returned to their places Julián absented himself for a moment and Victoria was left briefly to herself. Whether it was the wine and the food, or the music and the dance, or because she was surrounded by so many gay and gallant fellows, or because of the manifest happiness of her sister, or because it was the natural state of a normal young woman, Victoria now felt for the first time in many months the need (Orellana being now more myth than reality) for a husband. And this feeling made her both sad and happy; sad because of the absence of that husband, and happy because she realized that she had just passed out of a state of physical and emotional limbo and had taken possession of herself as a woman again.

At one point in the festivities Juanita was pleasantly surprised to see the elegant figure of Lord Fitzroy Somerset who had come, he said, to claim the English privilege of kissing the bride.

"What a lovely young woman you have become, Juanita," said his Lordship. "And, Smith, congratulations. You are a lucky—or perhaps I should say, clever—fellow. You realize, of course, that I have had the pleasure of knowing your wife since she was a child."

"And that wasn't very long ago," added Harry, frowning at Juanita in order to prevent himself from looking foolishly proud.

Seeing a vacant chair next to Victoria, Lord Fitzroy asked

permission to sit down beside her.

"How very pleased I am to see you well," he said. "Alexander Gordon and myself have been greatly concerned about you both."

Victoria and Lord Fitzroy did not have much time to renew their acquaintance before Julián came back to join them. Victoria was surprised that the two knew each other.

"Oh yes, Colonel Sanchez and I are good friends. We have been working together for some time now."

"Don Julián has been very kind," she explained to Fitzroy. "He has offered to help me try to find my husband. Jacinto has been missing, you know, since the battle of Ocaña."

"I would certainly like to help you myself if I could," replied Somerset. "I'll tell you what I can do; I will write to Miguel de Álava, who is our liaison officer, and see if he can make some enquiries from Spanish sources while he is down south. Meanwhile," continued Fitzroy, who was something of a diplomat, "I'm sure you could not be in better hands than those of Colonel Sanchez." And pleading urgent business elsewhere he took his leave.

Others presently followed, but the wedding party did not end then and there. In fact it did not end until five o'clock in the morning when the last of the *charros* and the last of the riflemen helped each other back to camp. For the gypsies, who went on singing round the camp-fires, it did not end at all until day dawned and the sun inhibited their native genius for celebration.

As for Harry and Juanita, when they got back to the tent that West had prepared for them they found that Jenny Cochrane had made up a wonderful double bed of blankets on top of a deep litter of straw.

"And there's thyme and rosemary under your pillows," Jenny said, "to give a sweet scent to your dreams." And she retired a little way off to where she had pitched her bivouac along with her goat and Garryowen the donkey.

But Juanita and Harry did not dream because they did not sleep. They were so ecstatic in the feeling of their awareness of being in love and so overwhelmed by the sheer astonishment of lying naked in each other's arms that they could not sleep. Their love was food, drink, sleep and everything that man and woman could desire, and they needed no other sustenance.

Nor had they slept when the silver notes of 'Rouse' sounded, suspending briefly their mutual enchantment.

Vente a la manta	Come to my blanket
donde por tu cariño	where for love of you
mi corazón canta y canta	my heart sings and sings
vente a la manta conmigo	come with me to my blanket
morena que me hace falta	my dark girl for it is you
	that I crave.

CHAPTER FIFTEEN

It was, in Johnny Kincaid's words, a fine, bright, butterfly morning when the Light Division broke camp and formed up to march in the direction of Salamanca. While waiting to move, some junior officers of the Rifles were, for the nonce, discussing that seven days' wonder, the marriage of Harry Smith. Inevitably some were openly critical of 'mixed marriages', while others expressed their doubts about the advisability of taking a wife of whatever persuasion on a campaign. All were pessimistic about the future of Harry's military career now that he was burdened with the liability of a pretty—above all a pretty—young wife.

"Shut up everybody!"

Kincaid, who had had his eye on an approaching horseman, brought the chat to a sudden end. Harry, who had just ridden over from Brigade Headquarters with orders for the move, was immediately aware of an unnatural hush on the part of brother-officers. Rightly he surmised that they had been talking about him.

"Morning, Harry," said Charlie Eeles. "We didn't expect to see you up and about so early."

"If," replied Harry, "you are trying to suggest that, because I was married yesterday, I shall be neglecting my duties, you are badly mistaken."

"Keep your hair on, old fellow," answered Beckwith. (He had picked up an American expression which referred to the Red Indian practice of taking 'scalps'.) "We all had difficulty in getting up this morning."

"Nobody," said Dan Cadoux when Harry had gone, "has a higher opinion of Harry Smith than Harry Smith—perhaps with some reason, though," he added generously.

Elsewhere in the lines members of Harry's old platoon were also predicting a falling off in their erstwhile Commander's performance, but for more rudimentary reasons.

When Harry eventually returned to his bride, briefly to acquaint her and Rifleman West that the Division was on the move, he found her in her tent sitting on an ammunition box, her face wet with tears. This was a double shock to Harry, first because it was so totally unexpected, and secondly because he had never yet seen Juanita in tears. It took a lot of soothing and coaxing on his part before he could persuade her to tell her trouble. Eventually she allowed him to see what she was clutching in her hand. It was a gold chain supporting a medal of the Virgin Mary. When asked why this had upset her so much she replied that she knew the person to whom the medal belonged. It was the property, she said, of dear Sister Rosario, the Basque nun who had taught her French.

"Look," said Juanita weeping anew, and she pointed to the back of the disc where the nun's name had been engraved together with the date of her name-day. Questioned further, Juanita said that a soldier—she knew not whom—had just been and given it to her.

Immediately grasping the horrible implications of this story, Harry was able to anticipate and counter Juanita's next reaction.

"Enrique, I know you have your duty to do, but so have I. I must go back into town and see if Sister Rosario is all right."

The chances of Sister Rosario being 'all right' under the circumstances, Harry knew, were very slim indeed. Juanita had experienced enough horrors. She was now his responsibility and enough, as far he was concerned, was enough. Harry was used to command, but a good instinct now told him that this was not the moment to assert connubial authority.

"Listen, Juanita, you are right to wish to see your friend and at any other time I would help you to do so. But we are just about to move—the vanguard has already left—and there is no one to escort you."

"But, Enrique, I must go. I shall never be happy until I know if Rosario and Madre Soledad are safe. Please, Julián Sanchez will send someone to go back with me."

"Julián Sanchez and his people left camp at five o'clock this morning," lied Harry. "They are well on their way to Alcántara by now. No, Juanita, in the army we never look back. Soldiers only look forward. You have joined the army now, *querida*, and it's on we go—by the left, quick-march."

Outside Harry Smith called West over to him.

"Who the hell was it came here this morning to see my wife, West?"

"Er—well, sir, I suppose it could have been Jackman," said West, fearful lest he had been guilty of some dereliction of duty, but at the same time anxious about giving away a mate.

"Thirteen platoon! I might have bloody well known," replied Harry savagely. "Look to it, West, on no account is Mrs Smith to leave camp or the line of march in order to go back to the town, understand."

From this April to the following July Wellington, the initiative being his, manoeuvred to make 'Pepe Botello', the usurper King Joseph, release his hold on Madrid. These manoeuvres, however, involved the Light Division in no serious engagements, and the time served Harry Smith to put his considerably enlarged household in order, and to break Juanita in to campaigning.

The idea of being a soldier, and the maxim of never looking back, appealed to Juanita and, however anxious she may have been about her nuns, she did not mention them again. She did not, in any case, have much time to ponder or speculate about the past.

For Harry the first essential was to teach Juanita to ride. At the beginning this girl, whom war had immured in the town of Badajoz since childhood, did not even know how to put her foot in a stirrup. For the next few days, therefore, she travelled sitting sideways on a blanket on the torpid Portuguese horse which West held on a leading-rein. But, through his friendship with Captain Ross of the Horse Artillery, Harry was introduced to a gunner who was harness-maker to the Troop, and this good man managed, for a small honorarium, to adapt an old saddle of Harry's into a side-saddle for Juanita.

But still Juanita, though lacking neither courage nor willingness to learn, took some time to realize that a horse was not a mere vehicle like a mule or donkey, but a potentially willing creature who needed a skilful pilot to put it to effective use. During these weeks it was only love that came between Juanita and Harry's short-fused temper.

This love was the sweeter for the fact that not only had neither partner ever had carnal knowledge of the opposite sex before, but that they had never even been in love. Harry, unlike many of his friends whose every waking—or even sleeping—thought was of the next possibility for sexual encounter, was that comparatively rare sort of man in whom sex lies dormant. When, with his marriage to Juanita, his sexuality was awakened it was for him a revelation and an epiphany.

For her part Juanita rejoiced in the love that was nightly consummated (when the exigencies of the service permitted) in their pretty little bell tent which had been a present from the regiment. It was for them love in a cottage with roses round the door—only ten times better because the tent was pitched in a new and fascinating place each night with the prospect of a new adventure each coming day.

The Smith equipage on the march had now become something of consequence. It consisted of Harry's two chargers, Chiquito and Old Chap; the latter on perpetual loan from a friend, James Stewart. (He had sold the Irish horse, Paddy, to a Spaniard for three doubloons.) Then there was the sluggish Portuguese horse ridden by Juanita; a mule which carried the bell tent, and Jenny Cochrane's donkey which carried her kit, cat, fowls and 'bivvy'. In addition there was also Jenny's goat, two more milch-goats recently acquired by Harry, and five greyhounds including the famous Moro who had bested Lord Wellington's Irish dog at Campo Maior.

All this (including Juanita) came under the command of Rifleman West and travelled with the baggage train since, on the march, Harry naturally rode with his formation. This was just the impedimenta of one junior officer, and by comparison a modest one. But it was not perhaps surprising that the Commander-in-Chief had fits of what he called 'Bengal Dog' when he visited the rear of his army.

But for Lord Wellington at this time there were certain bonuses. The main one was the fact, authenticated by Monsignor Curtis at Salamanca, that Napoleon's plans to invade Russia were well advanced. His Lordship felt confident that he could hold his own against any other Commander save Bonaparte himself. His daily prayer now was that the Corsican would catch a cold in the Russian snows.

While Juanita was learning to follow the drum, Victoria, having bade her sister a tender but, since they expected soon to meet again, not too tearful farewell, left with Frasquita under the auspices of Julián Sanchez. For their bodyguard the guerrilla leader had assigned to them Miguelín, and these three now made their way to a 'safe' village in country controlled by the *garrochistas*, the intention being that they should lie up there until Wellington had opened up the road to Madrid. Once in the capital they would be able to make specific enquiries as to the fate of the defeated Spanish army at Ocaña.

As to Juanita, the prognostications that this convent-bred flower would wilt under the rigours of campaigning proved to be quite wrong. The Spanish rose-bud blossomed, and became a fiercely Anglophile bloom. The Spanish señora of hidalgo consanguinity soon became ashamed to be seen sitting sideways on an old nag like a peasant-woman going to market. She decided that it would be altogether preferable to ride *a la grupa** behind West or, when he was available, Harry. This became a turning point in her equestrian career because it gave her the feeling for real horses since Chiquito and Old Chap were both thoroughbreds.

"Enrique," she said, "why can't I ride Chiquito, *querido?* After all, he is a Spaniard like me."

Harry laughed, secretly relishing the idea that she had so much spirit. "No, you can't," he replied, "but I'll make a bargain with you. When you can ride as well as you can dance and sing you shall have Chiquito. Meanwhile, I must have two horses in case we go into action suddenly and I lose one of them."

"But why can't I ride Chiquito until we do go into action?"

"No. And what's this 'we'? When we go into action 'we' are going back to the baggage-lines with Jenny Cochrane and Rifleman West. And in English the word baggage has two meanings, and one of them means a *sinvergüenza* girl like you."

**a la grupa* is the Spanish term describing the becoming style and practice of a lady who rides side-saddle on the crupper behind a horseman.

"*Sinvergüenza, tu,*" answered Juanita, putting out her tongue. But Harry was adamant.

As Juanita began to know horses, so did the men of the 95th begin to know Juanita. There is nothing a rifleman likes more than being chatted to by a pretty woman, and soon Juanita, although she always spoke to Harry in Spanish, began to learn a few phrases in English. The greatest abominations to riflemen on the march—indeed to any foot-soldiers—were horsemen who thought they had the right to bump or push through the columns of marching men. But never at any time did they object to the presence of Juanita who used to come alongside them and greet them with a "Guth morrning" or "guth afterrnoon," as the time of day dictated. Some of the soldiers, though knowing perfectly well who she was, would pretend ignorance and would ask her name. To this she would reply, "Meesis Esmeet". Whereupon the wicked riflemen would all call out to her "'Ullo, Meesis Esmeet", "Goose-morning, Meesis Esmeet", and so on to their great amusement, and hers.

Likewise the officers, none of whom had been opposed to Juanita herself, but only to the idea of Harry getting married, started to enjoy Juanita's company, the more so as her English improved. Her particular favourite was Dan Cadoux who teased her and always made her laugh.

"The trouble with you, Juanita," he said one day after they had become on Christian name terms, "is that you are seeing too much of the riflemen. You're getting a perfectly horrid Cockney accent, you know."

"What is it cockney?" asked Juanita.

"Well, how shall I put it? Let's say it's like an Andalusian peasant who thinks he talks Castellano."

"Ah si, comprendo. Un accento basto, eh? Then I will talk very much with you in future. Is that all right?"

"Capital!" answered Cadoux with a laugh, "but we must be careful not to upset your husband."

That night when they were in bed in their little bell tent she asked Harry a question. "*Mi Enrique*, why is it you do not like Dan Cardo?"

"That is a very difficult question to answer, sweetheart."

"Is it because he likes very much the women?"

Harry gave Juanita a questioning look before answering.

"No, I do not think it is that at all," he said.

Relations between Harry Smith and Dan Cadoux had of late deteriorated even further. On the death of Peter O'Hare, Cadoux had been promoted to Captain and had been given O'Hare's old company. Harry, though he was effectively senior to Dan, and now held a prestigious job as Brigade Major, had never had command of a company in his own regiment. Cadoux's promotion appalled Harry to such an extent that one day, at a casual mention of O'Hare's name, he was provoked into saying that he had never expected to see the day when that gallant officer's place should be taken by a tailor's dummy from the Burlington Arcade.

This remark somehow got back to Cadoux and it offended him deeply. From that time forward Cadoux never spoke to Harry Smith except on business, though his friendship with Juanita continued to flourish.

By the middle of June the Light Division was on the Rio Seco facing Marmont's army which stood between them and Salamanca. Juanita was very excited by the proximity of the French for, though she was accustomed to them from their occupation of Badajoz, she now saw them from quite a different point of view, namely from that of a British soldier: a threat to be feared and a menace to be eliminated as quickly as possible.

On 13 June 1812, almost the same day that Napoleon crossed the river Nieman to invade Russia, Wellington crossed the river Agueda and marched towards Salamanca. On 21 July, after seemingly endless marching and counter-marching, the Allied Army crossed the river Tormes just south of the city.

The crossing took place in an appalling thunderstorm of a sort not uncommon in Spain. At one point two troopers were killed by lightning, numerous horses broke loose and bolted, (greatly endangering the lives of Major and Mrs Dalbiac whose tent was brought down on top of them), and it was generally held in the army that it was the worst storm anyone could remember.

Juanita had got halfway across the river when there was a particularly loud clap of thunder; whereupon the Portuguese horse, up to his girth in water, stopped in his tracks and just stood there shivering. Nothing that Juanita could do would make him budge. West had gone forward with Harry's spare horse, Jenny Cochrane was behind with the baggage, and there was no one at that moment there to help. To make matters worse, some concealed voltigeurs started popping random shots in the direction of the ford and little spurts of water were shooting up here and there all round her. The situation was an unpleasant one, to say the least, and things might have gone badly for Juanita had not Tom Smith, who was now Adjutant of the 2nd Battalion, and who was on his way to get orders from the Brigadier, come up just then.

Seeing Juanita's predicament he rode in after her, seized the Portuguese horse by the bridle, and dragged it through and out the other side.

Harry was full of jocularity that evening, having heard the story from Tom.

"I hear you've had your baptism of fire, Juanita," he said, grinning.

"Have I?" answered Juanita who was still furious after her humiliation. "Fire! What's that to me, fire? All I know is that I was nearly drowned by that cow of a Portuguese horse and I'm never going to ride him again—never."

This wiped the smile off Harry's face.

"My darling, I am very sorry—" he began but Juanita did not let him finish.

"You think I am going to be made to look like a *tonta*—an imbecile—in front of the whole brigade? From now on I ride Chiquito, or I walk."

That night the clouds rolled away both inside and outside the Smith's tent. The next morning the sun shone and when Juanita came out she saw Rifleman West holding handsome little Chiquito with her side-saddle on his back. Then a feeling of great joy and love came over her and she turned round to look for Harry.

"The Captain's already gone," said West, "but he told me to saddle your horse." Allowing time for this to sink in, he continued. "There'll be a bit of fighting done today, I wouldn't be surprised," he said. "Anyway we've got orders to go to the rear, Ma'am, so I'll be striking your little tent now if you don't mind."

Once mounted on Chiquito, Juanita suddenly discovered, like one who for the first time finds they can swim, that she was at last a horsewoman. Harry had frequently told her that, though Chiquito was a brilliant performer, he was a difficult horse to ride. Mindful of this, Juanita was prepared for almost anything, but to her surprise she found that she had complete control from the beginning and, riding him on a light Andaluz curb, she could make him do anything she wanted. To mount, Chiquito even had the Andaluz trick of stretching himself out on his fore and hind legs, thus bringing the stirrup nearer to the ground.

"And now," she told herself, "I can go anywhere I want to."

That night in the rear echelon no one was permitted to pitch tents lest a sudden move became necessary. For the same reason nobody was allowed to tether horses or transport animals but all had to remain saddled and ready to march. West cut some green barley for feed and what was left over Jenny Cochrane made into a bed for Juanita, putting a bunch of wild lavender under the blanket she used for a pillow. Having been reassured by West that it was no unusual thing for the Captain to remain on duty all night when there was action afoot, Juanita lay down under the stars with Chiquito's bridle in the crook of her arm. And thus she went to sleep, breathing the sweet-scented lavender and feeling Chiquito's soft nose nuzzling her. Once or twice in the night she was woken by the feeling of Chiquito gently prodding her with his nose, but this she found comforting and, smiling, she went back to sleep.

The next thing she knew was West shaking her; the greeny-yellow light of dawn in the sky.

"How did you sleep, Ma'am?" enquired West with a grin.

"Very well, thanks," replied Juanita.

"Then all I can say is it's a miracle because that horse of yours has eaten away your bedding."

Sure enough Juanita saw that she was now lying on bare ground with only a few green stalks of barley left of what had been her mattress. But she could not help laughing when she caught sight of Chiquito standing there with a nonchalant look on his handsome arab face.

At that moment from the south-west came a drum-roll like distant thunder, but thunder it was not since there was no cloud in the sky. The noise, punctuated from time to time with kettledrum crashes, gradually increased in volume until it became a perpetual horizon of menacing sound.

"His Lordship likes to get started early," said West, "so that he can get through by supper-time."

"Do you think the Captain will be back by supper-time?" asked Juanita.

"I wouldn't like to say, Miss. There's no telling."

"I suppose those are the guns firing?"

"That's correct, Miss. The loud and nasties, them's theirs — coming this way, like. The soft and friendlies, them's ours."

By midday the sounds of battle had shown no signs of abating and Juanita began to get anxious. To conceal this she chattered endlessly with West and Jenny, asking questions about anything that came into her head, and laughing at anything that could be turned into a joke.

Some time later, when West had gone to collect rations from the quartermaster, Jenny produced some cold beef and bread, but Juanita could not eat it.

"I know how you feel, Ma'am," said Jenny. "I used to be the same myself when my Padraic, God rest him, was with us. I don't know how I could have gone on so long, year after year, battle after battle. Every time the duty bugler sounded 'Assembly' me stomach turned over and I wanted to be sick. And then the waiting . . . the other women will be up there now, as near to their men as they're let—waiting all day, waiting all night sometimes. And then the terrible searching of the battlefield when one of the lads doesn't come back with his mates. They say we women are the worst for looting, but I say most of the time we're on a battlefield it's only to look for our loved ones. The truth to tell, missis, I'm almost glad it's over. God and Mary forgive me if that's a terrible thing to say, but I couldn't be doing it any more." And the corners of Jenny's pretty mouth turned down and she began to weep. "May the Dear God rest his soul."

Seeing the state poor Jenny had got herself into, Juanita went over and put her arms around her, finding in the other's distress some alleviation of her own.

"You're a good, kind girl, missie," said Jenny, "and it's nice you're a Catholic. We're in the same boat, you and me, and that's a comfort."

Presently, feeling a little better, Jenny said "Well it's all over for me now. It's you has to do the worrying and waiting now, poor lamb. Thank God there's a God, or there wouldn't be much comfort in this world."

There came a point, however, some time between about four and five o'clock, with the din of battle sometimes crescendo, sometimes diminuendo, when Juanita found she could bear the inactivity no longer. Saying that she was going to exercise Chiquito, she mounted and made off at a walking pace towards the rear. Once out of sight, however, she turned round and galloped off in the direction of the battlefield as fast as she could.

The Light Division Commander was now the able German General, Charles von Alten, and the two brigades under him were respectively commanded by Andrew Barnard and John Vandeleur, the latter having more or less recovered from the wound received at Ciudad Rodrigo. Harry Smith was, as previously, Brigade Major to Vandeleur.

By five o'clock in the afternoon not a man among the 'Light-Bobs' had fired a shot, the Division being held in reserve to protect the right flank. Thanks to Lord Wellington's brilliant timing and his knack, amounting to genius, of being at the right place at the right time, the day was going well for the British. Ned Pakenham, Lowry Cole and the commander of the Heavy Dragoons, General Le Marchant, had particularly distinguished themselves during the day, whereas the French had had the misfortune to lose, wounded, Marshal Marmont, as well as his second-in-command, General Bonnet, who was killed.

It was at the moment of crisis when Wellington, alone except for Alexander Gordon and a dragoon, was galloping over to tell Stapleton Cotton, in command of cavalry, to give the French a final push into the river Tormes, that he was spotted by General Vandeleur.

"By Jove, Harry. There goes the Peer now," he said with his spy-glass to his eye. "It looks as if we're going to miss the fun. Quick, gallop over and see if he has any orders for us."

As Lord Wellington on Copenhagen (he had already worn out three mounts) galloped towards Sir Stapleton Cotton, Harry Smith on Old Chap was galloping towards General Wellington. At almost exactly the same moment, the two men saw, midway between them, a pretty lady on a little chestnut horse galloping towards the point where the battle was fiercest.

Lord Wellington reached Juanita first.

"Ma'am you're riding into hounds," said his Lordship. "Pray be so good as to leave the field." And he pointed in the direction in which she should go.

At the moment that she was being thus addressed by the Commander-in-Chief, Juanita, out of the corner of her eye, saw Harry galloping up with a look of utter astonishment on his face. Laughing, she made off as fast as Chiquito could carry her before any more could be said.

"Any orders for General Vandeleur, my Lord?" said Harry, his hand at the salute but, at the same time, half-turning to look towards Juanita.

"Pretty gal," observed his Lordship. "Who is she?"

"My Lord," answered Harry, red as a beetroot, and trying to avoid Alex Gordon's eye, "General Vandeleur—"

"Yes. Tell General Vandeleur and General Alten to stand-down where they are. I shall not be putting them to any trouble today."

And, when Harry had gone, Lord Wellington turned to Gordon. "Alex," he said "where have I seen that young lady before?" And without waiting for an answer he galloped on to win the Battle of Salamanca in time for supper.

CHAPTER SIXTEEN

"My Lord," wrote Wellington to the Minister for War, Lord Bathurst, "I hope you will be pleased with our battle at Salamanca, there was no mistake; everything went on as it ought and there never was an army beaten in so short a time."

Salamanca had been a city of rejoicing, pretty girls crowded the streets, and the troops crowded the pretty girls, and if there are *Salamanceses* today with unusually fair hair and blue eyes it is hardly surprising.

After General Wellington, the hero of the hour was the 'local boy', Julián Sanchez, together with his *charros* who, for the purpose of identification in the Allied Army, had been given the grandiose designation, with no good reason that anyone could see, of the Burgos Hussars.

While there Wellington lost no time in making the acquaintance of his fellow-countryman, Monsignor Patrick Curtis, who entertained him to dinner at the Irish College. It was after discussions with Dr Curtis that 'the Peer' decided to march immediately on Madrid, sending the Burgos Hussars in the direction of Palencia and the river Duero to 'feel' for the French and protect the British left flank.

For Juanita, with her new-found equestrian freedom, life at this moment was one glorious adventure. In her happy state she could not resist on occasion showing off a bit in front of the riflemen, putting Chiquito into a *pasa andaluz*, or making him caracole in front of them. This provoked a good deal of Cockney witticism, most of which passed over her head, but she knew it was entirely good-natured. If Juanita happened to pass by during one of the mandatory halts the riflemen would invariably call out to her to join in their brew-up of tea, and she would dismount and sit with them at the roadside, delighted to be accepted as part of the regiment.

One day at the beginning of August, they came to the Sierra de Guadarrama and crossed over by the pass of Alto de los Leones. The air was beautifully fresh there in the mountains and the hot sun brought out the smell of the pines. The next evening they were over the watershed and came down to camp beside the Escoriál. The following morning General Álava, who had become rather friendly with Harry, appointed himself cicerone and showed the Smiths round that huge, austere palace-monastery.

At one moment in his guided tour Álava stopped quite still and then snapped his fingers as if he was about to dance. "That's an extraordinary thing," he said. "The Escoriál is called El Real Monasterio de San Lorenzo, and St Lawrence's day is today—the tenth of August! A good omen, wouldn't you say?"

But none of them really had an idea whether it was a good omen or not. Madrid had now been ruled by a Bonapartist government for three years and nobody knew how the Madrileños would react to the arrival of Wellington's men. Would they be cold-shouldered as invaders or hailed as liberators?

They need not have worried. On August 12, when Lord Wellington led his army down the Paseo de la Castellana, Madrid decided to go *en fiesta* for three days and nights.

The appearance of the British army was one that obviously appealed to the Madrileños. Having fought their way in all sorts of weather from the Portuguese border, all ranks arrived in Castile more or less in rags. Red coats were russet brown, green jackets were darkish grey and there was not a man who had not a patch somewhere on his clothing. But the contrast between their shabby finery and their obvious vigour, high spirits, and pride of achievement, went straight to the hearts of the citizens of the Spanish capital.

Indeed, Wellington's men did make a fine showing after their fashion. Used to the feathers and flamboyance of the French military presence, the arrival on the scene of the British Commander-in-Chief in a plain blue coat, unadorned cocked hat, followed by a small staff with minimal plumage, was in its own way quite spectacular. So in reverse, was the presence of the ladies.

First to be seen, riding with her husband's regiment, the 15th Dragoons (as she had done throughout the campaign), was the gorgeous Lady Waldegrave, a fair-haired beauty who, despite her smart appearance, was more accustomed to the battlefield than the ballroom, though she could acquit herself admirably in either. Then came the intrepid Mrs Dalbiac whose latest achievement had been to search for, find, and rescue on a donkey her nephew who had been wounded in the Battle of Salamanca. No great beauty she, but her pleasant English looks together with her frail frame made a deep impression on the Spaniards.

Last of all came the Light Division. First into battle they may often have been, but on parade this was never permitted. The speed at which they marched invariably threw all other formations into confusion, and so there was a pause while the crowds waited in expectancy for the famous 'Light-Bobs' to appear. When at last the silver bugles of the 95th splintered the air with *Over the Hills* and the little 'Green Men' were seen bobbing along behind them, a spontaneous cheer went up from the crowd.

Who can say how a crowd obtains its information? But it does, and very often the information is correct. It certainly knew about Mrs Smith.

When Juanita appeared, riding with Harry behind General Vandeleur, prancing along on her handsome little horse, the crowd went wild. Shouts went up, "*Viva la guerillera estremeña!*", "*Viva los novios!*" and, "*Viva la heroina de Badajoz!*" Women rushed forward to squeeze and kiss any part of Juanita they could get hold of, and both men and women reached out to shake Harry by the hand and pat him and his horse with indiscriminate affection.

Although the official, public fiesta went on for three days, festivities of a private nature went on for much longer. On the first Sunday after the entry into the capital a bull-fight was given in honour of the British Commander-in-Chief who had now officially become Generalissimo of all the Spanish forces. As a mark of special esteem the great torero, Pedro Romero, who was then in his fifties, came out of retirement from his native Ronda to bestow on Lord Wellington the sword, cape and hat of a *matador de toros*.

The occasion was brilliant, particularly for those British who had been fortunate enough to obtain seats and who had never seen a gala bull-fight before. It was the heyday of the *maja* fashion and all the fronts of boxes and barrier seats were decorated with the colourful shawls of their decorative owners. When the matadors in their suits of lights came glittering into the arena, they stopped to bow to the British General who rose amidst cheers to return the compliment.

To return Spanish hospitality the British also endeavoured to entertain as lavishly as possible, which meant that the party-givers were senior, or otherwise wealthy, officers, since the army, as was often the case, was hideously in arrears with pay. The Generals certainly did their best. As Wellington remarked to a newcomer, "Cole gives the best dinners in the army; Hill the next best; mine are no great things; Beresford and Picton's are very bad indeed." His Lordship, however, was selling himself short: he was a charming and excellent host, and his invitations were much sought after.

Among the senior officers, General Vandeleur had the reputation of being a great gossip, particularly after he had had what he called a 'jar or two'.

"Since you are going to his rout, Juanita," he said one day after dinner, "let me tell you something about Lowry Cole. You see we Irishmen know all about each other. The Peer, you know, became engaged to be married to Kitty Pakenham and then he went off to India to make a name for himself, which he did. But it took a bit of time, and when he came back to Ireland he found that Kitty had been—was being—courted heavily by Lowry Cole. Yes, you see, the plot thickens, doesn't it? Well, to go on. As it happened Kitty had changed a good deal in the years while Sir Arthur was with the sepoys, and not for the better—though presumably Cole thought otherwise. What, therefore, was he, Arthur, to do? Call Lowry out and fight a duel over her? Hardly a nice thing to do as Lowry is, and was, a very decent fellow. Let the whole thing drop? Let Kitty drop into Lowry's lap, as it were? That would have been the crafty thing to do, but the Peer is not like that, is he? No. He did the gentlemanly thing and stated that he considered the engagement still valid, and that if Kitty wished they would marry at once. She did wish it, and they did marry, and he and Lowry Cole have been the best of friends ever since. You see, Lowry probably thinks he was lucky."

"Why lucky?" put in Juanita.

"Oh, I don't know," answered the other, helping himself to port, "but perhaps you have observed that our revered Commander does not care to lead a very domesticated life."

"Are they not happy then?"

"Frankly, they are not. His Lordship is a good mathematician, you see, and Kitty can never get the household accounts straight. This aggravates him no end, so it suits him pretty well to be away campaigning, or so I imagine."

"Oh, Enrique," said Juanita, turning to Harry and clutching him by the hand. "How terrible it would be if you did not always want me near you."

"My dear," went on the Brigadier with a meaningful look, "the circumstances are slightly different. You see, Kitty is a bookish sort of lady. I don't think you'd ever catch *her* riding across a battlefield in full view of the enemy—and certainly not without her husband's permission."

General Sir Lowry Cole had quite recovered from the bullet-wound received at the Arapiles and, on the night of his party, was in the best of spirits. The supper, as promised, was excellent and the company, numbering more than forty, good, despite a shortage of ladies, for no Madrileña could be expected to go out alone—that is without a husband or a suitable female companion.

At table a great many toasts were drunk and a general air of conviviality prevailed. Afterwards the company withdrew, some to a card-room for a rub of cribbage or a hand of whist, but the greater number went to listen to a group of musicians hired for the occasion. It was then that Lord Fitzroy Somerset, who of course knew her form, suggested that Juanita Smith be persuaded to sing.

Juanita needed little persuasion. Borrowing a guitar from a musician she sat down, put one foot on a stool and, to her own accompaniment, sang a short, sweet air from her native Extremadura.

Hearing her, Lord Wellington, who was fond of music and who could play the violin tolerably well himself, excused himself from the company of El General Odonojú who was boring him, and crossed the room to listen.

Having sung herself in, as it were, Juanita, responding to calls of 'encore', began another.

La plaza tiene una torre,
la torre tiene un balcón,
el balcón tiene una dama,
la dama una blanca flor.
Ha pasado un caballero
—y quien sabe por qué pasó!—
y se ha llevado la plaza
con su torre y su balcón,
con su balcón y su dama,
su dama y su blanca flor.

The square has a tower,
the tower has a balcony,
the balcony has a lady
the lady a white flower.
A gentleman passed by
—Who knows why he passed!—
and took away the square,
with its tower and its balcony,
with its balcony and its lady,
its lady and her white flower.

This song was sung with such sweetness and musicality (Juanita had a low, and surprisingly strong, voice) that it brought several people clapping to their feet. Lord Wellington turned to Fitzroy Somerset who was next to him.

"Haven't I seen that gal before, Fitzroy? Who is she?"

"That is Mrs Smith, my Lord."

"Mrs *Smith*? How very improbable! Introduce me, won't you."

"Oh, so you are married to that saucy fellow in the Rifles," said his Lordship (in French) after the introduction had been effected. "He's not one to let the grass grow under his feet. Do you by any chance ride a small, chestnut, arab-looking horse?"

"Yes, my Lord," answered Juanita laughing at what she knew would come next.

"Well, Mrs Smith," continued the great man, looking at her pretty teeth as she smiled, "I am delighted to make your acquaintance, and you may sing for me as often as you care to—you are very accomplished—but I do not want to see you on the field of battle again. . . . Now, tell me," he said steering Juanita to where dancing had begun in another room, "are you free tomorrow morning? I'll tell you why I ask. I am being painted by a rather grumpy little chap and really he should be painting someone like you, not me. But I am obliged to submit, though you can understand it is very boring for me, and I would be greatly obliged if you would keep me company for half an hour or so."

"I would like that very much. Who is the painter, my Lord?" asked Juanita.

"A fellow called Goya. Used to be Court Painter here, I believe."

"Oh, yes. Don Francisco Goya. There was something about him and the Duquesa de Alba. . . . "

"Was there, indeed! Tell me all about it."

The party went on until two or three in the morning—long after Lord Wellington and the Smiths had gone back to their respective billets. As a measure of its success it ended with some of the younger and more boisterous officers chairing the host, together with Generals Álava and Vandeleur, into the street—at which point they accidentally dropped poor Vandeleur, who remained very sore and out of sorts for two days.

It was, in fact, Miguel de Álava, Wellington's liaison officer, who had persuaded the two parties, painter and peer, to come together for the purpose of having the portrait painted. It had not been an easy business to arrange. Wellington was reluctant to sit, both out of natural modesty and because he could not bear the inactivity. Goya for his part had just embarked upon a series of horrific etchings entitled *The Disasters of War* and was disinclined to leave this work in order to go back to an oil-on-canvas portrait of a military hero. However, once the two men had met they liked each other well enough and the project was allowed to go ahead. Wellington, being nothing if not practical, further insisted on going to Goya's studio at 15 Calle de Valverde because, as he said, it was better for Goya to be in his own place of business where he had his equipment. Furthermore he (Wellington), being there, could get away from the bores and importunists who now abounded in his own headquarters.

"How now, Monsieur Goya? Will that do?" (The two men both spoke excellent French.)

"What's that?"

"Will that do for a pose?"

"Any pose will do. All poses are equal to me. People are best as they are."

"Quite so."

"How is that?"

"I said quite so."

"You will have to speak up," said the painter and pointed with a piece of red chalk to his ear. "I am deaf."

"They heard me well enough on the field of Salamanca," said Lord Wellington, projecting his voice a bit.

"I have the noise of battle in my ears all the time," replied the painter.

"Too bad, sir. Will it bother you if I speak to some of my people while you work? It will save me time."

"What's that?"

"I said would you mind if I did some work while sitting for you?"

"Work? If you want to work while I work that is good. We will both be occupied and that makes it easier for me to concentrate. Also you would look more natural if you are thinking about something. The great difficulty with some sitters is to stop them looking as if they have nothing in their heads. It is unlikely that you would have seen my group portrait of our late Royal Family. If you had, you would know what I mean."

On the morning after Lowry Cole's rout Harry got up with a pretty thick head to go on duty. This consisted in the main in attending on General Vandeleur who was suffering from multiple bruising and severe hangover. As soon as Harry had gone, Juanita turned over in bed and immediately fell asleep again. The next she knew was Jenny shaking her energetically.

"Ma'am, ma'am, the carriage is here waiting on you. It's at the door."

"Carriage? What carriage?"

"I don't know, ma'am. The cheeky humbug of a jarvey says he's from Lord Wellington and will I look sharp and get my mistress. 'Lord Wellington me Royal Irish,' says I—"

"*O Dios mio!*" said Juanita, leaping up as if she had found a scorpion in the bed, "It *is* Lord Wellington. Quick, Jenny, what can I wear?"

With Jenny's help Juanita scrambled into a tight-waisted, above-the-ankle black dress, put on white clocked stockings and shoes, threw a white lace mantilla over her hastily brushed hair and, snatching a pair of long white gloves, jumped into the carriage. Dishevelled, but no less attractive for that, she arrived pink and breathless at Don Francisco Goya's studio.

"This is my *guerillera estremeña*," announced Lord Wellington, effecting the introductions. "She has come to tell me of her experiences in Badajoz and I shall listen attentively, not only because of my interest in the matter, but in order that I shall appear less empty-headed when translated to canvas."

And so Juanita, tentatively at first, but with increasing eloquence as she became engrossed in her subject, told the story of her war as a child in Badajoz. She told of her meeting with Don Julián Sanchez, 'El Charro', believing him to be a priest; she told of the death of her brother, Cristóbal, defending La Trinidad gate; of the bravery and inspiring leadership of General Menacho; of the spirited Madre Soledad and her work as a spy, though saying little of her own part in the business. She told of the treachery of General Imaz, of Miguelín's capture and dramatic re-appearance, and of many things besides. It was only when she came to describe that moment when she and her sister Victoria realized that their gallant British liberators were behaving like brutal conquerors, did she falter, finding herself in a state of confusion between the remembrance of that awful experience and her overwhelming love for Harry Smith which had been the direct result of it. Lord Wellington, the liberator-in-chief, tactfully ignored the implied criticism of himself and took pains to put this very young person at her ease.

"Do not distress yourself, Juanita, if you will permit me to call you by your Christian name," said Lord Wellington. "Regrettable—unpreventable—things happened. There are no excuses. Unlike the French, our troops are not conscripted. Conscription calls up men of all degrees of upbringing and education, but ours are recruited from the ranks of those who can find no better calling. They are the very scum of the earth, but they fight like the devil—and there you have it."

"You have good officers and bad men; we have good men and bad officers," put in Don Francisco, who had developed a knack of following a conversation despite deafness and despite his concentration on the work in hand. "I am working on a series of etchings portraying the disasters of war," he said, "but I do not portray the Spanish army, though it is the biggest disaster of all. I have in my

Caprichos attempted to depict cowardice, arrogance, idleness and stupidity in the educated classes. But now I prefer only to portray the common people who are to me the true patriots. It is they who are the heroes. It is they who are fighting with their hearts and minds and bodies to deliver their country—not the army."

During all this time neither Lord Wellington nor Juanita had noticed that the painter had unobtrusively changed his attention from his official sitter to the girl talking to him, and in this while had done a sketch in Indian ink and wash* of a young woman with rather tousled hair whose bright spirit shone out of her big, dark eyes.

Goya signed the sketch, dated it 22 August 1812, and then handed it to Juanita.

"Señora," he said, "I have listened to your story with as much attention and interest as your gallant General here and everything you say has, as far as my experience goes, the ring of absolute truth. Please accept this little drawing as token of my admiration for, and pride in, a fellow-countrywoman, for, though a lady, you are of the people—one of the true patriots of whom I speak."

And turning to Wellington, he said, "I hope, sir, you will forgive me if I have wasted your time."

"On the contrary, sir, I consider my time well spent," replied Wellington, "in listening to such an edifying discourse as you and Mrs Smith have provided me with." And Lord Wellington always meant what he said.

When Juanita had left, her place in audience was taken by Dr McGrigor, Chief of Medical Staff, who had been summoned to receive a sharp reprimand for having routed the wounded after Salamanca by a road contrary to the one specified by the Commander-in-Chief. During this painful interview Don Francisco was able to proceed with the official portrait, though it now (and forever after) took on a rather more severe expression than when Juanita was present.

When the time came for Lord Wellington to take his leave, he

*This sketch is not listed in Gassier and Wilson's definitive catalogue raisonné. Their only reference is to 'a number of small drawings, some in sepia, some in ink-and-wash, not listed in the 1812 inventory'.

thanked Don Francisco. "As an invader, albeit a friendly one, it is useful to hear what the people of the invaded country are thinking and feeling, Monsieur Goya. I happen to think that painters are more reliable as witnesses than writers in this respect."

"Judge for yourself," replied the painter, turning his easel round. His Lordship looked at the canvas briefly.

"Hmm, yes," he said. I dare say that is pretty much what I see in the shaving-mirror every morning and I can't say that I care for it. But tell me, sir," he went on, turning his attention to an equestrian painting on the wall, "why do you paint horses with such fat blunt noses and little round ears. . . ?"

When Juanita got home to her billet she took out Don Francisco's sketch and studied it for the first time. She saw then what she had not, in her confusion at receiving the gift, seen before. Beneath the waist-length portrait Don Francisco, in his fine, thin hand, had written a caption. It read, 'A heroine of Badajoz'.

Then Juanita bent over and wept for love of this old painter and for all her fellow-countrymen who were, in their many and various ways, struggling to rid their country of an intolerable presence. And her tears fell and made wet blots on Goya's drawing.

CHAPTER SEVENTEEN

THE PAINT WAS hardly dry on Goya's canvas before his sitter, Lord Wellington, was off to the north with part of the army (excluding the Light Division) to invest the city of Burgos, the fortified city that lay directly in the path to France.

The remaining British troops under 'Daddy' Hill, the only one of his Generals to whom he could trust an independent command, were concentrated in Castile to contain the threat of Joseph Bonaparte advancing with Soult and Suchet from the south-east.

During this period of comparative inactivity Harry and Juanita made many enquiries about the fate of Jacinto Orellana and the Spanish cavalry after the battle of Ocaña. They found out remarkably little. It was generally known that many had been killed in that battle, but even more had been taken prisoner and removed to France. Such casualty lists that were thought to have existed had been sent to the Central Junta in Cádiz. News of Orellana there was none.

And news from Burgos, as it came in, was all bad. Casualties had been heavy, the fortress was well-defended and virtually impregnable without adequate siege-guns; and of these there were far too few, and the few too far away. On top of all this the weather broke early and rain and cold made life a misery for the besiegers.

On 21 October Wellington raised the siege and pulled out of Burgos. A return to Madrid was out of the question for fear of being caught in a pincer-movement between Joseph and Soult in the south and the 'Army of Portugal' in the north. Recalling the remainder of the army under Hill, Wellington withdrew the two forces in converging columns towards Salamanca. But what had started as a strategic withdrawal soon turned into a retreat.

Now it was the British whose lines of communication were extended and the French, under the redoubtable General Clausel, took full advantage. Too much time in the environs of Madrid had allowed the men—even the Light Division—to get soft. Then sickness set in and the Commissariat, as so often happened (since it was not directly under the Commander of the Forces), failed to provide adequate rations. The skies opened day after day over the hungry, sickly army, and the French cavalry gave them no respite.

Whitehall, so sluggish in matters of supply, reinforcement and pay, reacted like a probed nerve at the news of the failure at Burgos. To mitigate the implied censure, however, Lord Bathurst remarked that perhaps Lord Wellington had grown tired of success. Wellington in response drew his pen with more rapidity than he ever drew sword.

"It is a very common error among those unacquainted with military affairs," he wrote, "to believe that there are no limits to military success. Believe me, my Lord, that an army that has made such marches, has fought such battles, and in the doing has undergone such hardships, must need from time to time new boots, new clothing, good food, and what is owing in the way of pay. Given the foregoing, your Lordship may depend upon it that I am by no means tired of success."

To add to his aggravation, Lord Wellington now received a letter from his Kitty belatedly congratulating him on the taking of Madrid.

The Light Division now suffered as it had not suffered since La Coruña. Harry Smith worried about Juanita. But Juanita never murmured. Many nights when there was no chance to pitch a tent she slept out in the rain, or under the tail-board of a cart, or wherever else she or West could find in the way of shelter. She refused, despite much persuasion, ever to share Jenny's 'bivvy' since there was no room in it for two, and she would not deprive Jenny of her small comfort.

On one occasion, when Harry had been on duty for two nights running and had fallen asleep at the camp-fire in front of her, she woke up crying with cold and roused Harry to make him move. But almost immediately she apologized: "I am so silly, Enrique," she said. "You must have been nice and warm where you were, and that is enough for me."

Whenever possible Juanita opted to stay with Harry on the line of march. In retreat the baggage-animals always went ahead so that it often happened that night fell before they could catch up with their food and bedding. Then they would sit by the fire, and would chew a few biscuits before wrapping themselves in their cloaks and getting such rest as the cold and wet permitted.

Nothing seemed to depress Juanita. She laughed constantly at her own bedraggled condition and made fun of anyone who felt sorry for themselves.

"I don't know how she can keep so bleedin' cheerful," remarked Sergeant Prickett one day.

"Juanita is quite remarkable. If I didn't think it would raise hell at the Horse Guards," said General Vandeleur to Harry, "I would give her command of a platoon."

"She seems to have taken over my old platoon as it is," answered Harry. "She has taught them how to make a stew with chick-peas and they're all getting fat on it."

The next day the brigade was 'invited' to provide the rearguard consisting of the 95th Rifles and the Portuguese 1st Caçadores.

While the Caçadores were denying to the enemy a ford over the river Huebra, some French *tirailleurs* came on rather strong and a sharp skirmish ensued. Suddenly Juanita who, with Rifleman West, was watching the fight from the window of a cottage, saw what she thought was Harry's horse, Old Chap, galloping past dragging its rider by a stirrup. She rushed out of the cottage and managed to catch the bolting horse by its bridle, and then saw that the fallen rider was not Harry but the unfortunate Colonel of Caçadores, by this time quite dead.

Meanwhile bullets were flying about in all directions and West did the only thing he could, which was to push Juanita to the ground and hold her flat until a moment came when he could get her back to the shelter of the cottage.

When Harry heard of this incident he exploded. "You will never—and I'm giving you a direct order—" he said to his wife, "you will never attempt such a thing again, do you understand? If I am dead, I am dead, and there is nothing you can do about it."

"And if you're dead, I want to be dead too," shouted Juanita, "and there's nothing you can do about that either—*Estupido! Imbécil! Mierda! Poo!*"

That night the line of the River Huebra was held, the rations and the baggage came up, and Harry and Juanita were able to pitch the little bell tent. Once snugly inside they did not take long to make up their quarrel and they went happily to sleep listening to the croaking of the frogs outside and the occasional murmur of the sentries as they warmed themselves at the fire.

The following morning, much to Harry's dismay, an order came for General Vandeleur to take over a cavalry brigade immediately and to hand over 2nd Light Brigade to a Guardsman called General Skerrett. The latter, Harry knew, had a reputation for being personally courageous but timid and vacillating as a commander of troops.

The main body of the army was now falling back on Ciudad Rodrigo and 2nd Light Brigade, forming part of the rearguard, were ordered to hold the main bridge over the river. When Harry took his new Commander down to look at the situation he saw the Rifles occupying a small group of houses which commanded the bridge itself.

"General Skerrett," said Harry, quickly appreciating the situation, "unless we send down the 52nd to support the 95th the enemy will drive in those riflemen even though they fight like the devil."

"Do you say so?" replied Skerrett in a sarcastic tone of voice. "Then that is not saying much for your regiment."

"You will be of a different opinion, sir, in a minute," replied Harry shaking with rage. He knew the Riflemen would be expecting the customary support from their old comrades-in-arms, the 52nd, and if this was not forthcoming they would hold him responsible.

Already shot and shell were beginning to fall all around and a large French force could be seen forming up to attack in column. The attack came and, as predicted, the Rifles, though taking heavy toll of the enemy, were pushed out of the houses with severe losses to themselves.

"You see now what you have permitted, General," said the Brigade-Major (Harry was still only a Captain) to his superior officer. "Now we must retake those houses which we never need have lost."

"Well, perhaps we should. What do you—" But Harry had

already turned his horse's head and was on his way over to the 52nd.

"What the hell's happening, Harry?" shouted Colonel Colborne, their commanding officer, as Harry came in view. Why didn't you send for us before?"

"I'm sorry, Colonel, but General Skerrett would not have it."

"Well, what now? Does he want me to retake the houses covering the bridge? I don't think the French look very permanent there. Have we permission to see them off?"

"If you will accept it on my responsibility, Colonel."

"You mean the Brigadier might be sticky about it?"

"I fear so, sir. But I don't see how we can let them stay on this side of the river."

"Nor do I, Harry. Here we go then—permission or no."

Led by their Colonel, the gallant 52nd counter-attacked and soon had the French out of the houses. Firing then ceased for the afternoon.

The evening came on very wet. But everybody except General Skerrett knew that the enemy needed to take the bridge, no matter the weather or the cost.

"General," said Harry, "you saw what they did to us this morning. I would like to suggest that the whole battalion of the 95th occupy the bridge and the houses, and that Colonel Colborne should be close at hand with the 52nd to support them if necessary."

General Skerrett only laughed and said, "You may leave a picket of an officer and thirty men on the bridge. If the Rifles are as clever as you say they are, that will be sufficient."

Harry was astonished. "Is that an order, sir?" he said.

"I have just told you so, haven't I?"

"Then sir, I am going to take it down in writing. We shall repent this before daybreak."

Harry then galloped over to the 95th where he found his brother Tom, now Adjutant of the battalion, to whom he passed on the Brigadier's orders.

"You must be mad, Harry," said Tom.

"Not me, old boy. Those are the Brigadier's orders. Come on now. Find me the picket."

"It's Dan Cadoux's turn for the picket," said Tom. "Runner, go and fetch Captain Cadoux, will you?"

He was soon there.

"You know I'm down to fifty men, Tom," Cadoux said, ignoring Harry. "We had quite a few knocked down this morning."

"I'm sorry, Dan, but it seems there's nothing for it." answered Tom.

There was an awkward silence. Dan gave Harry a sort of nonchalantly interrogative look which the latter chose to avoid.

"Well then," said Dan after a pause, "off I go, but I'm not particularly keen on dying. For one thing one is bound to meet all those people whom one has been avoiding for years and hoped never to see again." He turned to go. "Anyway, I'll block the bridge as best I can and God help what's left of 'C' Company."

It was now dark and Harry rode as fast as he could to Colonel Colborne. When Harry showed him the written order the good Colonel was at first too astonished to speak. "Harry," he said at last, "There is only one thing I can do. I will have everybody sleep on their arms and at the first sign of an attack we'll get down there without waiting for further orders."

Harry returned to Brigade Headquarters with a heavy heart. He felt certain that disaster was imminent and he felt himself powerless to do anything about it. Apart from these gloomy preoccupations, he was sensitive to the hostility of the new Brigadier and was depressed at the thought of having to suffer it for the foreseeable future. He wished more than anything that he could resign as Brigade Major now, this minute, and go down and take his place once more in the comradely atmosphere of his own regiment.

In the early hours, Harry was lying wide awake near General Skerrett by the headquarters fire, when a dragoon arrived with a message from the Divisional Commander. Harry took it and read it aloud.

> "It is my belief that the enemy will make every endeavour to possess himself of the bridge on your front before daylight. Every precaution therefore must be taken to prevent him doing so.
>
> Charles von Alten, Major-General."

"Now, sir," said Harry, "we have the Divisional Commander's orders. Let me go at once and put them into effect."

"Just a moment," replied Skerrett getting to his feet and wrapping his boat-cloak round him. "You are hasty fellow, Smith. We will take this one step at a time."

"But General—this is an order."

"I am well aware of what is, or what is not, an order."

"Damn your eyes, General, you will lose the picket and the bridge."

"Damn your eyes, sir. You are insubordinate. This will mean a court martial for you."

"Or you, sir—the odds are on you!"

"Consider yourself under arrest, Captain Smith."

"Too late, General! You are too damn late!" Harry shouted, because at that moment they both heard—indeed nobody could help hearing—on the wind as it was blown towards them the dreaded rhythm of the French *pas de charge*. Then came the all too familiar shouts of "*En avant! En avant! Tuez—Tuez—Tuez!*" followed by the first crash of musketry.

Cadoux's little band held out till just before daybreak, but when they saw their Captain killed they lost heart, suffering yet more casualties as they withdrew. Despite every effort, the remainder of the 95th and Colborne's 52nd, on account of Skerrett's inept dispositions, had been just too far away to do more than redress the situation after it was too late. Dan Cadoux's company, saving a few survivors, had been wiped out.

Harry was at the bridge soon after first light. What he saw there made him rage. The French had attacked in brigade strength and the bridge was literally choked with their dead together with those of the riflemen who had paid the price of one man's foolishness and obstinacy.

When Harry found Dan Cadoux's bullet-riddled body he saw that a finger—the one that had always worn the ruby ring—had been cut off.

The incident of the bridge soon came to Wellington's ears.

"Do you wish to see General Skerrett, my Lord?" asked Fitzroy.

"No," came the answer. "I will have nothing to do with a blackguard."

"But you will not punish him, my Lord?"

"No. Is there any punishment that I could possibly give which would bring back those gallant fellows?"

And then, as Fitzroy was about to retire, Lord Wellington added in as angry a voice as the Military Secretary had ever heard him use, "I pray God and the Horse Guards that I may be delivered from such incompetents as General Skerrett!"

God lost no time in answering Lord Wellington's prayer. General Skerrett, who was a bilious sort of fellow, was so put out by what had happened that he developed a severe liver attack. Then, hearing of his father's death (he was heir to a great estate) he asked for leave of absence which the Commander-in-Chief had no hesitation in granting him. Colonel Colborne was given command of the brigade and all concerned were happy again.

Notwithstanding his satisfaction at working under so good a soldier as John Colborne, Harry could not get over Dan Cadoux's death. Dan, he realized had been a man with whom he could have had a firm friendship had not some form of jealousy, envy, or like distemper on his own part infected their relations. Dan had gone to his death, he felt sure, believing that he, Harry, had been instrumental in bringing it about. And Harry out of pride had done nothing to disabuse him of this misconception. Dan had died in the belief that Harry had callously failed to bring help to a brother-rifleman in his hour of need—of this Harry was certain. And to crown it all Dan's body in death had been outraged, almost certainly by his own countrymen, for the purpose of theft.

For days after the event not even Juanita's loving tenderness could cure Harry of his melancholy and black humour.

Not long afterwards the army reached Ciudad Rodrigo and retired once again safely behind the river Agueda. At the same time the French, believing that they had extended their lines of communication far enough, and mindful of the time of year, decided to go into winter quarters. Wellington's army happily followed suit and thus the campaign closed.

Second Light Brigade had not long been in their billets in the neighbourhood of Alameda when Harry was once again reminded of the affair at the bridge. By an act of inexplicable folly on the part of two people the ruby ring, once the property of Dan Cadoux, was offered for sale. This caused such outrage amongst survivors of that brave officer's company that the matter soon came to the ears of authority. An enquiry was immediately made and the men responsible found. Rifleman Doubleday was charged with the theft of the ring and of mutilating the body of an officer. Sergeant Prickett was accused of being an accessory after the fact. Both men were found guilty by court martial. Sergeant Prickett was sentenced to be reduced to the ranks, and Rifleman Doubleday was awarded five hundred lashes of the cat-o'-nine tails.

Sergeant Costello, who had been promoted soon after the crossing of the Huebra, described the execution of Doubleday's sentence thus:

> The square of the whole Battalion was formed for punishment, there was a tree in the centre to which the culprit was to be tied, and close to which he stood with folded arms and down-cast eyes in front of his guard. Surgeon Bowker stood by while the buglers were busily engaged in untying the strings of the cat.
>
> There was a solemn stillness on parade that was remarkable: a pensiveness on the features of both officers and men, deeper than usual, as though the honour of the profession was to suffer in the person of the prisoner.
>
> Flogging is at all times a disgusting subject of contemplation; in the present instance it seemed doubly so now that a brave and, until within a few days, a popular fellow was to suffer.
>
> The sentence of the court martial was read by the Adjutant, Captain Tom Smith, in a loud voice. Poor Billy Doubleday under the eyes of the whole regiment looked deadly pale. That countenance that had faced the fiercest battle with fortitude—that countenance which the fear of death could not change—was now blanched in dread of a worse fate.
>
> "Buglers, do your duty," exclaimed the Colonel in a voice husky with emotion, I thought, as the men seemed to hesitate in their business of stripping the prisoner and binding him to the tree. This, was however, soon accomplished, Billy only once

> attempting to catch the eye of his Colonel with an imploring glance.
>
> The Colonel betrayed much uneasiness—he had no stomach for flogging, but he knew his duty. I beheld him give a slight start at the commencement of the punishment, but his sense of duty became paramount the moment he beheld the bugler laying on rather lighter than was common.
>
> "Do your duty, sir, fairly!" he uttered in a loud voice.
>
> The first man had bestowed his quantum of punishment, twenty-five lashes, when he was succeeded by another. This man, as if determined that his reputation as a flogger should not suffer, however his victim might, laid on like a hardened hand. Doubleday's sufferings were becoming intense; he bit his lips to stifle the utterance of his pangs but nature, too strong for suppression, gave place more than once to a half-agonized cry that seemed to penetrate to the very blood in my veins.
>
> One hundred, two hundred, three hundred lashes continued in this way till on Billy's back no skin could be seen for blood and pulped flesh, some of which spattered upon the Surgeon who was obliged to withdraw a pace or two.
>
> At the three hundred and first lash the Colonel ordered the punishment to cease and the prisoner to be taken down. When this was done he addressed Doubleday: "You see, sir, how very easy it is to commit a blackguard's crime, but how difficult it is to face his punishment."
>
> So ended the most memorable punishment-scene I have ever witnessed.

There remained only one far from tangible result: the effect on Harry Smith. First, it brought him closer to his faith in that he took inner comfort and strength from prayer. Secondly, he became more compassionate, less abrasive, and less ready to condemn. He had even, much to some people's surprise, a good word to say for 'Worthy George' Simmons, declaring him to be a good old fellow and a credit to the regiment.

This amelioration of character, which had started with his marriage to Juanita, was now growing to its fullness. It was a purely inner process that did not declare itself to the world. In fact, to all outward appearances, Harry was still the same fiery and impetuous little fellow that he had always been, and his short-fused temper and unparliamentary language still frequently surprised those who did not know him, and kept in awe a number of those who did. Only Juanita knew what she knew and she had the sense to say nothing.

One day Jenny Cochrane was milking the goats when along came Sergeant Costello. Since his promotions the exigencies of the Service had not given him much chance to see her. Now he lost no time in pointing to three black, gold-edged chevrons on his sleeve.

"Oh, I am happy for you, Ted," said Jenny in all sincerity.

"And you know what," replied the other, "it makes a big difference on pay day, so."

"It does surely," agreed Jenny.

"And you know something else," went on the Sergeant, "I was just thinking, with my pay and your wages we could be quite well off—well what I am saying is, Jenny, you need someone to look after you and I'm the man to do it—that is if you will have me—if you will marry me, Jenny. There now, I've said it."

Jenny wiped the goat's teats carefully with a damp rag she kept for the purpose and stood up, the pail of milk in her hands.

"Best thanks to you, Ted, for the compliment you are after paying me," she said. "I appreciate that, so I do—and there's no better or kinder man in the regiment nor in the wide world itself. I know that. But . . . no, Ted. No, I could never marry again—not a soldier, that I couldn't. Not after what I went through for Padraic. And they killed him in the end, didn't they, while he was having a little drink, God rest him. And if I married you, sure to God, Ted, they'd kill you too, and I couldn't go through with that again."

The little Sergeant stood for a long moment in silence.

"Jenny Cochrane," he said, "I understand you well and it's God's truth I'm telling you, I respect the honest way you are after telling me what's in your heart. I will only say this one word more: that is, if we are spared, it may be that one day you will change your mind. I'll be saying strong prayers for that."

And Ted Costello left her there with the milk-pail in her hand, and he did not come to visit her again.

CHAPTER EIGHTEEN

When Lord Wellington took the field again in May 1813 he had under his direct command Julián Sanchez's force, the Burgos Hussars, now numbering two thousand trained men.

On Julián's own initiative—or more accurately on the initiative of Victoria De Los Dolores—a sort of mobile field hospital had been created for the *charros*, most necessary if casualties were not to be left to the negligible resources of the local population, or worse—to the enemy.

During the winter months, Victoria, being used to the bustle of a hospital, had become increasingly impatient with her secluded and inactive life. Eventually it occurred to her to put her nursing experience at Julián Sanchez's disposal. This he instantly accepted and wondered why neither of them had thought of it before.

From the outset Victoria seemed to have a good grasp of what was required and she soon discovered that she had considerable organizing ability. With the help of a young surgeon called Dr Echegaray and a number of medical students from the University of Salamanca—many of whom had joined Sanchez—she built up an effective unit staffed by patriotic volunteer nurses. Nor were they short of funds and equipment. Victoria was adroit in coaxing whatever was available from local Juntas, as well as from private sources in Salamanca, Ciudad Rodrigo and other towns. In short Victoria made an occupation for herself which served an important purpose as well as satisfying her own emotional needs. The arrangement also suited Miguelín. As fond as he was of Victoria, a taste for active service had got a grip on him and he was tired, as he put it, of being 'a lady's maid'. He was now freed to return to duty.

From Julián's point of view the initiation of a medical unit was highly satisfactory. He was growing away from his old image of Partisan hero with knives in his belt. Influenced by his British friends he liked to see things 'regimental' and properly done. For one who had started with a band of half a dozen desperate men living rough in the mountains it was a matter of prestige now to have his own Field Hospital.

Julián, unlike some guerrilla leaders, did his best to obey orders, though there remained one matter in which he still made his own rules. Julián had never 'fought dirty' like many of the *partidas* and as far as possible had respected the rules of war with regard to prisoners. But he made an exception where traitors were concerned. In the category of 'traitor' came all who had sworn an oath of allegiance to the pseudo-King Joseph, any *afrancesados* who had been active politically or who had taken up arms against their own people, and all Spanish soldiers who had deserted to the French. Traitors, therefore, if they fell into the hands of the *charros*, could only hope for a quick and painless death.

Wellington re-crossed the Spanish frontier on 22 May 1813. That morning his Lordship felt instinctively that he would never return to Portugal. He never did. Exactly a month later, on 22 June, he was able to write to Lord Bathurst as follows:

> I have the pleasure to inform you that we beat the French army commanded by the King in a general action near Vitoria yesterday, having taken from them more than 120 pieces of cannon, all their ammunition, baggage, provisions, money etc. Our loss has not been severe.

The Peer's despatch to the Horse Guards was, to say the least, an understatement. The booty captured from King Joseph's headquarters alone was spectacular. On seeing it, Wellington turned a completely straight face to his ADC. "By God, Alex," he said. "I have never seen so many whores in all my life."

The Rifles in general, and Harry Smith in particular, had played an active part in winning the battle of Vitoria and, towards the end of the day, Harry Smith found himself with some of the 52nd and 95th rounding up a heterogeneous collection of prisoners. Among them were two mounted hussar officers in the pale-blue uniform of King Joseph's Guards: one an arrogant-looking fellow with captain's rank, the other a mere boy. On being questioned by Harry, the senior admitted sourly that they were Spaniards and explained that many of the Spanish taken prisoner after the battles of Alba de Tormes and Ocaña had been offered the option of either enlisting under the colours of King Joseph, or being sent as prisoners-of-war to France.

During this discussion the Captain several times looked about him nervously, frequently passing his tongue over dry lips.

"Your name, sir?" said Harry, "What is your name?"

"Garcia," replied the Captain, looking furtive. "Diego Garcia."

Harry was about to pursue his interrogation when he was interrupted by the precipitate arrival of a party of *charro* horsemen led by a fresh-faced young man who clearly knew what he was about.

"There he is. There's Orellana!" the young *charro* shouted excitedly, pointing at the man who called himself Garcia. "That's the end to your gallop, Jacinto, you bloody traitor."

"Hold hard, you there, sir!" shouted Harry, nettled at this interference. He was about to question the *charro* when, to his amazement, the boyish-looking hussar leapt off his horse and grabbed hold of Harry's leg. The hussar then began to address him in a shrill urgent voice—a voice with a Portuguese accent.

"Senhor Capitano, Senhor Capitano. Please, we are *your* prisoners, please."

"And who the devil are you, sir?" cried Harry in astonishment.

"I am Sister Teresa, Senhor."

"Sister? Sister *who*?"

"Teresa—Teresa from the convent in Abrantes, Senhor."

Harry, his mouth open, stared down at the speaker who was undoubtedly a young and pretty girl beneath the well-cut uniform. She looked imploringly at him out of big dark eyes which possibly—yes, even probably—he had seen once before.

"I am his wife," she said, pointing to Orellana. "In the name of God don't let the *guerilleros* take him—please, please, Senhor!"

Harry, who had taken part in six major actions and countless equally dangerous minor ones, had never before had such a baffling experience. Here was his brother-in-law, a Spaniard called Orellana whom he had never seen until this moment of taking him prisoner, and with him a young hussar who claimed to be Orellana's wife and, at the same time, a nun who had fed him, Harry, pastries in a convent in Portugal. The matter was getting out of hand.

Suddenly there was some sort of scuffle and a horse cannoned into Harry from behind. There was a loud discharge of a pistol followed by Teresa's terrified scream. By the time Harry had his own horse under control Orellana was lying dead on the ground.

"Who the hell did that?" shouted Harry.

"Shot whilst attempting to escape, Señor Capitán," replied the fresh-faced *charro* holding a smoking pistol in his hand. He looked defiantly at Harry.

"And what the devil is your name, sir? El Coronel Sanchez shall know about this."

"I am known as Miguelín, Señor Capitán, and I know well who you are. You are the husband of Señorita Juanita, isn't that true?"

"And if I am, what is that to you?"

"That man on the ground there, he was a traitor. He deserted his country and he deserted his wife. People do not treat the De Los Dolores family that way—not while they still have friends."

"You shot my prisoner, sir."

"If by shooting your prisoner I have spared Don Julián an embarrassment and Doña Victoria a deeper hurt, I am glad of what I have done. Let me tell you, you who are the husband of Juanita, that *coñazo* there," and he spat at the body of Jacinto Orellana, "that man was long overdue dead."

By the time Miguelín had finished speaking, Harry's hot temper had cooled into something like respect.

"I tend to speak hastily, forgive me. We both have the same interests at heart—and I dare say the world can do without Orellana."

Harry turned to Miguelín. "Take the body of Orellana," he said, "with that young woman to El Coronel Sanchez. Tell him, with my compliments, that I will explain everything—but for God's sake, Miguelín," Harry added, "do not let Doña Victoria know what happened."

"At your orders, Don Enrique," replied the other. "*Vaya usted con Dios.*"

"Go with God," replied Harry then swung his horse round and

galloped off, thinking how true was Dan Cadoux's observation at Salamanca about the bizarre nature of society on a battlefield. . . . "Poor Dan," he thought. "Poor Victoria. Poor little nun."

The most effective rearguard for a defeated army is the loot it leaves behind. At Vitoria King Joseph, the beaten Bonaparte, had had his entire treasure and baggage train with him. This included not only the pay for three French armies but also the booty from innumerable Spanish churches, museums, and palaces. Apart from that, as General Wellington had already observed, there were literally hundreds of private carriages containing the wives and mistresses of government officials and officers, together with their gewgaws, fripperies and general pelf and paraphernalia. There was even a mobile brothel for the benefit of the ordinary soldiers. Over and above there were stocks of cattle and foodstuffs enough for several armies.

All this the victorious allies fell upon and Joseph and what remained of his armies were able to make good their escape towards France.

Since the Huebra Harry had given up sending Juanita to the rear before a battle simply because there was no means of keeping her there. But she had now learnt, like the soldiers' women, to hover on the outskirts of a battle, ready to go on to the field, or not, according to circumstances. At Vitoria the circumstances clearly dictated pillage. The news of the huge booty left by the French had spread like a prairie fire and the wives of the 95th were anxious to get their share of it.

Juanita, followed by the faithful West, was up forward even before the field had been cleared of the enemy, who were now more concerned to save their own lives than to take anybody else's. Juanita easily persuaded West that there was no danger. The only danger was in West himself. Though a man of long service and good conduct, he was now exposed like everybody else to the almost irresistible temptation of picking up whatever was going from the riches of King Joseph's baggage park. Juanita, on the other hand, was preoccupied with love, not loot.

Towards nightfall she came up with the headquarters of 2nd Light Brigade where she found Harry in an exultant mood for, apparently, he had led a successful attack on the village of Margarita. This was the hinge point of the enemy's position, and Harry had been congratulated by the 7th Division Commander, Lord Dalhousie, himself.

That night Harry and Juanita bedded themselves down in a large barn where West provided them with a dish of eggs which, to his chagrin, was about all he had had the opportunity to loot. Later, when they had laid themselves down on a pile of straw and wrapped themselves in their cloaks, Harry told Juanita of the strange events of the afternoon.

"Poor Victoria," was all Juanita could manage to say as she drifted off to sleep. Then suddenly, she was alert. "I think I can hear something up in the loft—Enrique!"

"Probably rats," grunted Harry.

"No, it sounds like some animal—and a little bell."

"Go to sleep," said Harry.

The next morning at first light, while they were waiting for the kettle to boil, Juanita said, "Harry, there is somebody or something up in the loft—I heard the little bell again."

With the assistance of West Harry managed to shin up to the loft and there, to his astonishment, were upward of twenty Frenchmen, all more or less severely wounded. One poor fellow who seemed to be at death's door was being cared for by a grieving lady, obviously Spanish. Beside her, snuffling sympathetically, sat a little pug-dog with a bell round his neck.

The lady and the wounded were much alarmed at Harry's arrival but took comfort when he assured them in Spanish that he meant them no harm.

"West," called out Harry. "The ladder's up here. Give me a hand, will you?"

And when they had the ladder in place he called to Juanita. "Juanita, come up here. There are a lot of French wounded. Explain to them that I will get help as soon as I can."

Juanita lost no time in doing as she was bid and, together with her fellow-countrywoman, she did what she could to ease the sufferings of the unfortunate Frenchmen.

Harry was as good as his word and in the course of the morning they were treated by a surgeon and removed to hospital.

When Harry found Juanita again that night he heard a tinkling sound as he approached their tent. Entering, he was immediately growled at by the little pug-dog who turned round and jumped on to Juanita's lap where he sat smugly twitching his twist of a tail.

The blow, when it fell, was a double one for Victoria. Jacinto had turned out to be a traitor, a turn-coat, probably a seducer, certainly a faithless husband. Further, having been taken more or less in adultery, he had died without benefit of priest. All this Victoria now took upon her own conscience and it weighed as heavy as her heart. After a day of reflection she went to Julián to ask to be relieved of her duties and to be sent back to Badajoz where she could find refuge in the Convent of Nuestra Señora de Soledad.

The story of Harry Smith's sister-in-law's husband being captured in enemy uniform, and his subsequent death under dubious circumstances, had gone the round of the messes. When Alex Gordon came to hear of it he begged brief leave of absence and went to find Victoria. When he found her at Sanchez's rear echelon she was once again wearing black as on the day he had first met her. Despite her pallor he now thought she looked, in some reflection of inner maturity, more beautiful than ever before.

After observing the formalities about Victoria's recent bereavement, Alex talked about Juanita and Harry and recalled old times in Badajoz. Victoria was genuinely interested to know how he had fared since their last meeting and was happy to be able to congratulate him on his knighthood and promotion to Major. They discussed the great victory that had just taken place, the brilliance of Lord Wellington's generalship, and the hopes for the early expulsion of the French and the usurper-King from Spanish territory. It was not until Alex looked at his watch to see that it was time for his return that he was able to draw Victoria a little aside and say to her, "Doña Victoria, I am well aware that this is not the time to raise matters of a personal nature and that it would be extremely ill-bred of me were I to do so. You are now returning to Badajoz, I believe to enter a convent, and I am going in the opposite direction. For that reason I would say, without wishing to be presumptuous, that I hope with all my heart that you will take no vows that would keep you immured for the rest of your life; a life that, when this war is over, may once again seem to have something to offer to a young and beautiful woman such as yourself."

"Thank you, Don Alejandro," Victoria replied, "for all your kind concern on my behalf. As you say, this is not the time for the discussion of personal matters. I can only say that my whole life is infinitely painful to me at present—more perhaps than you can imagine—and like most people in trouble and sorrow I need to go home, but I have no home to go to. The only place I know where I can get peace to revise my life a little—if that is possible—is the convent of La Soledad where I was educated and which has always been a second home for my sister and me."

"I very well understand how you must feel," answered Alex, looking very serious. "Let me only say before parting," he continued, "that my hand and my heart are yours should you ever feel you have need of both or either of them."

"I shall always remember what you have been good enough to say to me. It would be to my great regret if we were never to meet again."

And with that they shook hands and parted.

Sanchez, meanwhile, had been trying to deal with Teresa which was not entirely easy. He had provided women's clothes for her, insisting that she get rid of the hated turn-coat uniform. This Teresa was very reluctant to do since she was aware of how well the hussar outfit suited her. He listened to her story, though.

"And did you never realize that Jacinto Orellana had left the true Spanish army to join Joseph's *afrancesados*?"

"No, Senhor. I am Portuguese and he is Spanish. I thought all Spaniards were on the same side, as we are."

"And he never told you he was already married—to Doña Victoria, in fact?" asked Don Julián.

"No, Senhor. He never told me he was married to anybody—not even to Doña Victoria," she added with a hint of malice.

"Well, it is poetic justice—or something of the sort—because Doña Victoria is going to Badajoz and I am going to send you with her and, with the money I shall give you, you can cross the border at Elvas and go home."

"Thank you very much, Senhor," replied Teresa, her black eyes sparkling with amusement, "but I do not think I will go with the Senhora Viuda* de Orellana to Badajoz. And I certainly will never go home to my parents or they will put me in a convent again. No, I think I will stay here with Miguelín, if you please. He has promised to marry me when the war ends if his parents give their permission, and that is, I think, the best offer I have had to date. So . . . may I go now, Senhor Coronel?" she added with a sweet smile. "Miguelín will be expecting his dinner."

In the event, Teresa stayed with the *charros* as Miguelín's woman, Victoria went back to Badajoz and was made welcome at the convent of La Soledad, and Harry and Juanita marched on with Wellington's army to the Pyrenees.

*Lit. 'Lady Widow'. But the emphasis on the 'widow' is deliberately bitchy.

CHAPTER NINETEEN

SORAUREN, RONCEVALLES, San Sebastián; the Nivelle, Orthez, Toulouse. The place-names that distinguished the last campaign of the Peninsular War read like the battle-honours they subsequently became.

Juanita, at fifteen a veteran campaigner, now spent the greater part of her time when Harry was on duty caring for the wounded and sick. True, there were many occasions when there was little she could do for them but, as one of the riflemen said, no man was ever the worse for seeing Mrs Smith's smile.

The defeat of the French now seemed inevitable. The tragedy was that so many battles would have to be fought and so many men would have to die before the desired end could come about. And the Pyrenees in winter were inhospitable enough even when not defended by a stubborn enemy.

During a thunderstorm in the mountains during a night operation there is a picture, seen in a flash of lightning and held on the retina of the eye, of Juanita holding an umbrella over General Vandeleur. The poor man, suffering agonies from his old wound received at Ciudad Rodrigo, the pain now aggravated by rheumatism, incited Juanita's compassion even though she knew his condition was probably exacerbated by his fondness for port wine.

In kinder weather the sight of Juanita, mounted on Chiquito with the little pug-dog (a present from the Spanish lady at Vitoria) riding on the pommel, was familiar and popular with the Light Division. But no matter what the conditions, all ranks cheered up whenever Juanita Smith appeared on the scene.

For Juanita the crossing into France had been a strange experience. Not only had she never left her native land before: she had never even expected to leave Badajoz. Now all was totally alien to her.

Nonetheless, the local inhabitants where they passed were surprisingly friendly, being for the most part pro-Bourbon and anti-Bonaparte, and they regarded the British more as deliverers than invaders.

The only thing that worried Juanita was the thought that the child she was almost certain she was carrying, would be born a Frenchman.

"No fear, *querida,*" said Harry when she expressed this anxiety to him. "We'll hoist the Union Jack over the bed that it is born in."

"If it is born in a bed at all," added Juanita, laughing at the thought of one of the riflemen's 'campaign wives', a Portuguese woman, who had been taken in labour ascending La Rhune, one of the highest mountains in that part of the Pyrenees. The happy event did not seem to interfere with the lady's engagements in the least for, a short while after the alfresco delivery, she came screeching into camp on her donkey to present the lucky warrior with his son and heir.

"Well, if he's a true rifleman," said Harry referring to his own unborn offspring, "he'll be born in a wet ditch, for we're well used to that." And Juanita never gave the matter another serious thought, for she knew that if Harry was with her all would be well.

Very suddenly, on 10 December, about twenty miles east of Bayonne, the French mounted a heavy attack as determined as it was unexpected. 2nd Light Brigade, who were billeted in the château at Arcagues and in farms nearby, were for once caught almost literally with their trousers down. On the alarm being given Harry dashed off to bring up the 43rd who were in reserve and Juanita had just time to slip into her habit and mount Chiquito before the enemy broke through into the château grounds. In the scuffle that followed the little pug was left behind. It would have fallen into the possession of the enemy had not a bugler of the 52nd, who knew him, whipped him up and stuffed him into his haversack before dashing out of the back door more or less as the French came in by the front.

It was not till after midnight, and after some hard fighting, that the situation was restored. Getting back to the château exhausted, Harry found that his portmanteau had been ransacked by the French who had also made off with a goose that they had been fattening for Christmas. But obviously there was nothing to be done and seeing Colonel Colborne lying asleep on the floor just as he had got off his horse, and assuming that Juanita was safely in the rear with West, Harry threw himself down likewise and went instantly to sleep.

But for the daily presence of Harry and the permanent consciousness of the baby in her womb, it is possible that Juanita might have felt homesick. It was now seven months since Juanita, hearing from Miguelín of Victoria's impending departure for Badajoz, had ridden from Alameda to Gallegos to say goodbye to her sister. Victoria, accompanied by Frasquita, had soon afterwards left with an escort of *garrochistas* for the Extremeñan capital. The leave-taking had been miserable for all concerned. The two sisters had parted wondering if they would ever meet again.

It was a more joyful occasion when, arriving two days later at the convent of La Soledad, Victoria found herself clasped in the arms of the Reverend Mother. And there was no lack of happy tears when, at a summons from Madre Soledad, Sister Rosario came in carrying a fair-haired baby boy, fathered on her after the siege of Badajoz. In fact a nice damp time was had by all as the baby wetted its napkin as soon as it was given to Victoria to hold.

Madre Soledad let Victoria's first day pass in such frivolities as the routine of the convent allowed. There were still some girls in the school there (including Marie Carmen of the bad teeth) who had been in the same class as Juanita. Needless to say nuns and girls alike were agog to hear Juanita's news. Of course they had heard rumours. Was it really true, they asked Victoria, that she was married to a British officer? Was he handsome? What was the colour of his eyes? How tall was he? Was he a Catholic? Oh, dear! Did it matter? What was her wedding dress like? Who had made it? And a good deal more in the same vein.

The next morning after hearing Mass in the chapel Victoria and Madre Soledad sat down to a serious talk.

"I do not want to hear your confession, my child," the Reverend Mother began with the same phrase she had used so many times before. "That is not my job. But I know you are in some kind of trouble and I can only suppose that it is something to do with

Jacinto. So you can tell me all, or nothing, or just a little as you please. In any case you know your confidences will be as safe with me as in Padre Antonio's confessional."

Victoria looked at Madre Soledad's face, which radiated the intelligence of the antique Moors. She told her of Jacinto's double betrayal and his death. She told of Sir Alexander Gordon's gentlemanly proposal of marriage. What she did not tell, because she had not properly admitted it to herself, was that the man she really loved—it had come to her gradually on the journey—was Julián Sanchez.

"Poor lamb," said Jenny Cochrane one day in December. "There she is, only fifteen and going to be a mother. Sure, she still needs a mother herself."

The person Jenny was addressing was a snipe-nosed little Cockney called Joe Kitchen, a rifleman whom Harry Smith had taken on as servant now that West's responsibilities as groom and 'master of the menagerie' had so increased.

One bitterly cold and sleeting night on the French side of the Pyrenees Harry and Juanita were looking for a billet for themselves and Colonel Barnard. The day had been a messy one with the Light Division advancing fast behind the cavalry, leaving in their wake pockets of enemy, many of them ignorant of their own, let alone the British, dispositions. Eventually they found a house in the village of St Sever which had not already been taken over by Stapleton Cotton's cavalry.

That night, or rather in the early hours of the morning, Juanita complained of pains in the stomach. These became so severe that Harry got dressed and went to call Jenny Cochrane.

"I think what the poor dear needs is a midwife, Captain," said Jenny after talking to Juanita. "I'll go to find Mrs Keogh. She's had nine herself and delivered a good many more."

But when Mrs Keogh finally came there was little she could do except, later in the morning, explain to Harry that Juanita had lost her baby. This was a great sadness to them both, but they comforted each other.

In due course winter turned to spring again and by Juanita's sixteenth birthday on 27 March the sadness of the events at

Christmas-time had receded to a memory. On 10 April 1814 the battle of Toulouse was fought and won. It was not, from the British point of view, the most successful battle of the campaign. Sir Thomas Picton, commanding the 3rd Division, had, according to Harry, behaved with his usual crusty impatience and, in 'anticipating the off', lost an unnecessary number of men who might otherwise have seen their native land again.

Two days later Wellington was having a shave prior to attending an official function at the Préfecture in Toulouse when Colonel Frederick Ponsonby arrived hot-foot from the Royalist city of Bordeaux. He was immediately shown into the presence.

"I have extraordinary news for you, M'Lord," he said.

"Ay. I thought so. I knew we should have peace; I've long expected it," replied his Lordship scraping away at his chin.

"No, M'Lord. Napoleon has abdicated."

"How abdicated? Ay, 'tis time indeed."

Lord Wellington went on shaving reflectively for a moment. Then suddenly he put down his razor and straightened up. "You don't say so? Upon my honour! Hurrah!" And the Commander-in-Chief, still in his shirt sleeves, spun round on his heel snapping his fingers like a schoolboy.

The Allied Army was not slow to celebrate. In the next few weeks there was an outbreak of balls, picnics and parties given for the most part by the local French, who, being of the Royalist south-west, were only too delighted to mark the ascent of Louis XVIII to the throne.

It was a spring of rejoicing. Johnny Kincaid quickly fell in love again, Harry Smith obtained home leave, and his brother Tom, who had recently had a bullet removed from his knee (lodged there since Fuentes de Oñoro), was given sick-leave with permission to accompany his brother.

But it was also time for saying goodbye. All Spanish and Portuguese troops were to be sent home, and with them all non-British camp-followers including 'campaign wives'. Many and heartrending were the partings between the soldiers and the women who had faithfully taken care of them and shared with them the rigours of the campaign.

When the time came for the Iberian contingent to march off, a

British guard of honour complete with band presented arms to their old comrades, and thousands of men not on duty lined the route and cheered their 'dago' pals as they passed by.

At the rear of the column, with no music but the tinkling of a multitude of bells, proudly marched the little contingent of goat-boys and their many-coloured, yellow-eyed herd. The goats had all been given at Harry's instigation as parting presents to the boys so that they might earn a living on the long road home.

Having sent West ahead with the horses to Langon (Gironde), Harry and Juanita, together with Tom Smith and some other Rifles officers such as Jack Molloy and Orlando Felix (he of the theatrical fame), chartered a river-craft on the Garonne and, embarking at Castelsarrasin, made their way downstream in easy stages to their port of embarkation at Bordeaux.

This was one of the happiest times of their lives. The weather was fine, the river beautiful, and each evening they stopped at some new village or riverside hostelry for *la vraie cuisine bourgeoise* and a comfortable bed. Now at last, for the first time in many months, there was no 'standing-to' before first light, or 'rouse' at dawn. There were no calls to 'assembly', or shouts of "Stand to your arms!" Above all there was no daily expectation of wounding or death.

When, after this prolonged and agreeable picnic, the boating party finally reached Langon, a pleasant town in the Bordeaux district surrounded by vineyards, they found the trustworthy West waiting for them with the horses. What is more he had taken the precaution to get them rooms at a local inn renowned for its excellent food.

That night the party, appetites sharp-set from the river journey, sat down to the best of Bordelais cooking. Beginning with *lamproie à la Bordelaise*, lampreys cooked with leeks and red wine, they drank a fine fruity Entre-Deux-Mers. With the *entrecôte au poivre* which followed they drank the rare red Graves of Château Haut-Brion whose original proprietor, Tom Smith said, must have been an Irishman called O'Brien. Finally with the first strawberries of the season they had, on the *patron*'s recommendation, an old sweet Barsac.

"Barsac! Delicious! Where is Barsac?" demanded Orlando

Felix, filling everybody's glass.

"No idea, old boy," replied Harry. "Let's get Juanita to ask—and let's have another bottle." Harry turned to Juanita and noticed that her face had suddenly gone bright red. "What's the matter, *querida?*" said Harry. "Don't the strawberries agree with you? Or have you drunk too much wine?"

"No, no, Enrique—I will ask," she said turning to the *patron*. "*Pardon, monsieur, dites-moi je vous en prie, où est-il Barsac?*"

"*Barsac, c'est ici, Madame! Tous les vignobles de cette région tiennent l'appellation Barsac.*"

"Oh, Enrique," she turned to Harry, "this is something so strange—so strange. I will explain in a minute. And, again turning to the *patron*, she asked if he knew the family Soula.

"*La famille Soula du Château Montalivet? Mais oui, Madame. Je la connais très bien.*"

With all that had happened to her since the sacking of Badajoz, Juanita had not given a thought to Jean-Pierre Soula. The extraordinary accident of finding herself in his home town suddenly brought back memories of those pre-Harry days —memories which had in recent months almost ceased to exist. Now she told Harry about this Frenchman with whom she had worked for so long, and whom in her capacity as intelligence agent she had deceived so many times. And she told him how sad and guilty she had felt when, safe in the Rifle Brigade camp, she had seen him being marched off as a prisoner-of-war.

"Enrique," she said, "I would like to go and see old Monsieur Soula and tell him that we know his son is alive."

"But, *querida,*" answered Harry, "if he is a prisoner he will surely have had an opportunity by now to write a letter."

"Perhaps. Who knows? But as we are here it would be a kind thing to do, don't you think?" replied Juanita concealing, perhaps even from herself, that what she really wanted was to see what young Madame Soula was like.

After two years of marriage Harry had got pretty much into the habit of letting Juanita have her way in most things. The next morning, therefore, Harry and Juanita were on the road to Château Montalivet.

The 'château', when they got there, was no more than a large farmhouse with two long sheds, or *chais*, attached to it. It stood in the midst of well-cultivated vineyards where fragile sprigs of palest green were beginning to shoot from old black stumps.

At their approach to the house a dark-haired, rosy-cheeked woman, showing signs of pregnancy, rose to her feet from where she had been sewing on the porch. She answered Juanita's greeting with a suspicious look.

"Is it possible to see Monsieur Soula?" asked Juanita. The woman paused for a moment, looking intently at Harry's uniform, before answering.

"Which Monsieur Soula do you wish to see, Madame?" she replied.

At that moment a little boy of about seven or eight rushed out of the house shouting, "Maman, Maman—" before falling silent at the sight of strangers.

"Why, Madame," Juanita said, "I do not know how many Messieurs Soulas you have here, but that"—and she indicated the little boy—"is certainly one of them."

"Upon my word," said the pregnant woman without smiling, "you have the advantage of me, Madame. Pray be so good as to wait one moment."

In a moment there appeared a well set-up man, his black hair greying slightly, who came forward to greet his visitors with the usual French punctilio. "Soula is the name," he said. "Is there anything I can do for you?"

"Yes, indeed there is, *mon capitaine*," said Juanita laughing. "You can salute an old friend from Badajoz."

It is a well-known fact that some people, meeting old acquaintances outside the context of a mutually familiar venue, sometimes suffer confusion of identity. In this case it seemed an age before Jean-Pierre Soula could put a name to the face he now saw before him, and when he did, he went into such a pantomime of astonishment, slapping his forehead, and invoking the Deity a dozen times or more, that Juanita thought he would never have done.

After kissing her hand and holding on to it, and calling on God to be his witness several times over, he turned to Harry and said, "And who is this gentleman?"

"This is my husband, Captain Harry Smith," answered Juanita proudly.

"But, Juanita, you have married an *Englishman!*" he exclaimed. "But please forgive me," said Soula quickly, offering Harry his hand. "This wonderful surprise has quite deprived me of my manners. You must accept my apologies."

Soula then insisted that Harry and Juanita should leave their horses and come into the house.

"I was fortunate enough to be released in an exchange of prisoners," he explained as they went indoors. "I have now been back almost six months."

"So I noticed," said Juanita.

"Noticed?" replied Soula, eyebrows raised.

"Madame, your wife," replied Juanita placing, in a gesture typically Spanish, her hands about six inches from her own abdomen, a gesture which made Soula give out a bark of proud laughter in which Juanita joined.

"Micheline!" Soula called out to his wife. "Come, you must meet some old friends from Spain."

Madame Soula, having satisfied herself that the lively and attractive Juanita was married to—and probably in love with — the English Captain, made herself quite charming and agreeable, particularly when Juanita began to play with her little boy.

"You will of course stay to lunch with us," she said, "and while I go to make some preparations Jean-Pierre will perhaps show you round the *chais* and introduce you to Monsieur my father-in-law."

"I am delighted to make your acquaintance," said Monsieur Soula *père* with great courtesy. "Because of this silly war it is a long time since I was in England but I have been many times to London. You know Mark Lane? St Mary Axe? Crutched Friars? That is where I sell my wine. And now we shall have a little *dégustation.*" And the old gentleman led them to the end of the *chai* where he called for the *maître* to bring a number of samples to him.

Taking these one at a time, he poured each into a clean glass which he held first to the light of a candle, then to his nose.

"This," he said, touching his sharp proboscis, "is the most sensitive instrument on the whole property. No bad wine ever goes into my mouth because it never gets past my nose."

Finally, putting the glass to his lips, he sucked the wine noisily in through his teeth and, after holding it reflectively in his mouth for a moment, spat it out in a thin, white jet on to the floor. Having completed this performance to his satisfaction the old man then proffered the glass to Juanita with a slight bow.

"A good Barsac is like a lovely girl," said old M. Soula, looking at her, as much a connoisseur of women as of wine. Then continuing in a more matter-of-fact tone, "It is true that here at Montalivet we are only a *cru bourgeois*, but I assure you that we take as much trouble to make our wine as do the classic growths of Sauternes. Now I think it is time to have a bite to eat," he said, leading the way out of the *chai*.

At lunch—Arcachon oysters, chicken *en casserole* with *petits-pois à la Française*, a strong local cheese, and claret as if to acknowledge that there *were* other wines outside the Barsac district—the conversation flowed freely. Micheline Soula wanted to know all about Juanita's family and how she had met Harry. Jean-Pierre told of his release from prison at Lichfield via the big seaport of 'Soutanton', and old Monsieur Soula asked affectionately after various wine merchants of London of whom Harry had no knowledge whatsoever.

"One last thing," said Jean-Pierre Soula, when Harry and Juanita were about to take their departure, "I often wonder what happened to my black horse. I gave it to an officer who was, I think, of the same corps as yourself."

"Monsieur Barsac?" said Harry. "I can give you very good news—or bad—depending on how you look at it. Your horse is the favourite mount of my friend Johnny Kincaid and by now they are both well on their way to England."

At five o'clock that afternoon, with many protestations of goodwill and promises for future meetings in England, France or Spain, Harry and Juanita went on their way.

Two days later they were on board their transport at Bordeaux. Their vessel was just warping out from the Quai des Chartrons when the 1st Battalion of the 95th came by to board a 74-gun man-o'-war further down the quay. Seeing Sergeant Costello, Jenny Cochrane waved and having caught his attention, shouted out:

"A girl can change her mind, Ted."

"What?" replied Costello cupping a hand to his ear.

"I said, can a girl change her mind!" she shouted again.

But just at that moment the order was given to march to attention and Jenny never heard Ted Costello's reply.

CHAPTER TWENTY

NAPOLEON'S LAST ADVENTURE, the 'Hundred Days', was a massive but short convulsion. The news of Napoleon's escape from Elba came to Harry and Juanita in Cambridgeshire where they were staying with old Surgeon Smith, Harry's father, and the family. Together with some of Harry's younger brothers and sisters they were returning from a ride one day when they saw the stage from London approaching. As they drew abreast Harry, who knew the coachman slightly, called "Any news?"

"No, sir. No news," answered the other as they passed by. Then before he had gone the length of a cricket-pitch, the coachman turned round on the box and shouted something over his shoulder.

"What's that?" Harry shouted after the retreating stage.

"Boneyparter, I said . . . Boneyparter's back!"

And so he was. Napoleon was back in metropolitan France with the army rallying to his standard. And within a few days came an order posting Harry as Brigade Major to General Sir John Lambert at Ghent. Harry recorded the following in his memoirs:

> All was now excitement, joy, hope and animation, and preparation of riding-habits, tents, canteens etc., my sisters thinking of all sorts of things for my wife's comfort which we could as well have carried as our parish church. My youngest brother but one, Charles, was to go with me to join the 1st Battalion, Rifle Brigade, as a Volunteer, and his departure added to the excitement. [Tom had already rejoined the regiment as Adjutant to 2nd Rifle Brigade]. I never was more happy in all my life; not a thought of the future for my wife was going with me and all the agony of parting was spared.

But the agony of parting was not spared poor old Surgeon Smith who had hoped that Juanita, who had become such a close companion to him, might perhaps stay behind with the junior members of the family to keep him company. Instead he had to face parting from three sons and a much-loved daughter-in-law.

"Napoleon and Wellington will meet," he said, "and a battle will ensue of a kind never before heard of. I cannot expect to see you all again."

The Smith equipage was now so big—six persons including West, Jenny Cochrane and Joe Kitchen; eight horses, various dogs (including Pug) and several greyhounds—that they decided it would be economical to charter a small sloop to take them to Ostend. Within 24 hours of leaving Harwich they were landed in Belgium and the following day the whole Smith troop was on the road to Ghent.

It was not until they had passed Bruges that Harry began to see the size of the operation on which they were embarked. Troops from all over Europe seemed to be converging on the Belgian capital for what appeared to be a determined effort to rid Europe of Napoleon once and for all.

On the road they encountered many of the Dutch-Belgian troops—an unimpressive lot—under the youthful Prince William of Orange, known as Slender Billy, whose only qualification for high command, apart from his rank, was that he had been for a couple of years a supernumerary on Wellington's staff in the Peninsula. Then there were British troops recently disembarked, some of whom—but only some—were Peninsular veterans. Among them Harry was pleased to see the King's German Legion, regarded by the Light Division as good—or almost as good—as any of their own regiments. But Harry noted that, for the most part, they were newly raised 2nd Battalions of the 'scum of the earth' variety who had not yet been hammered into shape.

The old Light Division was now non-existent as such; the various regiments being distributed here and there throughout the army. When Charlie Smith left Harry and Juanita to join the regiment he found himself posted to the 1st 95th under Sir Thomas Picton. The 2nd and 3rd 95th were, with the 2nd Division under Sir Harry Clinton, brigaded with their old pals, the 52nd. Harry, of course, was with Lambert's Division which consisted of the 4th, 27th (Enniskillen), the 40th and the 81st. These were the troops, together with the Brunswickers, Prussians and Hanoverians, who were now to come under the command of Arthur Wellesley, 1st Duke of Wellington.

Harry was grateful that Sir John Lambert, whom he had got to know quite well in Spain, had asked for him as Brigade Major. He respected Lambert and felt a filial affection towards him much as he had for dear old Uncle Sydney Beckwith and, later, John Vandeleur.

Thus with Harry in the 6th Division with Lambert, Charlie with the fire-eating old Picton, and Tom in Clinton's 2nd Division, the scene was all set for the three Smith brothers to take part in one of the greatest battles of modern times.

Quatre Bras had been an indeterminate engagement favouring the French but, as far as the British Army was concerned, it had served the purpose of preventing Napoleon from first smashing the Prussian Army under Blücher before demolishing the remaining Allied forces piecemeal.

During this operation Harry attended to his duties as usual, but all the time there was a question in the back of his mind which nagged him as much as his hangover. Who was the portly civilian who had kept staring at him at the Richmonds' ball?

Harry hated hangovers. He wished they had never been to that damn ball but Juanita so loved dancing and danced so well and looked so animated and attractive withal and, moreover, was such a favourite with the Duke that there was no getting out of it. If the Duke had introduced her as 'my Spanish *guerillera*' once he had done it a dozen times. And this, Harry remembered with satisfaction, had made some of the English 'young marrieds' and peaches-and-cream débutantes (Brussels was at present the 'in' place of the smart set) fearfully jealous. In fact his Grace had at one moment called her over to present her to Slender Billy, who was suffering from having recently been jilted by England's Princess Charlotte.

"*Voilà, Prince,*" he said, "*ma petite guerrière espagnole, la héroïne de Badajoz.*"

And the young Dutch Prince bowed from a considerable height and popped his pale blue eyes at her.

That was eight hours ago. Now he was covered in mud

somewhere in the neighbourhood of Genappe with the rain trickling down inside his collar. Only the Duchess of Richmond, he thought, who was so grand that she didn't even consider that Napoleon might interfere with her social plans, would have had the face to give a ball at such a time. And only the Duke of Wellington, he concluded, as the wet infiltrated between his trousers and the saddle, would have had the wit to accept the invitation and to have made use of it. Harry almost laughed aloud when he thought of how the Duke had gulled the *bon ton* into a false sense of security while secretly making his pre-battle dispositions to the sound, not of kettledrums, but the waltz and minuet.

It was after midnight that Harry, who was drinking at the buffet, got the tip from Alex Gordon, who got the tip from pretty Georgina Lennox, who got the tip from Harry Webster, Slender Billy's ADC, that it was time to file quietly away. That was on 16 June.

At Mont St Jean on the morning of the 18th Harry was tightening Lochinvar's girth, at the same time observing a rain-soaked column of Netherlands troops slopping along in the mud. 'Bumpkins in uniform,' he thought. 'More danger to us than to the enemy.'

Less than a mile away, in a sand-pit near a farm called La Haye Sainte, Billy Doubleday was voicing much the same notion. "Good job old Nosey's here if you ask me," he said, looking with suspicion at some Nassau troops who had deserted from the French in Spain. "You don't know where you are with this lot, do yer? We was better off with the dagoes, I reckon, eh Pongo?"

Pongo Prickett, who in Spain, it will be remembered, had been bust for his complicity in the disgraceful business of Captain Cadoux's ring, had had two of his stripes restored for conspicuous gallantry in the Pyrenees. Here in Belgium he may have shared the views of his creature, Doubleday, but he was not, on this wet and muddy morning, much inclined to express them.

"When his Lordship wants your opinion, Doubleday, no doubt he'll ask for it. Meanwhile I want to see that bundook of yours clean, bright and slightly oiled, because at the moment it is covered in shit."

A moment later the sun cleared from behind the last of the

stormclouds and lit the sodden scene. It was nine o'clock in the morning of 18 June.

"What was that you was sayin', Corporal? About the Commander-in-Chief comin' to solicit my advice?"

Corporal Prickett was not slow to get the point. Among the medley of muddy troops marching and counter-marching across the open fields he had no difficulty in picking out a group of horsemen led by the conspicuously inconspicuous figure of the Duke himself. Wearing a plain black cocked-hat, white stock and dark-blue coat he appeared to be listening to what a podgy-faced man in a German uniform had to say. Behind these two could be seen the plumage of an enormous retinue some of whom, such as Lord Fitzroy Somerset, 'Daddy' Hill and Colonel Sir Alexander Gordon were well-known to the Peninsular men. Others such as that randy dandy, Henry Paget, Earl of Uxbridge and the pale-pink Prince of Orange—part of what their Adjutant, Captain Kincaid, called 'the smart International set'—were definitely not. At the heel of the hunt came a number of civilians, none too happy on horseback, whom Bob Beckwith had no trouble in identifying as 'Grub Street hacks, Members of Parliament, and other assorted arseholes'.

"E's coming over, look," said Doubleday.

"Of course 'e is. How could he commence battle without obtaining your appreciation of the situation?"

The Duke stopped at the back of the sand-pit where Shag Davies and Spider Brown had a camp-kettle of tea brewing. The cortège of royalty, nobility and gentry reined up behind him.

"Mug of tea, M'Lord?" called out Rifleman Davies.

The Duke looked as if he would be delighted to take a mug of tea with anybody, but the fat German was giving him such an earful in the most beastly English imaginable that he could do nothing but put out his hand, and Davies put the mug into it.

"Sorry we don't have enough to go round all your friends, M'Lord," went on Davies, turning to look at his mate. Spider, not much liking the look of the German and other foreigners present shook his head in agreement.

Still listening to the German who was going on repetitively about somebody called Gneisenau, the Duke gulped down the hot tea, handed back the mug with a word of thanks, and nudged Copenhagen to walk on.

At Mont St Jean a head poked round the door of the barn that served as Brigade Headquarters. "Ah, there you are Harry," said General Lambert. "I want you to go and find the Duke—no one else will do, mind. You're likely to find him at Hougoumont," and he pointed to a large farm complex clearly marked on the map. "Tell him with my compliments where we are and bring back his orders."

At that moment there was a crash of gunfire, the first of the morning, and it rattled the door of the shack. "I think it is going to be a busy day," said the General.

There was still baggage going back along the Ohain road when he came to it. Some of Von Wincke's *Landwehr* were trying to move up against the stream, so he decided to cut across country which helped him to avoid the cross-roads between La Belle Alliance and Mont St Jean, a certain traffic-block.

'French artillery fire all along the line now,' Harry thought. 'Boney's going to attack, depend upon it. And this will be my first battle with Napoleon actually in command! I may even get a sight of him. Thank God I decided to ride the thoroughbred. With the going like this I'll need at least three horses to get me through the day. Can't understand the reasoning of fellows like Ponsonby who ride a hack into battle for fear of getting their best charger hurt. You get dismounted and what happens? You stand there like an idiot and risk the chance of getting your balls cut off by any loose *Cuirassier* who might be passing!'

Just to the south he could now see Picton's Highlanders with some of the 95th in front of them moving up into position behind the sunken road.

'That should stop cavalry all right. Kempt must be there somewhere with the 1st Battalion and brother Charley. How will Charley like his first smell of powder, I wonder? Shall I cut across and have a quick word? No, that won't do. That wouldn't do at all.'

Lochinvar's hooves were making a sucking noise as each foot came out of the mud. 'God help me if he casts a shoe. That must be the Charleroi road there. Yes, it is.'

He could see a senior officer struggling to get his horse out of the road up a steep bank.

"You there, sir," shouted the officer. "You there, in the Rifles. . . . Oh, confound this bloody animal."

Harry, loath to be deflected from his chosen course, nevertheless bent left-handed to close with the officer who, he could now see, was Sir George Scovell, the AQMG, clearly no horseman.

Harry pointed to a lower part of the bank which Scovell managed to negotiate.

"I say, is the baggage clear at the back there, can you tell me?"

"No, sir, I'm afraid not. They're pretty well blocking the Ohain road."

"Confound it. The Duke will make a meal of me if he can't get his reserves up." And Sir George, putting his heels into his sweating mount, pounded off, saddle squeaking, in the direction from which Harry had come.

"Is the Duke at Hougoumont?" Harry shouted after him.

"Hougoumont. . . . Confound it! . . . Yes," Harry heard, or thought he heard, as the old gentleman squelched away through the mud.

Coming out of the sunken road in front of some Brunswickers Harry came into open ground that until very recently had been standing rye. Now the crop had all been trampled flat and a sickly sweetish smell was coming off it as if the grain had already begun to ferment. French artillery fire was coming thick and fast now and, looking due south to where most of it was coming from, he could pick out the woods by Hougoumont farm. The Duke, he thought, would be sure to be up the sharpest end.

There was no difficulty in finding the Duke, and Alex Gordon, courteous as always, immediately gave him permission to go forward. As he came up Wellington was addressing a podgy German General. "Very well, Müffling, I have heard all that you have to say and I thank you."

'Oh, so that's Von Müffling,' thought Harry. 'Blücher's liaison man. He looks as if he has a great deal more to say.'

"I shall now release you," continued the Duke, "so that you may inform me the better as soon as you have news from your chief. . . . Hullo Smith," he called over, "Where are you from?"

"Sixth Division, General Lambert, my Lord."

"What have you got?"

"The Fourth, 27th and the 40th, with the 81st in reserve at—"

"I know, I know. How are they?"

"Excellent, my Lord. Very strong."

"Good. There'll be work for them today."

At this moment one of the numerous ADC's, a new fellow, the Honourable Eric Gladwell, edged up full of self-importance. "The artillery has slackened off, my Lord. I think the attack is not going to develop."

"Nonsense, sir," said the Duke, much to Harry's amusement. "There's no question of it not developing. It is simply a question of where the weight of it will fall." And turning back to Harry, "Where are you now, Smith?"

"By the road junction at Mont St Jean, my Lord."

"Well, tell Sir John to remain where he is until I send for him. Now, are you aware of my dispositions?"

"Only what I can see on the ground, sir."

"Very well. Go back and tell your General that I am putting the Hanoverians, who are new to the game, under his command. Feel for the left of General Picton's division—that's where they will be. Inform their commanding officer to stand fast until your brigade comes up, then he is to place himself under General Lambert's orders. Is that clearly understood?"

"Perfectly clear, my Lord."

Realizing that he was now dismissed, Harry Smith saluted smartly, turning Lochinvar on his quarters. But he had not gone a length before the Duke called after him. "Now is it quite clear, Smith, that you will take General Lambert up to Picton's left, but only when you hear from me? That, if I am not mistaken, is where you are going to be needed."

At the sand-pit near La Haye Sainte the riflemen were making themselves as comfortable as possible. True, there'd been no proper meal for two days but clothes were now drying out a bit in the sun and most men had a few biscuits and some salt beef left to chew on. Also there was enough tea and sugar to go round. Archie Stewart, now commanding 13 Platoon, had been given young

Charley Smith to look after and didn't quite know what to do with him. It was a bit of a responsibility in view of the family connexion. Then he saw Prickett. If Pongo was not the most regimental NCO in the battalion, he was at least a survivor. Yes, he would do.

Pongo was sharing a cold partridge with his accomplice, Rifleman Doubleday, when Stewart and Charley Smith came up.

"You seem to have made yourselves quite at home here, Corporal Prickett," said the Platoon Commander.

"Quite cosy sir, yes—until the shit starts flying."

"That's a nice-looking partridge," went on Archie Stewart, trying to keep a sound of envy out of his voice. "Where did you get it from?"

"Well, sir, you know the way it is—no names, no pack-drill."

"Have a care, Corporal," said Stewart who was too newly joined to have known about the Cadoux affair. "We all know what the Duke's like about misappropriation of private property."

"Yes, we'll have to be very careful, won't we, Billy?" said Prickett tipping an unseen wink to Doubleday.

"I tell you what," said the Platoon Commander. "You'd better have Mr Smith with you. He's never seen a Frenchman yet."

"What, another Mr Smiff? You another brother, are you?" And when Charley nodded, Prickett turned again to Stewart.

"We'll pick a nice Frencher for him and he can shoot one for hisself. Go and take up a good comfortable position next to Doubleday, Mr Smiff. That's Sniper Jackman on your right and beyond him is Spider Brown and his mate Shag Davies—a right bunch of villains but they can shoot straight. The end man there, that's Bombproof Palmer—gallows-bait if ever there was—but you'll be all right with him."

Harry Smith had scarcely got back to brigade headquarters and dismounted to report to General Lambert when the Honourable insufferable Gladwell galloped up, splattering them both with mud.

"Are you Brigade Major here?"

"Yes," replied Harry, "you know I am".

"Then tell Lambert to move up to the position previously assigned to him."

"Tell General Lambert yourself. He's right here." The Duke's ADC ignored the snub but, on recognizing Sir John he put two fingers to his cap and repeated the order throwing in, "The Duke's compliments". Then he was away covering them again with divots of mud.

"Charming fellow," said Sir John.

At that moment there was a loud explosion behind them.

"Hullo, what was that?" said Harry.

"A shell, sir," replied Sir John. "Very animating. I daresay we shall get every delicacy of the season today."

Leading the Division up to its battle position it was soon obvious to Harry that a general engagement was well into its opening phase and that it was going to be very hard pounding indeed. The noise, which at first had been distinguishable between guns and musketry, had now developed into a heterogeneous roar like a perpetual thunderstorm, so much so that all voices had to be raised to a shout even to address a near neighbour.

Harry's reflections were interrupted by the shocking appearance of a great mob of Dutchmen who were, without doubt, in the act of running away. Many of them had thrown down their rifles and some were even struggling out of their packs as they ran. Very young they were for the most part, farm-boys and suchlike, but there were officers among them, too. One youth who passed close to Harry was snivelling audibly—sweat, snot and tears all mingling on his face.

Harry looked back to the General, but Sir John indicated that such troops were only trouble and better out of the way.

The next moment a Sergeant and three troopers of Ponsonby's Dragoons came towards them galloping crazily, men and horses wild-looking, accoutrements covered in mud, two of the men without helmets and spattered with blood.

"Good God! Not our Dragoons, too!" said Harry. But at that moment he saw the Sergeant, as he passed General Lambert, raise a French Eagle high in the air, and a cheer went up from the 27th.

As Lambert's brigade came up to their position behind the sunken road it became obvious to Harry how very right the Duke had been. But how could he have known so soon? Picton's Division had already withstood a heavy attack and were now reforming, but there was a wide gap left where the Dutch had run, and it was only covered by two companies of the Rifles in the sand-pit.

General Lambert immediately ordered squares to be formed in the gap and his two batteries of guns to be placed between them. The gunners he instructed were to take refuge inside the squares if attacked by cavalry, but once the danger was past, they were to run straight back and serve the guns again. Harry he now sent off to make contact with General Picton.

Making his way over to the 5th Division, Harry approached a fellow he knew called Tucker.

"Old Tom Picton's dead," said Tucker. "A stray ball knocked the poor old bugger down five minutes ago. General Kempt commands now."

Harry remembered hearing an exchange between the Duke and Marshal Beresford at Elvas after the battle of Albuera. "Tom Picton?" the Duke said. "When he came to me I found him a rough, foul-mouthed devil as ever lived, but in a fight he always behaved extremely well—no man better."

"I knew it was going to be a rough day," said Harry, thanking Tucker.

But as yet he did not know quite how rough. It was well, therefore, for his relative peace of mind that he had no inkling of the chain of events that had overtaken Juanita whom he supposed to be safely in her billet in Brussels.

CHAPTER TWENTY-ONE

IN ALL ARMIES and in all wars the same axiom obtains: the nearer the front the better human beings behave. Even in the best regulated armies it is impossible to maintain as high a degree of morale and discipline in the rear echelons as in the fighting units; and it is there in the rear, where rumours fly and skulkers lurk, that confusion will first manifest itself.

On the morning of 18 June Wellington's baggage-train had been ordered to withdraw to Antwerp. Accordingly Juanita, together with West and the rest of the Smith equipage, took their places and proceeded on their way.

At a village about five miles from Brussels Juanita stopped at an inn to get a bite to eat. While she was upstairs somebody galloped into the village shouting that Wellington had been defeated and that the French were descending on the capital like wolves on the fold. West quickly brought Chiquito round but the little horse was in a fidget, upset by the alarm. Juanita had no difficulty in mounting but, once up, she told West to hand her Pug and, in trying to grab hold of the little dog, she inadvertently dropped the curb rein. Chiquito, feeling himself improperly held, suddenly did an unheard-of thing: he bolted.

Chiquito galloped for eight miles down the Antwerp road with Juanita, the snaffle rein in one hand and the pug-dog in the other, barely able to keep her seat. Then she saw an over-turned cart lying in the middle of the road. Both alternatives, of jumping it or avoiding it, were certain to end in disaster.

But as Chiquito was gathering himself up to attempt the impossible the curb rein caught, pulling him up short, and throwing Juanita plus Pug on to his neck.

Juanita had just had time to regain her seat, but not her breath, when an odd assortment of horsemen—some of whom, perhaps, had no business to have been in the rear at such a time—came up shouting, "Come on Ma'am! Not a moment to lose!" Juanita had at first feared that they were French Dragoons but, relieved to find that they were not, she had no option but to follow.

Her mind was now in torment. If the Duke had been defeated, she thought, then Harry could be dead. But how could she find out for sure? In this agonized state of mind, covered from head to foot with mud except where tears of frustration and anxiety trickled down her cheeks, she arrived in Antwerp with no West, no money, no baggage and only a tired horse and a pug-dog for company.

At about this time Harry, unaware of Juanita's predicament, was returning to General Lambert, having made contact with units on either flank.

"Get inside the square, Smith!" shouted the gunner Battery Commander, Stephenson, or Sinclair, or Sinclair-Stephenson—Harry could never quite remember. And Harry joined the gunners running to the square which opened to let them in—just in time as a regiment of *Cuirassiers* came pounding heavily up the muddy slope shouting and brandishing their sabres. But to shout and brandish their sabres was about all the Frenchmen could do, first because of the heavy uphill going, and secondly because a British square, however badly mauled—and the 27th had been cruelly mauled by massed artillery fire—was more or less impenetrable to cavalry while there were still four men left to stand back-to-back with their bayonets fixed.

Inside the square Harry dismounted to rest Lochinvar who was bleeding from a shell-splinter in the fore-leg. Hearing above the din the unlikely sound of a child crying, Harry looked down and saw on the ground a wounded drummer-boy weeping noisily.

"Never mind, sonny, you're not too bad," said Harry, seeing that his wound was slight, "you'll make old bones yet."

"It's not for me, sorr," replied the drummer-boy, his face all screwed up with snot and misery. "It's me Daddy's dead." And he pointed to where an older man lay stretched out on his back beside him.

Confronted with this tragedy Harry could find no words of comfort to offer. Instead, he felt in his pocket and, discovering a coin, stuffed it into the lad's tunic-pocket.

"There, boy. There's a sovereign for you. It will come in handy."

Just at that moment there was a terrific cheer and a pounding of hooves as the Household Brigade (the Lifeguards and the King's Dragoon Guards) bore down with the full weight of heavy cavalry on the French *Cuirassiers*, driving those who had survived their abortive attack on the squares back to where they came from.

Then for a while there was an uncanny pause. To Harry, who like many had become deafened by gunfire, the battlefield suddenly seemed to have gone silent.

"Harry," said General Lambert in this weird lull, "go down and see how the Rifles are doing in the sand-pit. If they can stay put so much the better. If not tell them to fall back and join us here."

As he made his way out of the square, he saw Sinclair-Stephenson—as he believed him to be—back in business, his gunners double-loading with round shot and cannister, ready to take on the next comers.

Down in the sand-pit Harry came across Johnny Kincaid standing apparently nonchalantly beside his black horse.

"Good God, Johnny! Monsieur Barsac's lost an ear."

"Yes, and he's got two more holes in his hide somewhere, but it doesn't seem to worry him too much."

"Seen Charley?" asked Harry.

"Your Charley's the only one still standing up. Poor Charlie Eeles is dead and Charlie Beckwith will lose a leg. Andrew Barnard and Cameron are both wounded and Jonathan Leach has taken over the battalion. We're getting a bit thin on the ground, I'm afraid."

"Can you hold on?"

"We can hold on as long as the Brunswickers in La Haye Sainte hold on."

A bit further on Harry came across George Simmons who was taking advantage of the lull to write up his diary.

"Damn me, George," said Harry "but you're a cool fellow writing love letters at a time like this."

"You know me, Harry," replied George. "I never like to waste my time."

"You'll do, George," said Harry, and as he moved on he saw

George licking the point of his pencil and returning to his immortal work.

Coming to 13 Platoon Harry found Charley very pleased with himself having 'shot hisself a Frencher' and having been nicked in the neck by a bullet which had just missed the jugular vein. Apart from that the situation there was not so good. Davies and Brown were both dead. Archie Stewart had been bayoneted in D'Erlon's mass-infantry attack and several others had been wounded including, of all people, Palmer.

"What do you know, Mr Smith," said Sniper Jackman, "Bombproof Palmer 'ere is goin' to do a die on us."

"No 'e bloody isn't," said Palmer in a gasp which turned out to be his last.

"There you see," continued Jackman, "the poor bugger's gone. What a humbug!"

"If Palmer can make a die of it—well, I dunno!" commented Corporal Prickett, coming over. "'Ullo Mr Smiff, come to see your bruvver, 'ave you? 'E's 'aving a lovely time with that there bundook of his."

At that moment there erupted a new concentration of enemy artillery fire during which any attempt at conversation was useless. When it ended there came to the ear the awful sound that even the bravest heard with misgiving—French drums beating the *pas de charge*. When Harry saw that the full weight of this infantry attack was falling on the farm of La Haye Sainte, and when he saw that there was no longer any fire coming back from the Brunswickers in the farm, Harry passed on to Jonathan Leach General Lambert's orders to retire to the other side of the sunken road.

At this moment up came Gronow, a dandy little ensign in the Guards with a moustache like inverted eyebrows.

"Hullo Gronow," said Harry. "I thought you were on duty at St James's."

"Sir John's compliments, Smith," replied the other, "but the Brunswickers have run out of ammunition and can't hold La Haye Sainte. You're to withdraw the 95th."

"Already done, old boy, but the Rifles like to do it their own way—'Fire and Retire,' don't you know."

When Harry got back to Sir John Lambert, he saw an appalling sight. The massive concentration of artillery fire which Harry had supposed to have been mainly directed on La Haye Sainte and the sand-pit, had in fact landed on 6th Division—in particular on the gallant Enniskillen who were literally lying dead in their square. Harry noted one officer, Major Hume, and only about forty men still standing.

"Poor Alex Gordon's badly hit," said General Lambert. "He was down there at the farm trying to re-animate the Brunswickers. He didn't know that the poor devils had run out of ammunition.

"Dammit, General," said Harry, "I never yet heard of a battle in which everybody gets killed, but that seems—My God, look at that!"

"It's the Garde isn't it?" replied the General looking through his spy-glass.

The Division of the famous *Garde Impériale*, they both saw, was advancing in solid phalanxes, seventy abreast, directly towards them.

"They'll just walk through us. . . . Well, give the order to form line, Harry. I don't see why we shouldn't make it damned hot for them."

While Harry was facing the advance of the Imperial guard, Juanita was trying to resolve her own problems. It was an officer, one of the dubious fugitives from the Brussels road, eager enough to oblige a pretty girl, who put Juanita in touch with the British Town-Major. The latter kindly handed her over to his wife who gave her some hot food and dry clothes. The Town-Major meanwhile posted men to look out for West and eventually they located him. He arrived complete with Jenny, Joe Kitchen, the horses and all the baggage except Juanita's little jewel-box which had disappeared with all her money in it. This loss did not bother Juanita nearly so much as the latest rumour that there had been a big battle in which, although the Duke of Wellington claimed it as a victory, he had had to accept extremely heavy casualties. Juanita felt more strongly than ever that Harry had been killed because, as she reasoned, if there had been a heavy engagement Harry would have been in the thick of it, and she knew that the law of averages was no longer on Harry's side.

Despite the protestations of her host and hostess, therefore, Juanita determined as soon as possible to make her way to the battlefield.

It was perhaps as well for Juanita that she was not aware of Harry's situation which could hardly have been worse. Standing beside Sir John Lambert, Harry looked again at the huge mass of the *Garde* in their towering bearskins as they advanced towards 6th Division's thin red line.

It was an unbelievable sight, like a bad dream. When in war an irresistible force meets an immovable object, Harry thought, what is the answer—only death. But death in battle was straightforward and this was not. He stared again through the smoke straining to interpret what he thought he saw.

"General," said Harry. "Do you notice anything? I believe — they seem to be sheering off in echelon to the left."

"By God, Harry. I think you're right," replied the General. "You *are* right, Harry, and there's that humbug Ney out in front. What the hell is he up to?"

It was now after half-past seven and light was fading fast. Both armies had been pounding each other non-stop for over eight hours. Harry looked towards 'Wellington's tree' on the far side of La Haye Sainte and could see it well enough to note that the Duke was no longer there. He will have gone to join the Foot Guards, Harry thought, for that is where this attack will surely fall.

Harry was right. The Duke was with the Guards Brigade when Napoleon made his last ill-timed and fatal throw. The Guardsmen who had been lying down on the Commander-in-Chief's orders now, at his command, stood up. Then, at short range, they threw volley after disciplined volley into the serried ranks of the 'Immortals' while Colborne with the 52nd and 2nd Rifle Brigade, in a brilliantly executed manoeuvre, took them in the flank. It was too much for them and the 'Immortals' broke.

The Duke watched silently for several minutes. Then, snapping his telescope shut, he said, "Oh, dammit, in for a penny, in for a pound." Taking off his hat, he waved it three times in the air.

There was no mistaking the signal. A shout went up from those who saw him. They knew that the French were beaten and that now, at long last, it was their turn to go into the attack.

Harry heard the roar which gradually grew louder and nearer as each regiment in turn took it up. General Lambert heard the roar and interpreted it, correctly, as the rapid progress of the Duke from the right to the left of the line, indicating to each formation in turn that, for the survivors of the day, they had won the day.

Johnny Kincaid, however, back with the Rifles in the sand-pit, heard nothing because he had gone completely deaf. He knew soon enough what had happened, though, when the Duke himself appeared at the sand-pit—this time with his cocked hat raised in the air. The riflemen, dry-mouthed and hoarse from thirst and the smoke of battle that had enshrouded them all day, gave out a croaky cheer.

"No cheering, my lads," said the Duke. "Don't halloo till you're out of the wood. . . . Go and see those fellows off," he added pointing to a group of Frenchmen who seemed inclined to hold their ground.

And that is what they did, those that were left.

The Duke, alone with Fitzroy Somerset, was then within musket range of La Haye Sainte farm from which another French unit was now retiring. But some soldier, bolder than the rest, perhaps recognizing Wellington and thinking that he could win immortality by giving him his quietus, took a parthian shot. It missed the Duke but hit Fitzroy who was beside him, shattering his right arm at the elbow.

"Better get that seen to," said the Duke.

"My Lord, it is not my bridle-arm. I'll be all right."

"Fitzroy, I order you. Now go, pray, and find a surgeon . . . Smith," he called, "tell Sir John he may now advance—and return to me here."

Harry spurred the tired and wounded Lochinvar into a final gallop towards the 6th Division. Wellington, quite alone now, followed at a walking pace and arrived in time to see Major Hume and forty men of the Enniskillen walk out of the square where once they had stood six hundred strong.

"Forward, Enniskillen, and complete your victory," he called out to them as they passed.

When Harry returned to the Duke he was quite still, white-faced as he had never seen him, staring at the square of dead Irishmen.

There was one fellow, though, who was not quite dead. He had lost both legs and sat propped up against the bodies of his fallen comrades swigging a bottle of Hollands. He stared drunkenly at the Duke. "Arrah," he said, "maybe yer satisfied now, yer hookey-nosed vagabond!"

The Duke continued to stare at the Enniskillen square. Then, turning to Harry, "Do what you can for that poor fellow," he said and turned his horse's head towards his advancing troops.

Some time later, near La Belle Alliance farm where Napoleon had spent much of the day, Harry saw the Duke shaking the hand of an old man with a white moustache, whom he took to be Blücher. Blücher or no, Harry's first concern was for Charley. Charley, when found, was perfectly all right, sharing a cold snack with Prickett and Doubleday, and already rehearsing to himself his own Waterloo story for the benefit of former schoolfellows back home.

Nothing could be done for the thousands of wounded men, dead or dying who, for the most part, had to remain where they had fallen. It was best to try and forget about them till morning. Meanwhile there were fires to be lit, grog to be drunk and food to be eaten for those who had any. Then perhaps there could be sleep.

His duties done, Harry at last sat down by Sir John Lambert's camp-fire. He had not been there long when he heard a voice calling in the darkness.

"Anybody know where I can find Major Smith?"

"Smith? Why here," said Harry. "Who wants him?"

"It's me—Freer," came the answer, and the diminutive officer walked into the firelight.

"Forgive me if I intrude," said Freer tentatively, "but I was passing by and thought you would like to know that your brother Tom is safe and sound. Saw him just about the time of the general advance."

"Freer, you lovely little fellow, God bless you!" said Harry jumping up and clapping him on the back. "That accounts for all three of us now."

"And what happened to you today, Freer?" said Harry after they had refreshed themselves with a few swigs from his brandy flask.

"Hanged if I know," came the reply. "I spent the whole day being trodden in the mud and galloped over by every scoundrel who could afford a horse. To tell you the truth, Smith, I think I only owe my existence to my insignificance."

Back in the village of Waterloo the Duke of Wellington sat down to write his despatch to Lord Bathurst, His Majesty's Secretary of State for War.

From time to time he looked up wondering, hoping that someone of his personal staff, his 'family' as he called it, would walk in at the door. But the only ones to come in were Miguel de Álava and, later, the headquarters surgeon. In the next room, on the Duke's camp-bed, lay the faithful Alex Gordon. Alex's leg had been amputated two or three hours earlier and he knew, as his master knew—though they both pretended otherwise—that he would never see another dawn.

While the surgeon did his best to ease Alex's suffering, the Duke addressed himself once more to the last duty of the day: a duty in which he had little heart.

'My Lord,' he wrote, 'it gives me the greatest satisfaction to assure your Lordship that the army never, upon any occasion, conducted itself better. . . .'

It was not an easy despatch to write and in the end it was, from many points of view, an ill-written one. Small blame to the man who had just fought one of the most momentous battles of the age.

Later, after Alex Gordon had died, Wellington turned to Álava. "Thank God, Miguel, I don't know what it is to lose a battle," he said, "but certainly nothing can be more painful than to gain one with the loss of so many friends." And the Iron Duke, taking Álava's outstretched hand, did not attempt to conceal his tears.

So ended the battle of Waterloo.

After the Duke had laid himself down on the floor to sleep, a gibbous moon came out to shine over the wounded and the dead, and to illuminate the shadowy ghouls who emerged from God-knows-where to rob them. At this same hour Juanita rose, shivering, from her Antwerp bed. She had not slept much, but the Town-Major and his wife of their goodness had persuaded her that the horses needed rest and a feed to be of any use, and she had therefore agreed reluctantly to lie up for a few hours.

By three in the morning of 19 June Juanita and West, having left Kitchen and Jenny Cochrane in charge of the baggage, were out on the moonlit road to Brussels.

Some hours later, when they reached the capital, they found the centre of the city jammed with carts, wagons and carriages of every description bringing in dead and wounded from the battlefield. And when eventually they managed to get through to the Charleroi road they had to press their way forward through even more oncoming traffic of gun-carriages, limbers, ammunition wagons, and thousands of injured horses.

At one point, seeing some wounded officers in a chaise standing in a side street, West went off to ask if they had news of the 6th Division. He had no sooner gone than Juanita came across some walking wounded—men of the 44th Regiment in Pack's Brigade.

"Please can you tell me," she said to the soldiers, "have you any news of Brigade Major Smith?"

"Why, Ma'am," said one of them, "Brigade Major Smith was killed early on, along with old Tom Picton."

Juanita had anticipated this news; had tried to prepare herself for it. Now, forgetting entirely about West, she put her heels into Chiquito and forced him on through the throng.

Trying, despite the anguish, to keep her head, she only stopped to look at those bodies not in scarlet uniform, expecting at any moment to recognize the corpse of her Enrique.

It was afternoon by the time Juanita reached the battlefield proper. Little had changed since the previous day, though many corpses lay naked where they had been stripped by the local peasants during the night.

The dead lay there in thousands as far as the eye could see. When the realization of the sheer physical impossibility of finding Enrique finally got through to Juanita, only then in her utter despair did her courage fail. At that moment she remembered to do something which, as she afterwards admitted, she should have done long before.

"I remembered to pray," she said, "to appeal to God through Jesus Christ, and to Christ's Holy Mother who is one with God." And, with the reins clasped in her bridle hand, she crossed herself and prayed.

It takes those who have faith to believe in the power of prayer. Miracles are for the believers in miracles.

The recorded and authenticated fact of the matter remains that at this moment one Lieutenant Charles Gore, ADC to Sir James Kempt, who happened to be passing in the course of duty, saw a girl sitting quite motionless on a chestnut horse with her hands clasped before her.

"Why, Juanita Smith," exclaimed Gore riding up, "what in the name of all that's holy are you doing here?"

"In the name of all that's holy, Charlie Gore, I was praying for guidance. And you have come along, my dear friend."

At which Gore burst into laughter and Juanita, to his embarrassment, burst into tears.

"Where is he?" said Juanita, quickly pulling herself together. "Where is he? Where is my Enrique?"

"Why," replied Gore, "near Bavay by this time I expect, and as well as ever in his life—not a scratch."

"Oh, dear Charlie," said Juanita, "don't deceive me. The soldiers have already told me Brigade Major Smith is dead."

"Dearest Juanita, you must believe me. It is poor Smyth, General Pack's Brigade Major, who was killed—Smyth who spells his name with a Y. I swear it on my honour. I left Harry in perfect health riding Lochinvar. He was most anxious about you, though."

"Then God and Our Blessed Lady have really heard my prayers!"

"Good. Now come along, Juanita, we must get on if we are to get to Mons tonight. Have you the strength for it?"

"Strength?" replied Juanita. "I have strength for anything now."

Juanita and Charles Gore reached Mons just after midnight. Juanita had been on Chiquito since three in the morning and neither horse nor rider had had a thing to eat in all that time. The two had travelled a distance from point to point of over sixty miles.

The next morning broke fine and they were soon on the road to Bavay which they reached before midday. Charlie Gore led Juanita to 6th Division headquarters where almost the first person she met was Sir John Lambert himself.

"Juanita!" exclaimed the gallant soldier clasping her to him. "What on earth are you doing here?" You're supposed to be—"

"—in Antwerp. Oh, I know Sir John! But is he really all right? Is he? Please tell me where he is."

And the kindly General took Juanita by the hand and led her into a stable yard where, tending the wounded Lochinvar, stood Harry. The two stood staring at each other in silence for what seemed to Sir John an absurdly long time, and then Juanita could see Harry no longer for the tears of happiness that filled her eyes. She just stood with eyes shut until she heard Lochinvar move slightly and felt Harry's arms close about her.

It was another fine, bright, butterfly morning.

EPILOGUE

Because most people in this story actually took part in the making of history, the reader may like to know what fate had in store for them after the Peninsular and Waterloo campaigns.

Harry and Juanita Smith: The vow made by Juanita De Los Dolores to Harry Smith by the bastions of Badajoz, "I will be a good wife and true to you as long as I live," was kept in every particular. The only regret in a long life together, which may or may not have been due to the miscarriage that she had in the Pyrenees, was that Juanita never had children. But even this had its compensations since, being free from domestic ties, she was always able to follow the drum—and Harry's drum was no easy one to follow.

After Waterloo, for his part in which he was made a Companion of the Bath (CB), Harry returned to regimental soldiering, commanding the 2nd Rifle Brigade in Ireland.

In 1826 Harry and Juanita went to the Cape of Good Hope where, under his old friend Sir Lowry Cole, Harry served as Deputy Quartermaster-General of the forces. Subsequently, under Sir Benjamin D'Urban he played an active part in the Kafir wars, on one occasion riding alone from Cape Town to Grahamstown over rough, roadless country, a distance of seven hundred miles, in six days.

Harry, accompanied by Juanita, was posted to India in 1840 where he was knighted for distinguished service at the battle of Maharajpur, a battle at which Juanita assisted in the capacity of onlooker and medical orderly. Harry and Juanita were in the Punjab when the Sikh war broke out in 1845. Given his first divisional command with the rank of Major-General, Harry encountered at Aliwal a Sikh force very superior in numbers to his own. Taking a well-calculated risk Harry decided to attack and, leading the final charge himself, he inflicted a crushing defeat on that warlike people, driving those trying to escape into the river Sutlej. This beautifully judged and boldly fought battle earned Harry not only a baronetcy and the GCB but, what he prized even more, the praise of the Duke of Wellington in a speech in the House of Lords.

Harry returned to South Africa with Juanita for a second tour of duty in 1847. He was now Governor and High Commissioner of the colony at a time when the black peoples were resisting the encroachment of the whites. Moreover, the whites, notably the Boers, or Voortrekkers, were finding themselves at odds with their fellows. Considering that these problems still persist today after more than a hundred years, it is hardly surprising that Sir Harry Smith, who claimed to be a fighting soldier, not a colonial administrator, found himself in trouble. In 1852 Earl Grey, then Secretary of State to the Colonies, dissatisfied with Harry's progress in suppressing the native tribes, ordered his recall and replacement. Harry's 'sacking' hurt him badly, as his spirited and articulate rebuttal clearly shows. This was the first and only serious reverse in his otherwise impeccable career. There were, however, two consolations. First, Harry's and Juanita's personal popularity was unequivocally demonstrated by both blacks and whites at a tumultuous and emotional send-off from the colony. Secondly they arrived back in England just in time for Harry to be invited to the annual Waterloo Banquet at Apsley House. All the great old warriors still extant, many of them Harry's old friends and comrades-in-arms, were there. When the Great Duke himself rose to propose Harry's health, the toast was responded to with a spontaneous cheer. Thus was Harry vindicated in the eyes of the only people he cared about, his brother-officers.

It was the last Waterloo banquet ever held. Not long afterwards Harry was a pall-bearer at Wellington's funeral: a ceremony of opulent grandeur and solemnity, at the production of which the English are supreme.

It would be of little interest to the reader to chronicle Harry Smith's last official appointments in the United Kingdom. The Crimean War came with Charlie Beckwith writing to Harry: "I suppose, old boy, that our share in coming events will be reading the *Gazette* at breakfast, (and) shutting the garden gate. . . ." And they both fulminated over the press and the politicians' treatment of their old friend Fitzroy Somerset (now Lord Raglan) and they grieved greatly when he died. To George Simmons Harry wrote: '. . . Ah, poor dear Lord Raglan. He died, I fear, of a broken heart.'

But death was coming to all of them. On 12 October 1860 Harry himself succumbed to cardiac arrest and was buried at Whittlesey, his coffin born by eight riflemen who had served under him. Tom Smith, Harry's last surviving 'Waterloo brother' was there, 'young' Charley having predeceased them both. Juanita lived on for another twelve years, very much the grandmother of the family and still rolling her Spanish R's whenever speaking Harry's name. She was buried beside him.

There is a chapel in St Mary's Church, Whittlesey, dedicated to the memory of Sir Harry. In South Africa a town, Harrismith in the Orange Free State, still bears his name. But, by chance, it was for Juanita to be given the greater memorial. When, during the Boer War, in February 1900, a small dorp in Natal called Ladysmith was relieved after gallantly resisting a four-month siege, half the world came to know of it. How many people, though, knew that Ladysmith had been named after a Spanish girl called Juanita who herself lived through two memorable sieges of her own home town, Badajoz?

TOM SMITH: After Waterloo, as Adjutant riding at the head of the 2nd Battalion on 7 July 1815, Tom Smith led the British Army into Paris. That was the apogee of his military career. In 1817 he went on half-pay and soon afterwards became a barrack-master which, compared to commanding troops in the field, must have been a relatively humdrum occupation. He was good at his job, though, since in 1855 he was Principal Barrack-Master of the new model camp at Aldershot. Tom married and had a daughter, Alice, who spent much time with Harry and Juanita in their old age. Tom's long life came to an end in 1877, and he was buried in the military cemetery at Aldershot.

CHARLEY SMITH: For gallant conduct as a Volunteer at Waterloo

Charley was soon afterwards commissioned into the regiment as 2nd Lieutenant. But Charley, despite a promising start, did not care to pursue an army career. Three years after being commissioned he retired to lead the life of a country gentleman at Whittlesey where he married a Cambridgeshire girl. In due course he became a Justice of the Peace and eventually commanded the Cambridgeshire Yeomanry which, as a territorial unit, involved him in only part-time duties. When Harry and Juanita left for their extended tours of duty overseas Charley became the guardian of their much-loved mounts, Chiquito and Lochinvar, and the two animals lived out their herbivorous lives in juicy Cambridgeshire pastures. Charley died in 1854 at the early age of 59.

Victoria De Los Dolores: It is unfortunate that there is no first-hand evidence as to what happened to Victoria after entering the convent of Nuestra Señora de la Soledad in 1813. Juanita, from Whittlesey, shortly before Waterloo, wrote several letters both to Victoria and to Madre Soledad but, surprisingly, never received any reply. She never heard from either of them again.

There is one postscript to the story. When Sir Harry and Lady Smith returned to Cape Town in 1847 Juanita was sought out by a nun of the Dominican order. The nun, French by birth, politely wished to enquire if her Ladyship had been born in Spain and if her maiden name was De Los Dolores. The nun went on to explain that she had once been on a pilgrimage to Santiago de Compostela where she had met some nuns from Badajoz whose Superior had been of the same name. Could this, she wondered, be a relation? Before Juanita had time to reply the nun went on to say, albeit with some diffidence, that the Mother Superior had been accompanied by a fair-haired young man called Enrique, who—and here she blushed—some said was her son.

Julián Sanchez: Julián survived the war and retired in 1814 with the rank of General in the Spanish Army. Becoming disgusted with the internal squabbles and recriminations that broke out with the restoration of Ferdinand VII, he turned his back on politics and bought a bull-farm in his native province of

Salamanca. The wartime activities of Don Julián Sanchez, alias El Charro, are extensively recorded in the history-books of the period.

FRAY MIGUEL: 'El Fraile's' last act as a *guerillero* was to marry Miguelín and the former novice nun, Teresa. He then returned to his native Andalusia and entered a monastery of the Franciscan order at Jimena de La Frontera where he is believed to have died some twenty years later. The library and the records of the Franciscans at Jimena were destroyed during the Civil War of 1936–1939 and the graveyard has long since been ploughed up. But 'El Fraile' was not a man to have worried about his mortal remains.

MIGUELÍN and TERESA: At the end of the war Miguelín was offered, and was pleased to accept, employment by Don Julián on his bull-ranch. Teresa, who soon gave birth to a number of children in quick succession, settled happily down to country life rather to some people's surprise and, though her figure spread in direct ratio to the number of her offspring, her face never lost its prettiness nor her tongue its cutting edge. On certain occasions such as name-days and fiestas she could sometimes be persuaded by the children to take out of her cupboard a neat little Hussar officer's uniform and, giggling, she would pirouette round, holding it up against her middle-aged spread. In due course Miguelín, as a grizzled veteran in his forties, became *mayoral* of the Sanchez bull-farm. Apart from his family, Miguelín's only recreation was a weekly visit to his favourite bar in Santíz where, over a game of dominoes and a litre of red wine, he would recount his adventures as a *guerillero* and boast of his exploits with Wellington's men, in particular El Capitán Esmeet.

BROTHER JAMES DOYLE: Jimmy Doyle returned to Ireland in 1809 and was ordained priest the same year at Enniscorthy, County Wexford. He was there when he heard of the death of his twin brother Declan, killed with his regiment while retrieving General Skerrett's disastrous blunder at the bridge at Vera. Such was Jimmy's brilliance and energy in the ministry that, within ten years of his ordination, he was made Bishop of Kildare and Leighlin. In 1825 Bishop Doyle was summoned to London to report to a Parliamentary Committee on the state of Ireland and, while there, he was happy to be bidden to Apsley House to breakfast with his old chief, the Duke of Wellington. After a distinguished career both as prelate and political controversialist, Bishop Doyle died in 1834 and was buried at Carlow Cathedral.

LORD FITZROY SOMERSET: In August 1814, during the short peace between the Peninsular and the Waterloo campaigns, Fitzroy Somerset married Emily Wellesley, second daughter of Wellington's brother, the Earl of Mornington. To celebrate the occasion Emily gave her husband a ring which he very nearly lost together with his arm after La Haye Sainte. Fitzroy bore the amputation in complete silence and only gave tongue when he saw the orderly making off with the severed limb. "Hello," he called out. "Don't carry away that arm till I've taken off my ring."

Lord Fitzroy, who remained with, or close to, the Duke of Wellington for the rest of the latter's life, was promoted to a number of important appointments in the War Office, being raised to the peerage as Baron Raglan of Raglan in 1852. In the spring of 1854 when England and France declared war against Russia, Lord Raglan was sent to the Crimea as Commander of the British forces. How this brave and unostentatious soldier was made the scapegoat for the governmental mishandling of the British war-effort is well documented in the biographies and history books of the day. The failure of the (mainly French) attack on Sebastopol came at a time when Raglan was debilitated from the effects of dysentery. His health seriously impaired, this truly noble man, who had never flinched from danger on numerous battlefields, allowed contumely and disloyalty at home to undermine him yet further. On the evening of 28 June, with Emily's ring on his remaining hand, Lord Raglan died.

ANDREW BARNARD: Shot through the lung at the passage of the Nivelle, Colonel Barnard was back in command of 2nd Light Brigade—with a knighthood—in time for the battles of Orthez and Toulouse. At Waterloo Sir Andrew was once again wounded, though not badly, and finished the campaign as Commander of the division in occupation of Paris. Thereafter his career continued to prosper and he became variously Colonel-Commandant of the Rifle Brigade, equerry to George IV, clerk-marshal in the Royal Household of William IV and, on account of his life-long interest in the subject, Governor of the Royal College of Music. Rising to the rank of full General Andrew Barnard, at the behest of the Duke of Wellington, was made Lt Governor of Chelsea Hospital where the good man died in 1855. At his funeral the Peninsular Pensioners (Pongo Prickett among them), filed by his coffin, covering the body in laurel leaves which they had plucked from the Hospital gardens.

SYDNEY BECKWITH: 'Uncle' Sydney's health improved on return to England after Fuentes de Oñoro and he was promoted to Major-General with a knighthood in 1814. Sir Sydney saw no more active service, however, being posted to Bombay as Commander-in-Chief in 1830. Hardly surprisingly the climate of India suited him no better than that of Spain, and he died there of fever within a year of his arrival. Sydney Beckwith also had the distinction of becoming Colonel-Commandant of the Rifle Brigade and he will always be remembered as one of the most able Light Infantry commanders in the history of that arm.

CHARLES BECKWITH: (nephew of the above): Of all the Peninsular subalterns, Charlie Beckwith had the most unusual post-war career. Having left a leg behind at Waterloo poor Charlie was much concerned as an energetic man of 26 to know what to do with the rest of his life. One day, while waiting at Apsley House for an interview with the Duke of Wellington, he picked up a book in the library and started to read it. The Great Man having as usual many people to see, Charlie had plenty of time to peruse the volume in hand which he studied with ever increasing interest. It concerned a Protestant sect called the Waldenses, or Vaudois, who inhabited the valleys of Piedmont in Northern Italy. To cut a long story short, Charlie became so fascinated with the history of these poor, and much persecuted, people that eventually he went to live among them. He married a Waldensian peasant girl and, in the capacity of a sort of unofficial missionary, devoted the rest of his life to their welfare, building them a church and well over a hundred schools. Charlie had a gift for letter-writing, and his fresh and vigorous descriptions of life in the remote valleys of northern Italy fascinated Harry Smith, with whom he kept up a lively and affectionate correspondence. Charlie Beckwith died at La Torre, Piedmont in 1862.

JOHNNY KINCAID: Shortly after the Duke had told the riflemen at the sand-pit near La Haye Sainte to 'see them off' Johnny Kincaid had mounted the now one-eared Monsieur Barsac who almost immediately received a direct hit from a shell which killed the animal outright and severely wounded his master. Nevertheless Johnny recovered completely, and soldiered on until 1831 when he retired. In 1844 he was appointed exon of the Yeoman of the Guard and received an *ex officio* knighthood on becoming senior exon in 1852. Johnny wrote two books of light-hearted Peninsular memoirs: *Adventures in the Rifle Brigade* and *Random Shots of a Rifleman*, both of which make amusing reading, particularly in his references to Harry Smith and Juanita De Los Dolores. Johnny Kincaid, who in his youth had been so romantically inclined, died a bachelor in 1862.

GEORGE SIMMONS: During the general advance at the end of the battle of Waterloo George Simmons turned round to see how many men were following him and, at that moment, a ball entered his right side, puncturing the liver and fracturing two ribs on its course. A surgeon at a forward dressing-station extracted this bullet from his chest and George, suffering horribly was carried from the field on a horse being held on by a Sergeant who was himself wounded. It was a twelve-mile journey back to his billet in Brussels during which, as he afterwards noted, 'the motion of the horse made the blood pump out and the (broken) bones cut the flesh to a jelly'. After about six days George went into what was thought to be a final coma when suddenly the wound burst and, according to a letter to his parents dated 21 July 1815, 'the matter flowed forth as from a fountain. I knew in a moment my life was saved'. Johnny Kincaid, having himself recovered from his wound, recalled Simmons' return to the regiment the following year, '. . . George Simmons, with his riddled body held together by a pair of stays, for his was no holy day waist. . . .' Incredibly, George served on in the regiment for another 29 years, his girth (and presumably the stays) ever-increasing in circumference. In 1834 he married a Jersey girl, the daughter of one Sir Thomas le Breton. He retired as a Major after 36 years' service.

George Simmons, the plodding regimental soldier, was fascinated by the brilliant career of his contemporary, Harry Smith, with whom he not infrequently exchanged letters. From these it can be seen how a mutual affection and respect, which hardly existed in the Peninsular days, deepened as the years went by. George died in 1858, aged 72. His last recorded words—his mind wandering, no doubt—were: 'Where's the rigiment (*sic*)? . . . My word, the General and Sir Harry will soon be here.'

George's war-time letters and diaries were posthumously collected by another rifleman, Willoughby Verner, and published in 1899.

EDWARD COSTELLO: In the early hours of Waterloo a bullet tore the trigger finger off Sergeant Costello, at the same time as another one pierced his mess-tin. This disability did not keep him away from the regiment for long. At Cambrai, where they were stationed in 1816, Costello, who had obviously got over his passion for Jenny Cochrane, fell hotly in love with a French girl called Augustine Lourde, despite the strong objection of the girl's anti-British father.

So long as there was a war on the army medical authorities were quite content to keep much-wounded men like Costello in the service. But once the army had returned to peacetime conditions these men were weeded out. Towards the end of 1816, therefore, Costello was sent back to Shorncliffe where he was invalided out on a pension of sixpence a day, a near starvation wage.* It was just

*Sir Sydney Beckwith was one of the many compassionate soldiers who campaigned against the disgraceful way in which an ungrateful nation, as represented by the Government of the day, permitted its heroes to starve once they had ceased to be useful.

then that Augustine, having run away from home, unexpectedly arrived and almost immediately went into childbirth. Being unable to support himself, let alone a woman and child, Costello scraped together all the money he could lay hands on and took Augustine and baby back to France where he lodged them with an uncle. Augustine's subsequent fate is uncertain. Costello himself states that he received news of her death shortly after her return to France. The historian, Anthony Brett-James, on the other hand, states that Augustine married in France and had several more children.

As for Ned Costello, we do not hear of him again until 1835 when, possibly driven by necessity to ply the only trade he knew, he returned to Spain with the British Legion recruited to fight for Isabella II against the Carlist faction. In this hopelessly mismanaged conflict the unfortunate man from Mountmellick was once again wounded. Nevertheless he managed to return to England with the rank of Captain which at least must have improved his pension prospects. From this time on his fortunes improved and in 1838 he became a 'Beefeater'—more properly a Yeoman Warder—of the Tower of London. It was in this capacity that he came to serve once again with the man under whom he had scaled the walls of Badajoz in the Forlorn Hope—Johnny—now Sir John —Kincaid.

One day walking out on Tower Hill he saw a ragged and emaciated-looking man selling boot-laces on a tray. The fellow was staring hard at him. "Morning, Captain," said the ragged man. Approaching closer Costello soon discerned under the grime the familiar features of Billy Doubleday.

"What brought you to this, Billy?" said Costello after pleasantries had been exchanged. "Well, you know how it is, sir," said Billy. "Once they've done with you, they throw you away, don't they?" "I know only too well how it is, Billy," replied Costello, with sincerity, "and but for the Grace of God and His Blessed Mother I'd be in the same boat meself." And feeling in his pocket he took out all the coin he had on his person and gave it to Doubleday.

Ned Costello is known to have married a London woman by the name of Charlotte after his second return from Spain. Having an Irishman's gift for the use of language, Costello, during his leisure hours as a 'Beefeater', wrote his war memoirs, and *Adventures of a*

Soldier Written by Himself were published by Colburn & Co in 1852 and still make fascinating reading. Captain Edward Costello died at the Tower in 1869.

JENNY COCHRANE: It is pleasantly idle to speculate what might have happened to Jenny and Ned Costello had Jenny accepted the latter's offer of marriage. Jenny put her foot once again on the 'Oul' Sod' with the Smiths when Harry went to take command of 2nd Rifle Brigade at Downpatrick in 1825. But when the gallant Colonel was posted to a staff appointment in Jamaica the following year Jenny decided not to leave Ireland. Instead she married a rather drunken Sergeant called Murphy in the 43rd whose time with the Colours was nearly up. Considering the distressful condition of Ireland at the time, not to mention Sergeant Murphy's thirst, it is rather unlikely that the lovely Jenny, veteran of the Peninsular and Waterloo campaigns, lived happily ever after.

PONGO PRICKETT: For his gallantry in the field, and his sheer ability to survive, Prickett continued up the ladder of promotion, eventually reaching the highly respectable rank of Regimental Quartermaster-Sergeant. This was perhaps not the most suitable appointment for a man of Prickett's proclivities and disposition. Regimental records for 1819 disclose that Prickett was court-martialled for the misappropriation of War Department stores and once again reduced to the ranks. Having completed his service with the Colours, however, through the kind intervention of Colonel Harry Smith with Sir Andrew Barnard, Prickett was fortunate enough to be granted a pension at the Royal Hospital, Chelsea, where he died of old age in 1861. Pongo's funeral obsequies, however, were somewhat overshadowed by those of Albert, the Prince Consort, who went to his—possibly different—reward in the same week, month and year.

R.I.P.

ACKNOWLEDGEMENTS

It is my great pleasure to thank those who have supplied me with information or have helped me in other ways to write this book. First a former comrade-in-arms, John Baker (Colonel, MC, retd.), at the time of writing curator of The Rifle Brigade Museum at Winchester, provided me with a variety of detail concerning regimental matters which I had either forgotten or never knew. Another brother-rifleman, Mark Culme-Seymour, has been my literary litmus-paper in this, as in previous works. To the above my grateful thanks. My gratitude also goes to Victoria Guillamón and my son Anthony, both of whom have ransacked museums and archives in Madrid to provide me with information regarding the exploits of the Spanish partisans (*guerilleros* or *partidas*) during the War of Independence, 1808–1813. For information regarding the work of certain Irish clerics during the same Peninsular War (as we call it) *un abrazo* for my friend the erudite Father Gerard Rice of Navan, Co. Meath; likewise to my daughter Oonagh, a fond salute for her translation from idiomatic Spanish the lyric of a *sevillana*. My thanks are also due to the Librarian and staff of the London Library for their invariably prompt provision of books requested. I am happy also to acknowledge the estate of Antonio Machado for quotations from *Consejos, Coplas, Apuntes* out of the poet's *Poesías Completas*. And to Mrs Jan Siegler go my thanks for her ruthless, but necessary, excision of much dross. I bow likewise to my old friend, thespian, and fellow-scribe, Reed de Rouen, for a timely and valuable suggestion.

Four ladies have contributed to the typing and frequent re-typing of this fairly bulky work: Daphne Tobin, Joan Puryer, Sheena Pilkington (during the close seasons for steeple-chase jockeys), and my wife, better known as June Tobin. To them my sincere gratitude for their patience and their skill at interpreting my many long-hand revisions. As to the last mentioned, in addition to her time spent at the typewriter (when not running a large family and practising her own profession as an actress), my dear wife has also been of the greatest help in advising on ladies' costume and keeping me on the path through the wood of continuity in which an author (speaking for myself) of a large cast and of a fairly diversified work can easily get lost.

Finally, and affectionately, I wish to acknowledge the sharp perception and critical skill which my brother Michael brought and applied to the revision of this book.

Jimena de la Frontera P.L.

& BRUSSELS
N
K.G.L.
(Kings German Legion)
K.G.L.
Coleborne
Guards
Guards
HOUGOUMONT
FARM
QUATRE BRAS